Gary Stolkin is a British entrepreneur and novelist.

Raised in Essex and educated at Oxford, Gary founded the world's leading recruitment firm for the creative industries, has written for Fast Company and The Guardian, and is a five-time speaker at the Cannes International Festival of Creativity.

In 2018, Gary decided to make better use of the interminable hours he was spending on airplanes to write his debut novel, *Mykonos and Athena – A Furry Tale*.

He lives in Chelsea, South-West London, with Mykonos and Athena.

For anyone who has loved a pet more than people.

Gary Stolkin

MYKONOS AND ATHENA – A FURRY TALE

AUSTIN MACAULEY PUBLISHERS™

LONDON * CAMBRIDGE * NEW YORK * SHARJAH

A CIP catalogue record for this title is available from the British Library.

ISBN 9781398483033 (Paperback)
ISBN 9781398483040 (Hardback)
ISBN 9781398483057 (ePub e-book)

www.austinmacauley.com

First Published 2022
Austin Macauley Publishers Ltd®
1 Canada Square
Canary Wharf
London
E14 5AA

Chapter 1
The Holiday

As their plane made its descent over the Greek Islands, Harry and Amy stared out of the window at the turquoise sea below and the small, white-washed houses scattered across the arid landscape.

The plane's tyres hit the runway with a gentle bump and the engines roared as the captain brought the jet to a stop just before it reached the end of the precariously short runway.

Harry and Amy had flown for almost four hours from London, squeezed like sardines in an aluminium tube, and they couldn't wait a minute longer to get off the plane.

"Why is everyone taking so long?" asked Harry, impatiently, as the woman in front of them tried to retrieve her belongings from the overhead lockers.

Eventually they reached the door of the plane and as they stood at the top of the steps, the warm air hit them. It was a dry heat, the kind that makes you smile and let out a sigh of contentment, the kind that doesn't make you sweaty and irritable.

Turquoise sea, whitewashed houses and this gentle, white heat. Their friends had told them that they would *love* Mykonos, and now they were here.

Several miles away, on a building site outside Mykonos Town, a small tabby kitten climbed across the rubble and rubbish. The kitten didn't know that it was the only survivor of a litter born just seven weeks earlier. Its mother was born on this wasteland and had survived by foraging for scraps amongst the rubbish dumped on the site, and by visiting the dustbins at the back of a hotel just a hundred metres away.

But the wasteland had become a building site. Diggers had moved in a few weeks before and had started to clear away the rubbish that had accumulated on the site over many years. Eventually apartments would be built on it. What was once a sanctuary for feral cats was now a warzone.

The small tabby kitten had been weaned, but it wasn't ready to be separated from its mother. And it didn't know that its siblings were dead. Alone, hungry, and unable to see properly, it now had the infection that had been the downfall of the rest of the litter. One eye was already closed, lids glued painfully together. The other was congested and only partially open. The kitten hadn't ever ventured beyond the wasteland, but its instincts drove it towards the big white building on the horizon. And so it mustered the little strength left in its small, emaciated body to traverse the rocks and mounds of rubbish that had been its home, desperate to find refuge in a foreign land.

Back at Mykonos airport, Harry had gone to collect their car rental whilst Amy waited for their luggage. Harry figured that this would save them time. He didn't much like waiting in line and he wanted to beat the rest of the plane to the car rental desks. It worked, and by the time Amy appeared outside the terminal pushing their bags, Harry was waiting for her in a convertible Fiat 500. He beeped the horn to get her attention.

"Cute car," said Amy, peering over her sunglasses. "It looks like my father's lawnmower. Where shall we put the bags?"

"On the back seats," replied Harry, as he leapt out of the Fiat and threw their suitcases into the impossibly small space at the rear.

"Will they be safe there?" asked Amy, fastening her seat belt.

"Of course they will. It's only fifteen minutes to the hotel. I know where we're going," replied Harry.

And with that, Amy sat back and tilted her head to catch the afternoon rays. The sun felt good on her skin.

Shortly afterwards, Harry and Amy arrived at their hotel. They completed formalities at the hotel reception and downed a glass of complimentary sparkling wine before being shown to their whitewashed room. Harry opened the French doors onto their terrace, and they stepped outside to take in the view. Sunburnt arid terrain stretched out for a few hundred metres in front of them and then the land dropped away to a crystal clear sea in the distance. A warm breeze ruffled their hair.

"Bloody brilliant," said Harry, smiling. "Everything I hoped it would be." He wrapped his arms around Amy and gave her a hug.

"Not so sure about that," said Amy, pointing towards the wasteland over the ridge on their left. "It's a building site. Look at those diggers. We're on the wrong side of the hotel."

"Not a lot going on there at the moment," said Harry, hoping to pacify her.

"They're probably having their lunch," replied Amy, glancing at her watch. "I hope we're not going to hear them."

"Probably not," replied Harry. "Not from here at least, but if we do, I'll ask for a different room – okay?" He kissed her on the lips, and she smiled.

Harry and Amy had boarded their flight in London before seven that morning and all they'd eaten on the plane was an unappetising wrap filled with a mysterious curry flavoured mix. Harry had checked the label, which said that it was chicken, though he wasn't convinced.

"Let's order room service," said Harry, "and eat it on our terrace. While we wait for the food, I can check my e-mails and you can unpack your *ridiculously* large suitcase."

"Don't make fun of my suitcase!" retorted Amy. "I only brought the bare essentials."

"How many bikinis?" asked Harry.

"I refuse to answer that question," replied an indignant Amy, "but possibly four, or maybe five. Don't laugh."

Harry sat down on the bed and got out his laptop.

"Where's that piece of paper they gave us at reception with the Wi-Fi code on it?" he asked.

"Harry, you said you wouldn't work. You said this would be our time," pleaded Amy. "The code is written in the key holder I think."

"Got it. Thanks," he replied, logging on. "This will take me fifteen minutes and then I'll be able to relax. I'm going to sit outside on the terrace. Why don't you check out the room service menu. See if they have any grilled fish for me, please."

Harry sat at the table on their terrace and started to go through his emails.

"There's a fish brochette," shouted Amy from inside the bedroom.

"Perfect," he shouted back, "and vino. Let's have some vino. We're on holiday!"

Amy called room service to place their order, and then started to unpack.

"Hotel Wi-Fi is better than I expected," he shouted to her.

"Yipee!" she muttered sarcastically.

Harry didn't hear her. He was already working his way through his inbox, positioned facing the sun so he could see the screen and catch some rays at the same time. Harry loved the sun and tanned easily.

Less than thirty metres away, the tabby kitten had reached the edge of the wasteland. It was tired and dehydrated. All that now stood between the kitten and the hotel was a small access road that went up the hill along the side of the building.

The kitten could just about see Harry on the terrace and instinct compelled it to cross the road and climb the rocks to reach him. Local children had played on the wasteland before the trucks and diggers moved in. Sometimes they fed the kittens or picked them up and held them.

This kitten didn't know exactly who or what the children were. Their body language was not familiar. Maybe they were some kind of big, strange cat? The experience of being handled by the children had, however, gone some way to socialising the kitten. As the sun beat down relentlessly on its small, frail body, Harry, this very big cat, or whatever it was, was this kittens only hope.

Harry was rifling through his inbox to make sure that there was nothing else that needed urgent attention. He'd turned his out of office on and he told himself that people really shouldn't expect him to get back to them as quickly as he would normally do. He told himself that he needed to learn how to 'switch off'. He was going to have a proper holiday.

At that moment, Harry noticed something moving across the terrace. It was a bundle of fur not much bigger than his fist. It stopped and peered up at him.

Harry stood up. "Amy!" he shouted. "Look at this!"

"What?" she replied.

"Out here!" he shouted. "There's something you need to see."

Amy came out onto the terrace. They both stared down at the kitten, and the kitten stared back up at them, just able to see through its one eye that was barely open.

"Where did it come from?" she asked.

"I don't know," said Harry. "He just appeared."

"How do you know it's a he?" asked Amy.

"He, she. Whatever it is, it's not well," replied Harry.

They crouched down over the kitten. "Look at his eyes," said Amy. "The left ones all gunged up."

"I'm going to get a wet towel," said Harry. "We can clean his eyes."

Harry went to the bathroom and came back with a small moist towel. He then put the kitten on the bed and held it whilst he gently wiped its eyes. The kitten didn't flinch.

"Make sure you wash your hands after touching it," said Amy. "You know how allergic you are to cats. And they harbour all kinds of disease. You don't want to catch something."

"Why don't you fill that ashtray with some water?" Harry gestured as he carefully removed the gunge from the kitten's eyes.

The kitten's instincts had been vindicated as it opened both its eyes for the first time in several days. It was dazzled by the strength of the sunlight. It opened its mouth and tried to make a noise, but no sound came out of its larynx.

"He can't meow," said Harry. "He probably needs water."

Amy placed the ashtray on the floor. The kitten sniffed the water for a moment and then started to drink, its small tongue lapping up the cool liquid.

There was a sudden buzzing noise from the room bell which startled the kitten. It jumped back a few feet onto the terrace and crouched nervously.

"Room service!" a male voice cried from outside.

"Coming!" Harry shouted back. "Do you want to let him in?" he asked Amy, pointing at the door, "and I'll make sure this chap doesn't disappear."

"Sure," said Amy. She opened the door and let the waiter into the room.

"Mr and Mrs Parkman, welcome to hotel Helias Ambassador!" exclaimed the waiter in a heavy Greek accent. He was carrying a large tray and marched with this through the bedroom and onto the terrace.

"Mister Parkman and Miss Carter-Bowles, actually," said Amy, correcting him.

"Excuse me, miss," replied the waiter. "Where do you want your lunch?" he asked. "Should I put it on the table for you?"

The waiter then noticed the kitten cowering on the floor. "I'll put your lunch on the table here," he said, placing the tray on the table, "and I'll get housekeeping to remove the cat for you."

"Thank you," said Amy. "That would be great."

"The kitten's fine here," Harry interjected. "Housekeeping is not required. We like the kitten."

Amy scowled at Harry and the waiter looked confused. Harry signed the room service bill and the waiter shouted 'enjoy your lunch' as he closed the bedroom door behind him.

Harry looked at the kitten and looked at the fish brochette. "Maybe we can flake a piece of that fish and see if he'll eat it?" suggested Harry.

"Flake sounds very cordon bleu," joked Amy as she put fish on a side plate and mashed it with a fork.

Harry rinsed the hand towel and held the kitten gently whilst he gave its eyes another wipe. The kitten did not resist. It was starting to feel a little better thanks to the water it had drunk. It wanted to meow its approval but all that could be heard was the exhalation of air.

Amy handed Harry the small plate of fish. "That's amazing," she said. "His eyes are open."

"Cool, isn't it?" said Harry. He knelt down and put the small plate of fish under the table by the kitten. The kitten put its nose close to the fish and took a first, tentative mouthful. It went down easily, and it started to eat more quickly.

"He was hungry," observed Harry.

"Well, he seems a lot better now," replied Amy, glancing down at her watch. "It's not even three o'clock. Let's have our lunch and get down to the beach. Charlotte says they have a fantastic DJ and an awesome sunset party."

"That sounds great," replied Harry unconvincingly. He was crouched down, stroking the kitten whilst it finished the fish.

Amy re-appeared on the terrace in a yellow bikini. Harry glanced up at her and then took a second look. Somehow he'd forgotten how stunning she was. Amy had never been a huge fan of the gym, but she had been determined to be 'beach fit' for Mykonos and she was gratified that the time spent at the gym had paid off.

"Come on, Harry," said Amy.

"I'll be ready in a minute," he replied. Harry then picked up the kitten and put it on the bed inside. The kitten curled up and closed its eyes.

"Not on the bed, Harry!" protested Amy. "You don't know what terrible diseases it might be harbouring."

"We're not going to catch anything from it," replied Harry. "Do you think we should take it to a vet? Did you see how it was trying to meow before? It's in really bad shape."

"A vet?" replied an incredulous Amy. "I thought you didn't like cats. You're super allergic to cats, aren't you?"

"I am," confirmed Harry. "Actually, I can already feel my eyes itching. But we can't just do nothing."

"Of course we can," she snapped. "We've fed it and cleaned it up. He looks much better. Look. He'll be fine."

"He can't speak," replied Harry.

"He'll be here when we come back. He'll be waiting for us to give him more food. That's what cats do," explained Amy. "You can always take him to a vet tomorrow, if they even have a vet on the island, if you're that worried," she continued.

At that moment, the kitten sneezed, leaving a trail of mucous on the linen and hanging from its nose.

"He really is in bad shape," said Harry.

"Oh my God. We'll have to get the sheets changed!" exclaimed Amy.

"It's nothing," replied Harry, wiping the sheet clean with a towel.

"Look," said Amy, holding up Harry's wine glass, "you haven't even tasted your wine. Let's have a glass, put the bottle in the minibar for later, and get down to the beach, okay?"

"Actually, I think it's a girl," said Harry, stroking the kitten's tummy.

"What!" exclaimed Amy. "You're not listening to me at all, are you?"

"I am listening to you. Look, she's got nipples, a lot of nipples. It must be a girl," concluded Harry.

"Listen, at least come down to the beach club with me and get me a sunbed on the front line," pleaded Amy. "Charlotte says you've got to be on the front line and you're so good at that kind of thing. She said we have to ask for the manager, Yannis."

"Call me cynical, but I'm sure Yannis won't mind which of us presses a fifty Euro note into the palm of his hand to get a sunbed on the front line," responded Harry.

"You are *so* cynical," replied Amy. "But actually, you're right. Charlotte said give him one hundred Euros on the first day."

She kissed him on the cheek and asked, "Can I take the cash from your wallet?"

"Absolutely," replied Harry smiling. "It's in my bag."

"I just think it looks tacky for a woman to be greasing the palms of the manager," explained Amy.

"It's tacky, full stop, regardless of who's greasing the palms. Ed told me to bring lots of cash. Apparently it works wonders. You'll be fine," said Harry.

"Okay. I'll go down to the beach and you can join me once you've sorted out what's her face," said Amy, packing creams and sunglasses into a beach bag. "But promise you won't be long."

"I promise I won't be long," replied Harry, whilst gently stroking the kitten.

"Okay, see you at the beach!" said Amy as she opened the bedroom door.

"Let's call her Mykonos," suggested Harry.

"Call her whatever you like, Harry. Your eyes are red, and you have snot running down your lip. Maybe the vet can tell you where you can get some antihistamines. *Please* get to the beach for the sunset party," begged Amy. "We're on holiday, for goodness sake!"

Harry was conflicted. He knew that Amy was right and that the kitten would probably be there when they came back to the room from the beach. And he couldn't wait to get some sun to replenish the faded remnants of his Easter

Florida tan. He had wanted to get a few hours tanning on their first afternoon there so that he wouldn't be the palest man on the island. But there was something about this kitten. It was an adorable ball of fur. And it needed him.

Harry opened his laptop and googled cat images. It wasn't long before he found a cat that resembled the kitten. He learnt that the 'M' pattern on the forehead meant it was a tabby. He was definitely going to call the kitten Mykonos.

By now, Mykonos had curled up under the table on the terrace and was sleeping. Harry wondered whether they even had vets on the island, so he called the hotel front desk to find out. Yes, there were vets. The nearest practice was some two miles away and it would be open from four o'clock for a couple of hours. Harry looked at his watch and pondered the consequences of not making it to the beach that afternoon. Amy would get over it. He'd take her out for dinner that evening. And they had another nine whole days on the beach. He was going to take Mykonos to the vet. He sent Amy an apologetic text.

Harry found a small linen basket in the bathroom which contained spare towels, a hair dryer and complimentary slippers. He emptied the basket and placed Mykonos in it.

He carried the basket to their hire car and put it on the floor in front of the passenger seat. Using a map provided by the hotel front desk, he found his way to the vet's practice. He drove with one hand on the steering wheel whilst using the other to make sure that Mykonos didn't climb out of the basket. In fact Mykonos spent most of the journey sitting quietly in the basket. Being enclosed in the basket made the kitten feel safe.

Harry entered the small reception area of the vet's practice carrying the basket. The walls were lined with shelves stacked high with different brands of litter, pet food and all kinds of pet supplies. Harry surveyed the shelves. This was a strange world which, under normal circumstances, he would have actively avoided.

"Do you speak English?" he asked the middle-aged woman who stood behind the counter.

"I do," she replied, with a slight accent.

"I found a kitten and I'd like the vet to have a look at her," he explained, gesturing with the linen basket.

"We have a lot of cats on the island," she told him. "It's a great pity but, you know, half of them die every winter." She peered into the linen basket. "You can help this kitten, but if it is not well, it will probably not survive the winter. Please don't misunderstand me. I think it is a good thing that you want to help the kitten. It is just that we have a lot of tourists trying to help the animals in Mykonos, but they cannot take them home at the end of their holiday. Sometimes it is better to, how do you say, let nature take its course."

Harry liked this woman. There was a compassionate honesty about her. Her name was Lyra.

"I understand what you're saying," said Harry, "and I'm happy to pay to get Mykonos – I call her Mykonos – the medicine she needs. At least she'll have a better chance of surviving after I go home. I'm happy to spend the money to help her."

"I see," replied the woman. "I am the assistant," she explained. "Please take a seat. The vet will be able to see you in a few minutes."

"Thank you," replied Harry.

The vet's assistant took the linen basket and examined Mykonos. "It is a very handsome kitten mister, but you said you called her Mykonos?" she asked.

"That's right," replied Harry.

"Would you call her Mykonos if she was a male kitten?" she asked.

"Yes, I would, but I'm sure it's a girl. She has a lot of, er, teats, you know nipples. It must be a girl," explained Harry.

"Mister, all cats have eight nipples, male and female, just like all humans have two nipples. See what the vet says, but I think Mykonos is a boy," she said.

At that moment, the vet appeared and took Harry into the consulting room where he examined Mykonos. He told Harry that Mykonos was indeed a boy and that he was probably seven to eight weeks old. The vet explained that Mykonos was undernourished but his physical condition was not too bad – and that his teeth looked healthy. He had some kind of infection in his eyes and nasal passage which could be treated with an injection of antibiotics. The infection had affected his vocal chords, but the vet said that he would get his voice back once the antibiotics kicked in.

The vet administered an injection in the scruff of Mykonos' neck. Mykonos flinched, but he didn't complain. He was overwhelmed by this new world and sat quietly.

"Are you going to be feeding him?" asked the vet.

"I guess so," replied Harry.

"Well you should feed him dry food, because wet food will make it more difficult for him to clear the mucus," explained the vet.

"Dry food, right," confirmed Harry. "Can I buy some dry food from you?" he asked.

"Yes," replied the vet, "Lyra will give you a dry food for kittens."

"Great. Thanks," replied Harry.

"Where are you staying?" asked the vet.

"The Helias Ambassador," replied Harry.

"Very nice hotel," commented the vet. "Now, he is infested with lice," said the vet. "Look."

Sure enough, as the vet pulled Mykonos' fur back, Harry could see a lot of very small parasites.

Harry winced. "Could I have caught them when I've been stroking him?"

"No," replied the vet, "but we need to get rid of them. There's a treatment that's like a mild electric shock which paralyses the lice. They'll fall out in the next day or two. The anti-biotic is forty Euros and the lice treatment is thirty Euros. Is that okay?" asked the vet.

"Yes, of course," replied Harry.

Harry purchased dry kitten food and a small plastic carrying case to keep Mykonos secure when he drove him back to the hotel, and a small toy mouse for him to play with. The total cost was one hundred and fifty Euros.

The vet's assistant, Lyra, escorted Harry and Mykonos out of the surgery. "You look like you have a bit of a cold yourself," observed Lyra.

"Oh, it's nothing," replied Harry, "I'm allergic to cats."

"You are allergic to cats, and you are helping this kitten? I think it is a wonderful thing that you are doing, mister," said Lyra.

"Thank you," replied Harry.

"The vet would like to see Mykonos again in a couple of days to make sure the infection has cleared," explained Lyra. "This is included in what you have already paid. There is no extra charge."

"Okay," said Harry, "I'll bring him back in a few days."

Harry placed Mykonos' carrying case in the back of the car. Mykonos pressed his nose against the meshed side of the case and gazed up at Harry.

Harry's first thought was that Mykonos was the most adorable thing he had ever seen, and he was so, so happy that he might have saved Mykonos' life by taking him to the vet.

Harry's second thought was what the hell was he thinking? He didn't like cats, he was allergic to cats, and his holiday had been hijacked by a kitten.

Harry and Mykonos arrived back at the hotel. As Harry walked through the hotel reception with the carrying case, the staff looked on incredulously. Harry released Mykonos on the terrace of his hotel room and gave him fresh water and the newly purchased kibbles in a couple of saucers. Mykonos ate the kibbles with the ferocity of an animal that had been hungry for much of its short life. Over the coming week, Mykonos consumed whatever he could when the opportunity presented itself.

Harry watched Mykonos eat. When Mykonos had finished the kibbles, he sat on his hind quarters, a little bundle of fur no bigger than Harry's fist and started to clean himself. Harry was impressed by how meticulously Mykonos cleaned himself and wondered if he was ingesting the lice which must have all been dead by now.

Harry sat at the table on the terrace and started to go through the messages on his phone. There were several texts from Amy. She was angry. Where was he and why wasn't he on the beach? She had been put on the third row. If he had been with her, he would have made sure they were on the front row. Amy liked that Harry was good at getting the best table in a restaurant or the best seats in the house. He had an authority about him which she found incredibly attractive.

Harry replied to her series of texts: *Sorry. Ended up at vet. He's a boy! On my way to beach now. Love you.*

It was five thirty in the afternoon. Harry quickly changed into his swimming trunks and went back out onto the terrace to check on Mykonos. The kitten had gone. He was nowhere to be seen.

"Mykonos!" shouted Harry several times, as he surveyed the landscape. He realised how foolish this would sound to anybody who could hear him. Mykonos had seemed like the obvious name for the kitten, but as he shouted his name, he did wonder if it might have been less confusing if he was called Collin or Eric.

Harry locked the terrace doors and paused momentarily. Would he ever see the kitten again? And if he didn't, would it be a good thing or a bad thing? He sprinted down to the beach and joined Amy for sunset cocktails.

Amy and Harry had been living together for over three years. The connection between them had been strong and Amy had assumed that at some stage they would become engaged, marry and have children. Harry had been promoted to partner around two years ago in the management consultancy where he worked.

With his promotion came more travel, more people to manage, more targets to deliver on, and more emails to answer in the evenings. Harry's work had become all consuming. Amy enjoyed Harry's success and the lifestyle it afforded them. But she had started to worry about whether he would get around to marrying her. Her anxiety had been fuelled by her married girlfriends who kept telling her that she needed to get a ring on her finger. Amy, however, was concerned that pushing Harry too hard to get married might ultimately push him away. So she was resolved to playing the long game, provided it wasn't all that long. Amy wanted to have children and whilst she waited for Harry on the beach, she consoled herself with the theory that Harry's interest in the kitten might be a positive sign. Perhaps this meant that he was getting broody? Nevertheless, it did seem peculiar to her that he had taken to the kitten, given his general disinterest in animals and his allergic reaction to cats.

Harry and Amy enjoyed sunset cocktails on the beach and then returned to their hotel. Mykonos was nowhere to be seen.

That evening, they explored the narrow, whitewashed maze of passageways in Chora – the town – and had an early dinner in a small tavern on the water's edge. It was bliss. They had been up early that morning and it had been a long day, so they got back to their hotel by eleven o'clock. It had been a wonderful evening. They had laughed, they had held hands and Harry had been relaxed and attentive. Amy had almost forgotten what he was like when he wasn't distracted and constantly checking his emails on his phone. The evening reminded Amy of how things used to be.

As they drove back to their hotel, Harry began to think about the kitten and whether he would be on their terrace waiting for them. When they got into their room, Harry went directly onto the terrace. His face lit up. There was Mykonos, curled up like a tiny, furry croissant on the chair. Mykonos looked up at Harry, he yawned, and he stretched, he stood up, and he jumped from the chair to the floor.

"He's here!" said Harry. "He's come back."

"Of course he has," replied Amy, joining Harry on the terrace. "You fed him. He's back for more food."

As cats go, Mykonos was not a particularly brave cat. Indeed, he was, by nature, something of a scaredy cat. Leaving the wasteland and venturing to the unknown was courageous, but it was driven by a fundamental instinct to survive. He had understood that he was very sick, and when cats are reconciled to death, they find a place to be on their own so that they can die in peace. But this kitten was not ready to die. He had chosen the possibility of life, and some kind of miracle beyond the wasteland that would save him. It was the impossible dream. And Harry was the miracle.

Mykonos looked on in awe as Harry, the miracle maker, produced more kibbles and fresh water. Mykonos crouched down next to the saucers and ate until he was full. Once he had eaten, Mykonos ventured through the open terrace door and into Harry and Amy's room, where they were getting ready for bed.

"Oh my God!" exclaimed Amy, looking down at Mykonos. "Why don't you just join us in bed?"

She then shouted to Harry in the bathroom. "He's in the bloody bedroom!"

Mykonos was exploring the bedroom when Harry came out of the bathroom.

"He's so cute, isn't he?" said Harry.

"Adorable" – Amy grimaced – "but he's not sleeping in here."

"Oh we can't kick him out," pleaded Harry, watching Mykonos playing with the loose cord hanging down from a hotel bath robe. The antibiotics and the food had started to take effect. Mykonos was beginning to feel much better.

"What's he going to do, you know, 'his business'?" asked Amy. "It better not be in here," she protested.

"I don't know," replied Harry. "We can leave the sliding door to the balcony open a few inches so he can sleep in here or go outside if he wants. You hate air conditioning anyway, and if he needs to do 'his business', he can go outside."

"Well I hope we won't be murdered in our beds by some intruder because *you* left the terrace doors open," fretted Amy.

"I'm sure we will be safe," responded Harry.

"If he poos in here, you're cleaning it up," insisted Amy.

"Actually, they're very clean, according to this website," said Harry, waving his mobile phone at her.

Amy rolled her eyes and got into bed.

Harry left the terrace door partially open and joined her under the crisp white sheets. A warm breeze wafted around the room and then Harry felt the patter of tiny paws as Mykonos pulled himself up onto the bed, walked up the bed between them, and then curled up between their pillows. Harry looked at Amy. She was already fast asleep and snoring loudly. Harry smiled. Amy would be mortified if she knew that she had been snoring like a pig. It was so not Amy. He also felt exhausted. It had been a long day.

Harry turned his head sideways to look at the kitten. He could already feel his nose starting to run and his eyes watering a little. Mykonos was used to sleeping outside, under a rock or inside a container that had been dumped on the wasteland. He had never slept somewhere where he felt completely safe. His ears would swivel whilst he was asleep on the wasteland, constantly listening out for danger, so he never slept for long. But now he was curled up between the pillows, just a few inches away from Harry's face, and he felt totally safe. Harry lifted his hand and stroked Mykonos. Mykonos closed his eyes and fell into a deep sleep.

A shard of light cut across the bedroom when the sun rose early the next morning. Harry opened his eyes and stretched his arms above his head. *Mykonos!* He thought. He sat up slowly in bed and looked around. Mykonos was not there. He slid back down into the bed, disappointed that Mykonos had gone, but also relieved that Amy wouldn't wake up to find the kitten curled up next to her.

Amy opened her eyes and stretched. She smiled and Harry kissed her on the lips. She responded with a long, lingering kiss.

"Good morning," said Amy.

"Good morning," replied Harry, smiling.

Amy sat up and looked around the room. "No cat?" she asked.

"I don't know," replied Harry casually. "Must have spent the night on the tiles."

"Cool," said Amy as her head fell back into the soft pillow. As she rolled over to face Harry, Amy noticed what looked like grains of rice scattered around the sheet. She sat up slowly to survey the bed and realised that there were hundreds, if not thousands of tiny specks scattered across the bed linen. She picked some up.

"Harry, what are these?" she asked, showing him the grains in the palm of her hand.

Harry sat up. The bed looked like it was covered with them. The penny dropped.

"Amy," he said, apprehensively.

"Yes?" she replied.

"Don't freak out. But I think they're lice," explained Harry.

"What!" she cried, jumping out of bed as she threw the dead lice she was holding back onto the duvet cover.

"What the!" she exclaimed.

"The vet gave Mykonos some kind of electric shock to kill the lice," explained Harry. "Looks like they're all dead."

"But there are millions of them," said Amy, taking a closer look at the sheets. "They're everywhere. You're telling me all of these were in his fur?"

"Must've been," replied Harry.

"I need a shower!" cried Amy, running into the bathroom.

Harry put a bath robe on and stepped out onto the terrace. It was a glorious, sunny day. Mykonos was curled up on one of the chairs, the warm breeze caressing his fur. He stretched out his paws and yawned before jumping down from the chair onto the terrace, where he sat attentively. He looked up at Harry.

"Morning Mykonos," said Harry, leaning down to stroke his head. Mykonos then rolled onto his back and stretched again. Harry smiled and rubbed Mykonos' tummy. "I guess you're ready for breakfast, mate?"

Harry refilled Mykonos food saucer and got him some fresh water. Mykonos managed a squeaky meow.

"You can meow!" exclaimed Harry.

Harry went to the bathroom to tell Amy that Mykonos was able meow.

"Yipee!" exclaimed Amy sarcastically from behind a shower curtain.

Over the next three days Mykonos spent each night with Harry and Amy. During the days he never ventured far from the terrace that had become his home. Harry's nose ran like a tap at night, but during the day he was fine. Once she had put the lice incident behind her, Amy was relieved to discover that Mykonos was actually a very clean kitten. She took every opportunity to tell Harry how wonderful he was with Mykonos and that he was clearly 'a natural' when it came to parenting.

By day four of the holiday Mykonos appeared to have fully recovered from his infection. Nevertheless, Harry took him back to the vet for a check-up.

Mykonos sat crouched low in his carrying case on the back seat of the car, meowing in a full, high-pitched voice, while Harry drove.

They entered the ramshackle vet's surgery and Lyra greeted them with a broad smile. She escorted Harry into the vet's small consulting room behind the reception area.

"Hello again," said the vet. "Please get him out and put him on the table. How has he been?"

"Good, thanks," replied Harry, lifting Mykonos out of the carrying case.

The vet examined Mykonos, who stood patiently.

"Well, he seems much better," said the vet. "It will take a few more days for the infection to clear completely."

"That's great news," said Harry, stroking Mykonos.

"When do you go home?" asked the vet.

"At the end of the week," said Harry.

"And what will you do with the kitten?" asked the vet.

"I don't know," replied Harry. "I would like to take him home but need to discuss it with my girlfriend."

"She doesn't like cats?" asked the vet.

"I think she's starting to warm to him," replied Harry, "but she would prefer to have a baby."

The vet laughed.

"Is it difficult to take a kitten from here to the UK?" asked Harry.

"For the UK you will need to get him microchipped and he'll need a pet passport before you can move him. He also needs to have a rabies vaccination," explained the vet.

"I see," said Harry.

"And he cannot be moved until three weeks after the rabies vaccination," added the vet.

"Well I can't stay in Mykonos for another three weeks," explained Harry, "but I don't want to abandon him."

"I see," replied the vet. "Listen," he continued, "if you're serious about taking him back to England, Lyra might agree to look after him for three weeks if you promise you'll come back for him."

Harry looked at Mykonos and Mykonos looked up a Harry.

"How much will all of this cost?" asked Harry.

"I can do the microchip, pet passport and the rabies vaccination. It is one hundred and eighty euros," said the vet. "Lyra has a house full of cats and dogs that she has rescued. If you give her some money for his food, I think she will look after him. I can tell that she likes you."

The vet explained the situation to Lyra, and she agreed to keep Mykonos for three weeks provided Harry promised that he would return to collect him. Before he knew what he was doing, Harry had promised Lyra that he would be back.

"You can leave him now," said Lyra. "He is called Mykonos, right?"

"Yes," replied Harry, stroking Mykonos.

"I will take very good care of Mykonos," said Lyra, "and you will come back in three weeks."

"Thank you," said Harry.

"I just need some information about you for his passport," explained Lyra.

"Information about me?" asked Harry.

"Yes," replied Lyra. "Please write down your name here for his passport, and your e-mail," she continued, handing him a pen. "If you let me have your e-mail, I will ask my daughter to send you pictures of him."

"That would be great. Thank you," replied Harry. "How much money do I need to give you for his food?"

"I do not want money for his food," replied Lyra. "Just promise me you will come back for him. Many tourists fall in love with the kittens, but they do not come back for them."

"I'm definitely coming back," insisted Harry, "but I would really like to give you some money for looking after him."

Harry felt embarrassed that Lyra would not accept any money for herself. He could afford to pay her, and he didn't want her to be out of pocket. But he didn't want to insult her either by insisting that he paid. In the end he left enough cash to cover the vet's fees so they could prepare Mykonos for his journey to the UK.

Harry knelt down and looked at Mykonos through the bars of his carrying case. Mykonos' looked at Harry and blinked twice.

"Don't worry," Lyra reassured Harry, "I'll take good care of him."

With tears in his eyes, Harry turned his back on Mykonos and left the surgery.

Back at the hotel, Amy was in the bath shaving her legs as Harry entered the hotel room and shut the door behind him.

"I'm in here," shouted Amy.

He went into the bathroom.

"So what did the vet say? Is he better?" asked Amy.

"Yes, all good," replied Harry. "The vet says he's fit and healthy."

"Cool," said Amy. "So why do you look so glum?"

"I left him at the vet," replied Harry.

"Did they find a family on the island to take him?" asked Amy. By focusing on her legs she was able to conceal her relief. Her conscience was clear. They had managed to offload the kitten rather than abandon him.

"Apparently the island is overrun with cats – the last thing anybody wants is another cat," continued Harry.

"Oh," responded Amy. She was confused. "So what is the vet going to do with him?"

"He's doing a load of stuff so we can…so we can bring him to London," announced Harry.

"What!" exclaimed Amy, sitting bolt upright as she dropped the razor in the bath.

"I'm going to take Mykonos back to London," reiterated Harry. "He has to stay here for three more weeks to be microchipped and have his rabies jab, and to get his passport…"

"Passport!" exclaimed Amy.

"Yes, passport!" proclaimed Harry. "He needs to have a pet passport to travel."

Amy was flabbergasted. "And how will you get him back to London when he has this, er, passport?" she enquired.

"I need to check out my options. Either I arrange for him to be brought to London or I come back myself, I guess. I've got a couple of weeks to figure it out, make the arrangements," explained Harry.

"But what about your allergy?" protested Amy, grasping for reasons not to bring Mykonos to London. "And do we really want the responsibility?" she asked.

"I'll look after him," replied Harry, emphatically. "We can't leave him here for dead."

That night Mykonos went home with Lyra. She lived with her husband and teenage daughter, Christina, in a small whitewashed terraced house off a remote road in the North of the island. The house was also occupied by three other cats and a dog that she had rescued. Her husband put his head in his hands when she came through the front door with a new kitten, but she explained that she was looking after Mykonos for three weeks until a very charming Englishman would come to collect him.

"He had better," replied her husband.

Lyra's husband didn't much like cats, but he cast an eye over Mykonos and nodded approvingly.

"It's a better looking kitten than you usually bring home. He's actually quite handsome, this one," he observed.

Mykonos peered through the side of his carrying case. He was confused. He thought he'd found a place to live in Harry's hotel room and he felt safe with Harry. He knew that he had been sick, and that Harry had made him well again. But just as he had got comfortable in his new home, he'd been torn away and taken to a strange place with strange smells and strange bedfellows. He caught a glimpse of the dog as he was carried upstairs. He'd seen one before on the wasteland and didn't know exactly what a dog was, but he thought it must be an odd looking, dirty sort of cat that had a long tongue which it didn't use to clean itself.

Lyra was concerned that Mykonos wouldn't be safe with the other cats (not to mention the dog) so she decided that he would have to stay in her daughter's room. Christina, her 12-year-old daughter, was delighted to take responsibility for the adorable little kitten and she smothered Mykonos with love. Her room was small and cosy, and Mykonos felt safe there. Christina fed him and spent many an hour entertaining him, dangling shoelaces above his head and flicking a toy mouse across the bedroom floor. But despite all these distractions, Mykonos missed Harry. Each time the bedroom door opened he'd jump to attention and look up, hoping that it would be Harry who walked through the door. But Harry didn't come for him.

Lyra took Mykonos with her to the vet's surgery twice over the next few weeks. Mykonos was less anxious in the car than he used to be. He was compliant when the vet microchipped him and gave him his rabies injections.

And strange though it may sound, his instincts told him that Christina's room was not going to be home for very long and that this strange routine was a precursor to a much bigger journey. He hoped that whatever it was would reunite him with Harry.

Chapter 2
The Journey

Harry and Amy lived in a large and comfortable apartment in Chelsea, an upmarket neighbourhood in central London comprised mostly of Victorian houses that had been converted into apartments. Theirs was on the first floor and had a charming balcony that ran along the entire length of the apartment. Amy had filled the balcony with pots and troughs full of summer flowers, and there was also a table and chairs so they could eat dinner al fresco, looking down at the street below. At the rear of the house was a communal garden that ran the entire length of the street.

Amy was a graphic designer and cared deeply about how things looked. When she had moved in with Harry two years before, she turned her hand to making the apartment more stylish and more comfortable. Over time, picture frames of the happy couple, family and special friends had appeared, perfectly arranged, on top of the piano in the living room (or what Amy called the drawing room). 'Scatter cushions' were purchased, but rather than being scattered, they were perfectly placed on sofas and armchairs. Candles were chosen for their complementary scent of tangerine and jasmine.

Amy's precise placement of cushions and *objets d'art* verged on an obsessive compulsive disorder and fuelled an ongoing feud between Amy and Harry's long time housekeeper, Maria. Maria had been with Harry for almost seven years and had lasted longer than any of his girlfriends who, before Amy, had come and gone. None of Harry's previous girlfriends had moved into his apartment. Amy was the first, and Maria didn't much like it.

However many times Amy showed Maria where to place the picture frames after she had dusted them, or how to plump up the sofa cushions, or where to place the scatter cushions, Maria seemed incapable of executing Amy's instructions. It was unclear whether this was because Maria had no sense of the aesthetic, or whether she was venting her dislike of Amy by deliberately frustrating her.

And so it was with this in mind, that Amy anticipated the arrival of a cat and what that would mean for her perfectly designed interior.

Amy's biggest concern was where to place the litter tray. On their first weekend back in London, Harry had wanted to go to the local pet store to buy provisions for Mykonos. This included a medium sized plastic litter tray. Amy was determined that she wouldn't have to re-balance the apartment's subtle smell of tangerine and jasmine to camouflage the acrid odour of cat pee, so she persuaded Harry to buy a small kennel at the pet store that could be placed out of view in a corner of the terrace off the drawing room. This would house Mykonos' litter tray and be his outside toilet.

Harry went along with the idea to keep Amy happy. He knew little about a cat's toilet habits anyway. Harry therefore arranged for a small cat flap to be fitted in the bottom of the large pane of antique glass in the floor to ceiling French doors behind the piano in the corner of the drawing room. Amy insisted that the cat flap had to be out of sight and hidden by the piano, so it didn't compromise the aesthetic she had so thoughtfully created. This meant that Harry also had to have that corner of the terrace caged off with chicken wire to create a small outside pen for Mykonos that could not be seen from either the drawing room or the street, so the kitten would be able to go outside to use his bathroom.

Because of his busy work schedule, Harry reluctantly concluded that he couldn't possibly return to Greece to collect Mykonos, so he got his Australian assistant, Patricia, to do some research and she found a company in Greece that specialised in animal transportation. Harry spoke to Panos, the owner of Aegean Animal Movers, and Panos re-assured Harry that he'd made the arrangements to transport several cats to the UK. He would liaise with Lyra and personally collect Mykonos. He would take the kitten in the cabin on the short flight up to Athens, where he would put him in the cargo hold of the Aegean Airlines jet for his flight to London. All Harry would have to do is collect Mykonos from the Animal Reception Centre at Heathrow Airport. Panos sent through a quote which came to three thousand Euros in total.

'You could have bought one of those pedigree Bengal blue cats in the UK for all that money!' Wrote Patricia when forwarding Panos' quote to Harry.

"Three thousand Euros!" exclaimed Harry, reading the email. "That's ridiculous."

"I could try to organise it for you, I guess," replied Patricia, "but you'd have to go back to Mykonos to collect Mykonos and take him up to Athens yourself."

"I don't have time to go back to Mykonos," reflected Harry, "so you better get Mr Panos' bank details so we can send him some money. I mean, Christ, we haven't even met him. He could be a total imposter."

"What's the alternative?" asked Patricia.

"I guess we don't have any choice," replied Harry.

"If you're kissing off three thousand Euros," remarked Patricia, "he must be one *special* cat."

The next day Harry got an email from Lyra's daughter, Christina, saying that her mother wanted him to know that Mykonos was well and that Panos had contacted them. By now it was almost three weeks since Harry had returned from his holiday. Christina reported that Mykonos had been microchipped and vaccinated for rabies. He also had a pet passport and would need to be wormed the day before his trip to London. She confirmed that Mykonos could be moved on Saturday, 22 September, and that Panos would be collecting him and taking him to Athens that day.

The flight from Athens would arrive in London at seven in the evening and there were some complicated instructions for Harry on the process for collecting Mykonos at Heathrow Airport. Harry gave the instructions to Patricia and asked her to work out what he had to do.

As luck would have it, Amy would be away at a hen party in Florence on Saturday, 22 September. Harry thought that this was probably a good thing, given her lack of enthusiasm for the new arrival.

It was the evening of Friday, 7 September, and Harry was taking Amy out for dinner to celebrate the third anniversary of their first date. London was enjoying a late summer heatwave and Harry had booked the restaurant that he and Amy had gone to on their very first date. It was a French bistro with a lovely outside terrace and Harry had arranged for them to have the exact same table outside that they had occupied three years earlier.

As they arrived at the restaurant, this romantic gesture was not lost on Amy. She wondered whether an engagement ring might be presented in a champagne flute or at the centre of a Tarte Tatin, but she hadn't picked up any marriage signals from Harry since they had returned from Greece. Indeed, she told her best friend Charlotte that all of Harry's parental instincts seemed to be channelled into 'that bloody cat'. Charlotte agreed that all she could do was flatter Harry as far as his parenting skills with Mykonos were concerned and tell him what a fantastic father he would make. Charlotte offered Amy plenty of reassurance. Cats were famously aloof, after all, and not remotely interested in their owners. In fact they usually cheated on their owners by disappearing for days and hanging out with the neighbours. Dogs, on the other hand, were man's best friend. If Harry had got a puppy, "Now *that* would be a disaster," said Charlotte, but a cat could never be 'man's best friend'.

Charlotte had messaged Amy earlier that day;

"Darling, cat must pave way for baby, otherwise cat destined to be gloves or cushion cover. nice fur? Xxx."

"Tiger print. rather nice, actually." Amy messaged back. *"What if cat is proxy child? He's never going to propose :(xxxxx."*

That evening, Harry and Amy arrived at the restaurant and were shown to their table.

"It's the same table as we had on our first date," said a smiling Amy.

"Absolutely," said Harry. "Champagne?"

"Lovely," she replied.

They clinked their glasses and ordered their food.

"So have you decided when you'll be going back to Mykonos to collect, er, Mykonos?" asked Amy.

"Actually, I'm not going to collect him," replied Harry, tucking into his steak tartar appetiser.

"What do you mean?" asked a confused Amy. *Could he have given up on the idea?* she thought to herself. *Could there have been some kind of miracle?*

"I don't have time to do it. The vet's assistant wants him collected by the twenty-third of September and I fly back from New York on the nineteenth, so I have arranged for some animal transportation firm to do everything, and he arrives in London on Saturday the twenty-second," explained Harry.

Bugger! No miracle then, thought Amy. *No miracle and no bloody ring.*

"Fantastic," said Amy through gritted teeth. She wasn't very convincing. "How much did that cost then?" she asked casually, picking at her endives and Roquefort salad.

"Three thousand Euros, give or take a few Euros," replied Harry, nonchalantly. "Turning out to be a bloody expensive pet."

"That's over two thousand pounds!" exclaimed Amy, choking on a salad leaf.

"Tell me about it," muttered Harry, attempting to shrug it off.

"It's your money, Harry, but this is costing you a fortune," continued Amy, clearing her throat with the best part of a glass of Chablis. "I mean," she spluttered, "you could have got some pedigree Bengal bloody blue for that."

"I could," replied Harry, "but we have a kitten that found us. We saved his life. It's like he was meant to be with us."

Amy felt nauseous. "Twenty-second of September, right?" she asked.

"Yes," replied Harry. "You're in Florence for Charlotte's hen party that weekend."

"Well I don't want to come home from Florence to find the apartment smells of cat pee," pleaded Amy. "Promise me you will get some kind of kennel for the balcony, so we can put the litter tray out there?"

"I'm on it," replied Harry.

"You mean Patricia's on it," quipped Amy.

"We're both on it," confirmed Harry.

"I hope that French door will take a cat flap," continued Amy. "That's nineteenth-century glass, you know."

"Apparently the glazier says it will," he reassured her. "It's all organised. The cat flap will be hidden behind the piano, so it won't compromise the exquisite design of the drawing room."

"Don't tease me, Harry," said Amy in an irritated tone of voice. "It took a lot of time and great taste to get the apartment looking that good. I really don't want to see it go to pot because of some tabby."

"It won't," he replied. "In fact I think his fur will go rather well with the sisal carpet and it will certainly talk to the scatter cushions."

Amy grimaced and then lightened up. "And what will it say to the scatter cushions?"

"I've no idea," chortled Harry.

The next morning Charlotte messaged Amy;

"Darling, how was dinner? Kitten now gloves? Wedding bells ding-a-ling-a-ling? Xxxx."

Amy messaged back;

"No bells, no babies. Crazy for kitten, not me. Him destined for life of antihistamines. Me destined for life of cat hairs and smell of pee. Just googled. Kitten may live twenty years. Aaaagh! Xxxx."

Charlotte replied;

"Maybe kitten will escape, go missing? London dangerous place for cats. Maybe void will be filled with baby?"

Amy messaged back:

"Kitten actually quite cute. Wouldn't wish that on him. Maybe we can find nice home for him in London that isn't ours."

Over the next two weeks Patricia liaised with Panos so that all the arrangements were in place. Harry understood that Panos would email a copy of the paperwork so that Harry could get this stamped at the cargo centre at Heathrow airport and then walk to the animal reception centre where he'd have to present the paperwork so they could hand Mykonos over to him.

In the meantime, Harry organised a cat flap in the French doors, put a kennel on the balcony to house the litter tray, and had the entire balcony caged in with wire so that the kitten had a small outside enclosure.

The neighbours in this rather grand row of Victorian houses were somewhat perplexed. Their first floor balconies were dressed with window boxes, exotic trees and sun loungers for late summer al fresco drinks. Harry's, on the other hand, was enclosed with chicken wire.

Having secured the balcony, Harry was anxious that Mykonos might fall out of an open window, so he had window locks installed throughout the apartment that prevented the sash windows from being lifted more than a few centimetres.

Mykonos had spent the last three weeks largely confined to Christina's bedroom. He'd got used to Christina's odour and the smell of teenage perfume. He'd become accustomed to the sound of teenage music and the chatter of the teenage girls who visited Christina and who doted on him. He was scrupulous in his use of the small litter tray that Christina kept in the corner of her bedroom. Occasionally he was allowed to venture into the corridor. He longed to interact with the other animals that he knew were in the house but, for the most part, this small room was his home. And when he wasn't being entertained by Christina and her friends, he slept, and he stretched, and he yawned, and he thought of Harry.

Mykonos had grown during the three weeks he spent at this foster home. He may have been suffering from malnutrition when Harry found him (or he found Harry), but the kitten food he'd been eating during the last couple of weeks had fuelled his growth. His limbs were longer, and his ears didn't look quite as ridiculously big on his head as they had done when he was eight weeks old. His fur had thickened, and he spent hours each day grooming himself. He looked like a miniature tabby tiger cub. Of course, he didn't know it, but to the human eye, he was a handsome boy. So handsome, in fact, that even Lyra's husband grew quite attached to him and questioned whether they should let him go.

Mykonos was woken early in the morning of Saturday, 22 September, by a loud knocking noise from downstairs. It was barely light outside and Panos was banging his fist on the front door. He had come to collect Mykonos and take him to Athens. The dog started barking and Mykonos could hear voices, so he stretched out on Christina's bed, stood up and then stretched again. He was hungry. Christina climbed out of bed and looked at him. He looked back at her. He could feel her sadness. She picked him up and held him for a moment, and then left the room.

He used his litter tray and drank some water, and then jumped back onto the bed, curling up against Christina's pillow. It was then that the bedroom door opened, and Lyra entered the room. A tall man with a goatee beard stood behind her. He was carrying a small kennel like cage which he rested on the floor. It was Panos. He approached Mykonos.

"I'll get him," said Lyra, tears welling in her eyes. "He's special, this one," she said. "Take care of him, won't you?"

"Of course I will," said Panos.

"He hasn't had anything to eat this morning, has he?" asked Panos.

"No, nothing since last night," replied Lyra. "Just water."

"Good. His stomach should be empty. That way he won't throw up when he's on the plane to London. Sometimes the animals are sick, and they choke," explained Panos.

"I understand," she said, wiping tears from the corner of her eyes.

"Do you have his documentation?" asked Panos.

"Yes," said Lyra, handing him an envelope. "Pet passport and vet's certificate."

Panos looked at the documentation. "Good, everything is in order."

Mykonos crouched on the bed. Lyra leaned forward to pick him up. He struggled. He had a bad feeling about the man with the goatee. Lyra put Mykonos into the kennel and Panos closed the door firmly shut. Mykonos huddled in the back of the kennel. Christina peered in through the bars. She was crying as well. As Panos carried Mykonos downstairs and out of the house, the kitten bleated like a lamb and Lyra and Christina were sobbing. Even Lyra's husband welled up. They were all inconsolable.

Mykonos' bleating continued in the taxi to the airport but as he and Panos waited to board the plane to Athens, he stopped making a noise and sat patiently at the back of the kennel. He was exhausted from his bleating and resigned himself to his situation. The kennel was small, but he could stand up and he could turn around. Panos carried the kennel onto the plane and pushed it under the seat in front of him for the short flight to Athens. At Athens airport, Panos transferred Mykonos into a bigger kennel and gave him some water. Mykonos could move more easily around the bigger kennel, and he felt calmer. They took a bus to the cargo area where Panos produced the paperwork, paid the cargo fees, and deposited the kennel. All this time Mykonos sat patiently. His view of the world was through the caged door of the kennel. He could see lots of people running around, shouting at each other. Eventually somebody lifted his kennel, and it was placed onto the back of a truck. The truck took the kennel to an aircraft where it was loaded into a dark hold.

Mykonos continued to sit quietly at the back of the kennel. He was hungry, he was frightened, and when the door of the hold was finally closed, he was in complete darkness. After a while he could hear a noise the like of which he had never heard before. It was the deafening sound of the engines roaring as the plane sped down the runway. After a while, the noise wasn't as deafening but the kennel started shaking as the aircraft encountered some turbulence. This seemed to last for an eternity, but he sat patiently, crouching low in the back corner of his kennel. Eventually, he needed to go to the toilet, and he fretted that there was no litter tray and that there was nowhere to bury his poo. He scratched the floor of the kennel, but it was hopeless. In the end he made a neat mess in the opposite corner of the kennel and then fell sleep.

A few hours later Mykonos was woken by a bump that shook the kennel. It was followed by the roar of the engines and then silence. A short time afterwards, this dark space was flooded with light.

Mykonos stood up and stretched, touching the roof of the kennel. He could hear people's voices. And then he saw several men who lifted his kennel out of the hold and placed it in a truck which sped across the airport perimeter to the cargo area.

Normally Harry slept well – but he woke up early that Saturday morning. It was all the more surprising, given his antics the night before. Amy had travelled to Florence for the hen party on the Friday afternoon and Harry had taken the opportunity to spend the evening with some old university friends from Oxford. The all-male party had ended up in a somewhat sleazy nightclub in Soho drinking shots with a female Russian dance troop until the early hours of the morning.

Harry's friends teased him mercilessly once they understood that he had rescued a kitten from Mykonos (called Mykonos). The Russian dancers, though, appeared to enjoy the story. Women, Harry concluded, rather liked men who rescued kittens. Women, that is, other than Amy.

However, now Harry lay in bed slightly hung over, wondering whether this was a stupid thing to have done. It would disrupt his life. It would disrupt their lives. It was too much responsibility. And what did he know about cats?

In fact, Harry had learnt quite a lot about cats from the internet since rescuing Mykonos, and he had spent the previous weekend stocking up on kitten food, kitten toys, clumping litter, hairbrushes and antihistamines.

Harry's research had taught him that for the first day in its new home, a kitten should stay in one room to acclimatise itself, and he had decided to keep Mykonos in the kitchen for the first night. This meant that the litter tray would have to be in the kitchen as well. Harry figured out that that it would fit easily and discreetly in a corner behind the kitchen door. It would be out of sight and in nobody's way. In any event, Amy would never know because Mykonos would have been trained to use the outside facility by the time Amy returned home from Florence the following evening. At least that was the plan.

Harry set off for the airport at around five o'clock in the afternoon. He had checked the status of Mykonos' flight and it was scheduled to arrive shortly after five-thirty. Panos had emailed him the airwave bill (the receipt from the cargo company) which recorded an ominous description of the goods to be transported as 'One Live Cat'. As instructed, Harry went to the cargo centre at the airport to get the paperwork endorsed and then he walked for around twenty minutes to the animal reception centre, where all animals that arrived at the airport had to be inspected by a vet before being released to their owners.

Harry sat in the animal reception centre, surrounded by adults and children waiting to be re-united with their family pets. It was a window into a world that was totally foreign to him. A parallel universe in which animals were family members and tearful reunions were accompanied by yelps, barks and meows. Tails wagged and grown men fought back tears of joy. Harry had a realisation. He didn't belong here. He didn't belong in this world. He wasn't like these people. He wasn't cat man.

Meanwhile, Mykonos was upstairs being examined by a vet. He'd been allowed to leave his kennel for a stretch, and he had been given some food and water. A nurse cleaned away some dried poo that was matted in his tail and generally freshened him up by giving him a brush. His kennel was cleaned, and he was put back in it. Mykonos was entirely cooperative throughout the process. He was apprehensive, but he instinctively understood that these people were taking care of him.

Downstairs, the door behind a counter from which the animals were delivered opened and a nurse appeared with Mykonos in his kennel.

"Parkman?" said the nurse loudly.

Harry stood up. "That's me."

He walked over to the counter and peered into the kennel. Mykonos stared back at Harry through the bars and meowed. Harry put a finger through the bars and Mykonos rubbed his head against it.

"He's very well," she told Harry. "Sometimes there's a problem with the paperwork from Greece, but everything's fine with him. Just sign here," she said, pushing a form across the counter.

"Great. Thanks," replied Harry, and with that he signed the form, picked up the kennel and wandered out to the car park, where he had a mini cab waiting. He climbed into the back of the cab, and they set off home.

This was Harry's first opportunity to re-acquaint himself with the refugee kitten whose life he had saved. During the four weeks that had elapsed since he had last seen Mykonos, Harry had reflected on his actions and concluded that they defied logic. But reunited in the back of the cab, Harry's heart melted in an instant, and he was reminded of why he had become so attached to Mykonos.

Mykonos had grown during the past four weeks. His limbs were longer, and his ears appeared less comically big compared to the size of his head and body. He was undoubtedly a handsome boy and a prince amongst kittens. His fur had got longer, especially on his tail, which was starting to resemble a fox's brush. The markings on his coat were even more tiger like. His eyes were a piercing green. His only imperfection was a small, raised clump of white fur just above his nose. The vet in Mykonos thought that it was scar tissue. Harry thought it was the perfect imperfection.

For his part, Mykonos knew that he was a long way from the place where he was born. It was almost dark outside, and flashes of light shot across the back of the cab from streetlamps and other cars on the motorway. Mykonos was disorientated but his overwhelming emotion was joy. His instincts had told him all along that Christina's room was a temporary shelter, and despite the time that had elapsed, he had not stopped hoping upon hope that Harry would come back for him. Forty-five minutes later they were home in Chelsea.

Harry unlocked the front door and turned the hall lights on. He took Mykonos into the kitchen and placed the kennel on the floor. Once the double doors into the kitchen were closed, he released Mykonos from the kennel. Harry picked Mykonos up and held him for a while. Mykonos re-acquainted himself with the smell of Harry that he loved so much. Eventually Harry put Mykonos down and the kitten started to explore the kitchen whilst Harry filled two chrome bowls with water and kibbles. To Harry's surprise, Mykonos found the litter tray in the corner of the kitchen and did his business, neatly burying it.

How did he know how to do that? thought Harry. Lyra must have trained him well.

Whilst Mykonos ate, Harry took photos of Mykonos and emailed one to Christina, so she could show Lyra that the kitten had got to London safely. (Lyra did not have an e-mail address of her own.) Harry also sent a photo of Mykonos to Amy.

Christina replied immediately, saying that they loved the photo and that her mother said, *"Mykonos is the best."* Amy, on the other hand, did not reply.

Mykonos sniffed his way across every surface in the kitchen, jumping onto a chair and then onto the table, and from there onto the granite work surface that ran the entire length of one side of the room. Mykonos was a small kitten but had the dexterity of a monkey. It didn't take him long to work out that no other animal had been living in this space. His sensitive nose didn't pick up the slightest residue of animal scent, but there were plenty of smells he didn't recognise; the acrid odour of floor cleaner and the sweet jasmine and orange of the Jo Malone candles. The kibbles had tasted good. After eating a little more and drinking some water, he made his way back up onto the work surface, where he found the remote control for the small television in the kitchen. He started to push the remote control to the edge of the work surface, so that it fell onto the floor. Harry quickly moved kitchen knives, cakes and glass ware from where Mykonos could reach them. *Amy's going to freak out,* he thought.

Harry was going to follow the tips he'd gleaned from various websites for introducing a kitten to its new home by confining Mykonos to the kitchen for at least twenty-four hours. Mykonos, however, had explored every corner of the kitchen within a few minutes, so Harry decided to open the kitchen doors into the hall and to give him the full run of the apartment. The moment the doors were open, Mykonos moved cautiously out of the kitchen and into the hall, looking back at Harry as if to say, *"Are you coming with me?"*

A human refugee might have experienced severe psychological trauma from being moved from pillar to post. Mykonos, however, had become accustomed to being thrown into new, strange environments, and he was more adaptable. Deep down, though, he longed to have a safe place where he could stay and make his home. He hoped that this would be it and started to explore.

From where Mykonos was sitting outside the kitchen, he could see down a long hallway towards doors that opened onto other rooms. Across the hall, directly opposite the kitchen, he could see a huge room. Oversized double doors were pushed back to create a grand entrance. The drawing room beckoned like an adventure playground. Mykonos looked up. The ceiling was high. Much higher than in the hotel room or Christina's bedroom.

He walked tentatively across the hall into the drawing room. He surveyed the room. The furniture looked enormous. There were oversized sofas and armchairs and armoires stacked with artefacts.

A baby grand piano sat in the bay window and there was a strange hole in one of the walls that had a dark tunnel above it (the fireplace). After four weeks in Christina's tiny bedroom and almost the entire day trapped in a small kennel, he threw himself into this space. At first he ran around the room with Harry in close pursuit, but then Mykonos started to work his way around the room more meticulously, rubbing his scent against every surface, mapping out and memorising its layout. That mental map included the position of every piece of furniture and every ornament and artefact in it. Soon he would be able to sprint around the apartment whilst not colliding with any of its contents.

As Mykonos leapt from sofa to table to piano, Harry thought again about how Amy would be stressing out right now. But Mykonos was respectful of the picture frames and candles that Amy had placed very precisely on every surface. He weaved his way around the dozens of photos of Harry and Amy that adorned the piano without touching one of them. And he didn't attempt to push anything to the floor. Harry breathed a sigh of relief. In the coming years, Mykonos would not displace a single previous ornament, however loose change and the TV remote control would always end up on the floor. Like Amy, Mykonos liked clear work surfaces.

It had been a long day for both of them. Harry had made himself dinner and was ready for bed. Every now and then Mykonos would return to the kitchen to make sure Harry was still there, before resuming the exploration of his new home. Occasionally Harry would check up on him, lifting him into the air and then holding him close to his chest for a while. The bonding was mutual.

By now Mykonos was a very tired kitten. He was ready to sleep, but he didn't know where to sleep. There was so much space. So he followed Harry around the bedroom and the bathroom until Harry finally climbed into bed. Mykonos pulled himself onto the bed and curled up between the pillows, as he had done back in the hotel room. There were only a few centimetres between Mykonos and Harry's face, and Harry could feel his nose itching and starting to run. He despaired at the thought of a night's precious sleep being disrupted by his cat allergy, but he didn't have the heart to put Mykonos outside the bedroom. He resolved to keep Mykonos off his pillow and grabbed a handful of tissues from his bedside cabinet drawers. He took one last photo of Mykonos sleeping between the pillows but thought twice about sending it to Amy. He had messaged her a couple more pictures earlier in the evening – Mykonos on the piano, Mykonos on the sofa – and Amy's response verged on the hysterical. *'How did he get onto the piano?'* and *'you need to train him keep off the furniture'*. She probably wouldn't appreciate the way Mykonos had sharpened his claws on the corner of the George Smith sofa, thought Harry. And she certainly wouldn't appreciate his sleeping on the bed.

Harry lay on his side and looked at Mykonos. The kitten appeared to be fast asleep, but his ears still moved occasionally from side to side. Harry took one more photo before reaching for a tissue, blew his nose quietly, and then turned the bedside lamp off.

Chapter 3
The Patter of Tiny Feet

Harry worked hard during the week, and at the weekends he and Amy would lie in bed until late. Once up, they would don their jogging pants and walk to a local brasserie for breakfast or brunch. It was therefore a rude awakening at five in the morning when Harry felt small, sharp claws scratching at his feet. He leapt out of bed.

Mykonos had slept like a baby until four in the morning. Once he had woken up, he climbed off the bed without disturbing Harry and explored the apartment in the dark. By now he had mapped out all the rooms and his scent was everywhere. He loved that there was so much space and so many places to hide.

Christina had always got up as the sun was rising and she would begin her day by feeding him and playing with him. Mykonos was therefore impatient for the sun to rise in London and by five o'clock he had decided that it was time for Harry to get up, even though it was still dark. Harry's feet were outside his duvet and an easy target.

Having leapt out of bed when he felt the sharp nails running along the soles of his feet, a bleary eyed Harry wandered to the kitchen. His inner monologue said, "*What was I thinking?*" But his heart trumped his head every time he looked down at the little kitten, looking up at him. Mykonos was the cutest thing he had ever seen at five in the morning.

Harry decided to try wet food for Mykonos. He had bought sachets of tuna and salmon blended especially for kittens after researching kitten food on the internet. He'd also read that wet food wasn't great for the gums, and that dry food helped to promote healthy gums and teeth. So he'd decided to give Mykonos a mixed diet of wet and dry food.

Wet food was a revelation for Mykonos. It was like living off crackers for several months and then digging into a moist and juicy stew. Mykonos ran his nose across the food momentarily to verify the contents, tested a small amount on his tongue, and then tucked in with the voracity of a person who had been living on crackers. He ate the entire contents of the bowl, breaking for a minute to visit the litter tray, and then resuming his meal immediately thereafter. Harry looked on, fascinated.

After eating, Mykonos went into the sitting room and jumped onto an armchair. There he sat, cleaning his fur meticulously. Harry decided to go back to bed and managed to sleep for another hour before Mykonos joined him. Shortly before nine o'clock, Mykonos woke Harry again by scratching his feet. Accepting defeat, Harry got up, showered and dressed. He wanted to go out to get some breakfast, but he was worried about leaving Mykonos in the apartment on his own for the first time. He scoured the apartment to look for things that might get a kitten into trouble. Kitchen knives were now in drawers, razor blades out of reach, toilet seats down so he couldn't drown, washing machine, tumble dryer and dishwasher doors firmly closed, so he couldn't inadvertently become trapped in one of them.

Harry had read something online about somebody who had accidentally microwaved their cat, and this wasn't going to happen to his boy. Like a first-time parent, he was anxious about all the things that could possibly go wrong. Could Mykonos get his claw into a socket and electrocute himself? *Don't be ridiculous. Get a grip,* he thought. As Harry put on his trainers, Mykonos pulled and chewed the laces. He wanted to play, but Harry needed some space.

Mykonos sat in the hall staring up at Harry as he opened the front door. It was a stare that Harry would get to know well. It said *please don't go.* Although he didn't entirely grasp the concept of time, Mykonos knew that the last time Harry left him, it was a long time before they were re-united. Eventually, though, a rhythm would be established which meant that Mykonos got used to Harry's comings and goings, and it would be altogether less distressing to see Harry go out of the front door. But for now, Mykonos curled up like a mini-croissant on an armchair and went to sleep, home alone and not knowing how long he would have to wait before Harry returned. It was Harry's favourite armchair and it smelt of him. This was of some comfort to the kitten.

Harry walked down the Kings Road and grabbed a coffee and a pastry for breakfast. On a typical Sunday he and Amy would have a late brunch, do some shopping and maybe go for a run, or visit the gym. But it didn't feel right to leave

Mykonos at home alone. Harry felt anxious and he felt guilty. So he skipped the gym and walked back to the house.

As Harry turned into his street, he could hear somebody's house alarm ringing loudly. As he got closer to home, he realised that the ringing was coming from his building, and as he raced up the stairs to his apartment he realised that he had set the alarm without thinking about how a small kitten moving around the apartment would be picked up by the motion sensors. He opened the front door to the apartment, deactivated the alarm, and closed the door behind him. He looked for Mykonos. The kitten wasn't in the kitchen or either bedroom. He wasn't under any of the furniture in the sitting room. He wasn't up the chimney. He couldn't be in any of the bathrooms because Harry had made a point of closing the bathroom doors before he went out. He'd got it into his head that maybe Mykonos would climb onto a sink and turn a tap on.

"Mykonos," Harry cried, moving from room to room. And then, as he stood in the sitting room, he saw a face appear from under the lid of the grand piano. The lid was down but Mykonos had managed to squeeze inside. The kitten had never heard anything as deafening as the sound of the alarm. Petrified, he had looked for a place to hide. A small, enclosed space that might protect him from whatever was about to happen.

Harry scooped Mykonos up in his arms and held him close. Mykonos looked up at Harry and purred enthusiastically. He felt safe.

Harry spent the rest of the day playing with Mykonos. Harry learnt that, for Mykonos, everything was a toy, or had the potential to be a toy: the charger cable for his mobile phone, shoelaces. In fact anything that resembled string.

Mykonos passed what was later coined 'the string test' and would dance on furniture and tables if there was something that resembled string dangling above him.

Harry had bought various furry and feathery toys at the local pet store the weekend before Mykonos arrived and they played with these for much of the afternoon. Mykonos pounced like a ninja, legs splayed, before he landed on his target. He practised his hunting skills as Harry flicked and kicked furry and feathery toys around the bedroom.

Harry also managed to gently nudge Mykonos through the cat flap and into the cage that had been built on the terrace. He coaxed him back in by holding the flap open and offering him treats. Mykonos was too small to propel himself through the flap in a single leap, so he pulled himself up through the flap and soon got the hang of it.

Mykonos would regularly go and sit on the terrace, but he didn't much care for his outside cage. It was a window to a world that he couldn't explore and didn't understand. What he had learnt in his short life was that every time he started to feel like he was in a safe environment, he was torn away from it. It would be several weeks before he got used to the idea that this place would be a permanent safe haven.

Harry sensed Mykonos' anxiety and took every opportunity to hold him and play with him. Harry's feet had discovered that Mykonos had nails as sharp as needles. Now it was the turn of his hands and forearms. When a paw struck out to grab a cable or a furry mouse, a claw would leave tiny scratches on any flesh that happened to get in its way.

The sun was setting that Sunday evening and Mykonos was sitting on the piano looking through the French doors at the street below when the sound of a key in the front door could be heard. He turned around.

"I'm home!" shouted Amy.

She stepped into the hallway and looked across the drawing room. There was Mykonos sitting on the piano, looking at her. Harry came out of the bedroom and walked down the hallway towards her.

"Hi! How was it?" he asked, embracing Amy and giving her a kiss on the lips.

Amy was distracted.

"He's on the piano," she said, waving her finger towards Mykonos.

"Yes, I know," replied Harry.

"You allowed him on the piano?" asked an incredulous Amy.

Mykonos stood up and stretched, and then weaved his way through the picture frames, without touching a single one of them, before jumping onto the piano stool and then down onto the floor.

"You see, he's very careful," said Harry. "Very…precise."

Amy stared, jaw agape, as Mykonos walked across the sitting room floor towards her.

"So how was it?" enquired Harry again.

Amy wasn't going to be diverted. She walked into the kitchen and found Mykonos' litter tray behind the kitchen door.

"It was great, thanks, yeah great," she replied. "Why is his tray thing inside?"

"Oh, we can't really expect him to go outside so soon," explained Harry. "I mean, he hasn't even been here for twenty-four hours."

"What's that got to do with anything?" Amy retorted.

"Well, I bet you couldn't smell anything when you came into the apartment, could you?" said Harry, leaning down and picking Mykonos up. He held Mykonos at arms' length and moved towards Amy. "Stroke him. He's super cute."

Mykonos looked up at Amy. She stroked him gingerly. "He won't scratch me, will he?" asked Amy.

"Just small scratches. My hands are covered in them from playing with him. Look!" said Harry, putting Mykonos back on the floor and holding up his hands.

"Great!" said Amy in a sarcastic tone. "I'm going to unpack and jump in the shower."

"I want to hear about your weekend," said Harry, following her into the bedroom.

"No you don't," replied Amy, "you want to play with Mykonos. Play with Mykonos whilst I shower. Do we have anything to eat in the fridge? I'm starving."

That night Harry locked Mykonos out of the bedroom so that he and Amy could be on their own. The hen weekend in Amsterdam had taken its toll on Amy and she soon fell into a deep sleep, snoring loudly as usual. Mykonos sat outside the bedroom door. He couldn't understand why he had been excluded. He started to meow. Long, sad, high pitched meows.

Harry lay in bed awake, listening to Mykonos bleating outside the bedroom door like a lamb. He thought of all his married friends whose dinner party conversation revolved around why you mustn't allow your infant into the bed and the virtues of self-soothing. Eventually, Harry got out of bed and opened the door. Mykonos slipped into the room and pulled himself up onto the bed. He quickly learnt that if he cried for long enough outside the bedroom door, he would be allowed in.

Mykonos curled up between Harry and Amy, nestled in Harry's armpit. Mykonos loved this feeling. His stomach was full. He was warm. There was Harry's familiar smell. And he felt safe. And so Mykonos and Harry drifted off to sleep, despite the pig-like noises of Amy's snoring. Mykonos felt secure enough to fall into a deep sleep. His ears were completely still – not a twitch –

denoting a state of deep unconsciousness. He dreamed of mice and birds and sunshine and Harry.

The next morning Amy got up before Harry and took a photo of him and Mykonos curled up together in bed. She messaged it to Charlotte on her way to work – Charlotte replied,

'Shocker. Cat meant to be aloof and independent. Not man's best friend'.

Chapter 4
The Gilded Cage

Maria had cleaned Harry's apartment, made his bed and ironed his shirts for many years before Amy came on the scene. She was a beautiful woman in her mid-forties whose face showed the stress inflicted by an abusive husband and two ungrateful teenage children. Her roots were grey, and her fingernails cracked from scrubbing other people's homes, but she had a wonderful smile, melancholic eyes, high cheek bones, and a slim, firm body.

At first Maria had resented Amy's candles and scatter cushions, and general remodelling of the home, but she was generous enough to acknowledge that the apartment did look better, and that Amy had a certain style. She was protective of Harry and didn't much like the way in which Amy tried to organise his life, but she was generous enough to recognise that Harry did seem happier since Amy had moved in. They were by far the tidiest people that Maria worked for, and this did make her life easier.

Maria liked cats. She had wanted to get a cat when her children were younger, but her husband had forbidden it. And now that her children were older, she wouldn't have been able to trust them with a kitten. Her initial reaction when she received the text from Harry saying that the kitten had arrived was that this was going to mean a lot more work for her; endless hoovering of cat hair and emptying of litter trays. But when she opened the front door of the apartment to be greeted by Mykonos' little face beaming up at her, it was love at first sight. She lent down and picked him up. Mykonos didn't resist. Harry and Amy had gone to work a few hours earlier and Mykonos was very pleased to have some company. He had slept a little and briefly ventured through the cat flap onto the terrace, but it was raining outside and so he quickly came back in.

Maria played with Mykonos and gave him some treats. She then started cleaning whilst he followed her around the apartment. At first, when Maria vacuumed, Mykonos would run and hide. Within a week or two though, he had got used to the sound. Over time, the vacuum cleaner and the floor mop became his great adversaries, and he would stalk them, sometimes pouncing, making one of his ninja moves, before retreating. Maria's three mornings a week were packed with treats and fun. They were highlights of the week for Mykonos. He raced to the front door when he heard the sound of her feet in the hall outside and the turning of the key in the lock. Conversely, his little heart sank when she put her coat on and left the apartment, closing the door behind her.

He would go onto the terrace and watch Maria disappear down the street and out of view, at which point he'd climb through the cat flap and back into the drawing room. He was on his own for much of the day and he was lonely. As the weeks passed though, and the daily routine was established, he became less distressed by the departure of Harry, Amy or Maria, and drew comfort from the fact that they all re-appeared in what felt like a short space of time – although he was never quite sure how much time had elapsed.

The next weekend Harry and Amy were going to stay with some friends out of town and Harry asked Maria if she would pop into the apartment on the Saturday and Sunday to feed Mykonos and to play with him. Maria's husband needed the car that they shared, so he gave her a ride and came into the apartment to view the kitten. Mykonos was waiting attentively as she opened the front door. He looked up at her and then slid back on his heels when he saw the strange man behind her. Even Maria's callous husband managed the semblance of a smile when he looked down and his eyes met Mykonos'.

"He's a tiger," grunted Maria's husband.

"I told you," she replied.

Mykonos appreciated Maria. She had great instincts when it came to where he liked to be stroked and where he liked to be scratched. Over the coming months she also learnt how he liked to have his back massaged along his spine. There were occasions when Amy arrived home unexpectedly during the day to find Maria crouched over Mykonos, with Mykonos stretched out on his tummy and Maria working her fingers along his back.

"He likes me to massage him," explained Maria. She knew from Amy's disapproving glare that Amy would prefer her to focus on the cleaning, but Maria adored Mykonos and Mykonos had grown to adore Maria. For three days a week she was the only person that he saw during the day – and for only three mornings at that. He had boundless energy and nowhere to channel it for most of the time.

He would hunt his toys – in particular the leather mouse and the cotton fish – but for much of the time he was bored, and his boredom turned into loneliness. He would sit in the caged area on the terrace from time to time and stare at the cars and occasional pedestrian below. He would quiver at the sight of the blackbirds in the beech trees that lined the street. He longed to chase those blackbirds, but he was a prisoner in a gilded cage.

The highlight of Mykonos' day, of course, was when he heard the sound of Harry's feet in the hall outside and the front door opened. When Amy came home, he got a pat on the head, but when Harry came home, he would scoop Mykonos up into his arms and walk around the apartment holding him close to his chest. Once released onto the bedroom floor, Harry would then flick the leather mouse or the cotton fish up high into the air off the side of the bed and Mykonos would launch himself in the air to grab them. No mouse or fish could get past Mykonos, no matter how fast it travelled through the air and no matter how high its trajectory. And then he would return the toy back to Harry as if to say, '*Do it again, do it again.*' And Harry did.

"Hey, Amy!" cried Harry from the bedroom. "Watch this!"

Amy came into the bedroom to find Mykonos crouched on the floor at the end of the bed, eyes fixed on Harry, who was crouched on the bed and about to launch the leather mouse.

"Are you ready?" said Harry, looking at Mykonos.

Mykonos shuffled his hind quarters as Harry flicked the mouse, propelling it through the air. Mykonos launched himself vertically, jumping out of his skin, and intercepted the leather mouse, pulling it to the ground. He then returned it to Harry at the side of the bed.

"Isn't that cool?" said Harry. "Chelsea should put him in goal. Nothing gets past him. And he brings the toys back to me. He fetches. Like a dog."

"Very impressive," replied Amy. "You should film him and put it on You Tube. It's full of stuff like that."

"Good idea. Mykonos, you're going to be famous, mate," said Harry.

"Dinner's ready," shouted Amy from the kitchen.

"Coming," replied Harry. He headed for the kitchen with Mykonos following close behind.

Dinner was already plated up on the kitchen table. It was a kind of chicken stroganoff from a low carb cookery book that Charlotte had rather pointedly gifted to Amy at the start of the year. Harry looked at the plate. There was no rice or potatoes or pasta. Amy had put on a few kilos after she moved in with Harry, and Charlotte felt it was time to share her secret to staying as thin as a whip. Harry was delighted to have his dinner prepared for him, but he missed the carbs and found himself waking up hungry at three o'clock in the morning.

Mykonos jumped onto the kitchen table and started to sniff around the plates. "Off!" screamed Amy.

"Maybe it would be easier if we just put his bowl on the table," suggested Harry. "That way he eats with us and doesn't bother us."

"You're kidding, aren't you?" asked Amy.

"Actually, I tried it yesterday and it worked. Didn't bother me at all," replied Harry as he placed Mykonos food bowl on the table. Mykonos crouched in front of his bowl and started to eat his food.

"You are mad, you know," said Amy. "We'll never get him off the table now. It's bad parenting. I can't believe I said that, because we're not parents, but you know what I mean."

"I'm just trying to make life easier," replied Harry. "We're never going to keep him off the table, so we might as well get used to it."

"What's it going to be like when he's bigger? He's growing like there's no tomorrow and Maria thinks he's going to be a big cat. Just look at the size of his paws!" exclaimed Amy.

"Well I hope he's a big cat. I don't like those skinny, slinky cats," retorted Harry.

"You didn't use to like cats, full stop," continued Amy.

"I know, but have you noticed that my allergy seems to be wearing off? It's weird. I must ask Doctor Marcus. Some nights my nose doesn't run at all." Doctor Marcus was one of Harry's best friends from Oxford – and a respiratory consultant at the Chelsea and Westminster Hospital.

"Yes, I did notice that you're not snivelling quite as much in bed," said Amy. "Thank heaven for small mercies."

"Delicious chicken by the way," said Harry, changing the subject.

"Thanks," replied Amy.

"Do we have any bread?" asked Harry.

"No, we don't," replied Amy. "Are you trying to ruin my diet?"

"No, of course not!" protested Harry.

"I was thinking of getting rid of that horrendous cage on the terrace," continued Harry.

"Hurrah!" she cried.

"Yes, well it does look awful," he conceded, "and Mykonos barely goes out there, and we don't need it for his toilet, now we know his litter tray doesn't smell."

"It does smell sometimes, Harry," interjected Amy.

"Occasionally, when he does a real stinker, but most of the time you wouldn't notice. Anyway, I'm going to get that cage removed next week and maybe let him go onto the terrace," continued Harry.

"But aren't you worried that he might disappear?" asked Amy, feigning concern for the possible consequences of releasing Mykonos onto the terrace. Charlotte had told her that cats in the city live for under three years if they're allowed to roam the streets. On the one hand, Amy felt guilty for contemplating the curtailment of Mykonos' life by giving him access to the street, but on the other hand even three years sounded like an awfully long time to her.

"Well, you'd like that wouldn't you?" protested Harry.

"Of course not," Amy replied defensively. "Actually, I'm getting quite fond of him."

"I've had a look outside. He can walk along the terraces, but he can't get from the terraces onto the street. I'm shit scared that the little fella might fall off the terrace," continued Harry, "but I think he's old enough to try it. I'd take him downstairs and put him in the garden, but he needs to have some injections before we can put him out there."

"Aren't you worried that he'll get out of the garden?" asked Amy, feigning further concern.

"No, the wall runs the length of the back. I can't see how he'd get out, other than through the door the gardeners use, but that's locked all the time," explained Harry. "Anyway, I can't try him in the garden until he's older."

"I see," said Amy.

Mykonos stepped down from the kitchen table onto Harry's lap, where he curled up. Harry looked down at Mykonos.

"I suppose we'll have to have him neutered in a month or two as well," said Harry.

"Too bloody right!" concurred Amy. "Charlotte said that they had to get rid of their cat because he was squirting all over the furniture. Terrible smell, apparently."

"Well they should have had him neutered," suggested Harry.

"They did," insisted Amy, "and it still squirted. It was an absolute nightmare."

"That's ridiculous. They couldn't have had him neutered. Anyway, I'm not entirely happy about it," said Harry, gently stroking Mykonos on the top of his head and along his back. "Such a horrible thing to do to him. I hope he doesn't end up like some ladyboy." Harry was not transphobic. He was instinctively liberal and had a wide spectrum of friends. It was simply him projecting how he would feel about the procedure and wondering whether it might in some way change Mykonos' character.

"Well better that than some hormonal Tom squirting all over our furniture," insisted Amy. "Bad enough that the corner of the beige armchair in our bedroom is starting to fray from where he's been scratching it. We don't really want it stinking of piss as well…"

"Okay, okay, I get it," said Harry. "He'll be neutered, and I've ordered a scratching post online to give him something else to sharpen his claws on."

"That George Smith armchair wasn't cheap, you know!" interjected Amy.

"I know," Harry responded. "I paid for it!"

Chapter 5
The Cage Is Opened

That weekend Harry had the cage he'd built on the terrace removed. He also decided to seal the cat flap, at least for the time being.

However, after much fretting, Harry made the decision on the Sunday afternoon to open one of the floor to ceiling French doors onto the terrace. Having done so, he stepped outside onto the terrace and beckoned Mykonos to follow him. Mykonos watched attentively. At first he wasn't sure what to make of the open door. He had *so* wanted to step out of his gilded cage, but now the opportunity presented itself, he was unsure. And so he took a few tentative steps towards the open door and peered out.

Now, it is probably the case that most cats would have sprinted out of the apartment and onto the terrace the moment the door was just a few inches ajar. The smallest opening in the French doors would have been an invitation to scarper. But Mykonos wasn't like most cats. Yes, he was curious and keen to explore, but his curiosity was tempered by an anxiety born out of his fight for life as a kitten and having been moved from pillar to post since then. He'd shown great courage to escape the wasteland. But, ironically, his life to date had actually made him the proverbial scaredy cat.

And so Mykonos poked his head out of the door and stepped gingerly onto the terrace, moving tentatively towards the edge of the balcony. An equally anxious Harry looked on. Mykonos poked his head through the stone balustrade and looked down at the street below. He was old enough to gauge that this was a significant drop and not a distance that he could jump. Directly below him was the well of the basement and slightly forward were pointed metal railings that would surely skewer any falling object. On the other side of the railings was the sidewalk, where Mykonos could see a woman and child strolling down the street. A small dog followed them on a lead. Mykonos was not sure what to make of this strange looking creature. If it was a cat, it was an odd looking one. Mykonos didn't know quite what this was, but he suspected that it wasn't actually (a cat) like him at all. He looked up at Harry, who was looking down at him, and pulled back from the edge of the balustrade, much to Harry's relief. However Mykonos then jumped up onto the ledge that ran along the top of the balustrade, with the sheer drop beneath it.

Harry held his breath. He wanted to grab Mykonos from the ledge. It felt as though Mykonos was walking on a tightrope, with a seven metre drop on one side to the floor of the basement.

For Mykonos, however, this was no tightrope. It was a promenade that ran the length of the street and he had absolutely no concerns that he might fall. Harry kept telling himself, *he's a cat, he knows what he's doing*, and so Harry followed Mykonos as he walked along the ledge that continued from their balcony onto the balcony in front of the neighbour's drawing room. Mykonos then jumped down onto the floor of the neighbour's balcony and started to sniff around their terrace.

Harry climbed onto the neighbour's terrace, peered through their French windows to make sure that nobody was in, and then followed Mykonos, who had by now ventured onto the balcony of the next building in the street and was sniffing around some plant troughs.

It was easy for Mykonos to traverse the balconies, moving from one building to the next. Harry, however, had to clamber over the balustrade that divided one house from the next, trying to keep up with Mykonos. Two houses down the terrace, a woman appeared at the French windows and confronted Mykonos, gesturing wildly with her arms. She then opened the French doors, as Harry climbed onto her terrace.

"Shoo! Shoo!" she cried, lunging at the kitten. Mykonos cowered for a second and then sprinted along the ledge until he reached the safety of his own apartment. Harry was left standing on this women's balcony. "Get off my property," she shouted, "or I will call the police!"

Even though Harry and this particular lady had both been living on this street for thirteen years, he had never spoken to her. There hadn't even been an exchange of pleasantries in all that time. But Harry knew who she was by reputation.

The woman was commonly referred to as 'Agro Attwood'. Agnes Attwood had previously been Lady Baring by dint of her first marriage to Sir Ian Baring.

Much to her chagrin she had to revert to being plain Mrs Attwood following her marriage to Charles (Charlie) Attwood. Charlie had been a Lloyd's underwriter, with hopes back in the day of being Knighted for his charitable works. However, an underwriting scheme that Charlie had fronted turned sour. It transpired that he had recruited investors off the back of his claimed association with some minor members of the British royal family and the inference that they were in his syndicate. When the syndicate failed, it emerged that Charlie's association with these minor royals was much exaggerated, and that the inference that they were members of his syndicate was, in fact, a lie. Charlie's hopes of getting a knighthood were dashed, and so, therefore, were Agnes' hopes of re-possessing her title.

Neighbours speculated as to Agnes' age. She was as thin as a whip, with long blond hair that covered her shoulders. She dressed in flowing, lacy whites and creams, no matter what the season. And she never left home without donning a wide brimmed hat. Harry and Amy had joked that she always looked as though she was off to Henley Regatta. When Agnes' head turned, however, she had a face pulled taught by a lifetime of facelifts, caked in white powder to give her a smooth and deathly pale complexion. Agnes lips were thin – almost non-existent – and Amy's friend Charlotte, who knew Agnes' niece – said that Agnes had had *'a collagen catastrophe, darling',* many years earlier when she had attempted to plump up her lips but suffered a nasty reaction. As a result, according to Charlotte, *"She can't touch her lips anymore."* Amy had observed that Agnes had *'an old lady's neck and hands',* and guessed that she was probably in her seventies.

It was Charlotte who had originally told Amy that Agnes' nickname was 'Agro Attwood' because of her aggressive temperament and social climbing. Charlotte had explained that Agnes was a dreadful snob who behaved as if she lived in a stately home, rather than a maisonette in Chelsea.

And so Harry had to explain to Agro quite what he was doing on her terrace.

"Hello!" said Harry. "Apologies for bothering you, I was trying to retrieve my kitten."

"Well you and your kitten are trespassing on my property," replied Agnes. "You're lucky that I haven't called the police."

"Actually, the kitten has bolted back to my apartment," said Harry, pointing towards his building. "I live two houses down. I have the first floor lateral across twenty-seven and twenty-nine. I'm terribly sorry for the intrusion. It's the first time that I've let him out."

"Do you rent your apartment?" asked Agnes. She was riled. He was living in *the* first floor lateral conversion.

"No," replied Harry, somewhat confused. "I own it. I've been living there for thirteen years."

"Well just make sure I don't see you or your cat on my property again," Agnes continued, "or there will be trouble." And with that, she turned around and stepped back through the French doors into her apartment.

Harry climbed across the series of dividing balustrades to get back to his apartment and found Mykonos sniffing around the terrace outside the main bedroom. He picked Mykonos up and took him inside, closing the French doors behind him.

Mykonos had stepped out of his gilded cage and although he hadn't gone very far, he'd got a taste for this strange, elevated outside world that expanded his territory. Over the next couple of weeks, Harry let Mykonos onto the terrace on a daily basis and would watch him walk along the ledge in front of the neighbours' buildings and sniff around their terraces.

It was easy to get him back into the apartment. The shaking of a set of keys or a bag of treats and he always appeared within seconds. And as the weather turned cold at the end of November, Harry would start to leave the cat flap open when he and Amy went to work. It was nerve-wracking at first but when he or Amy came home in the evening, Mykonos' head would be poking through the balustrade, looking down at the street, waiting for them. And as they entered the building and walked up one flight of stairs to the first floor, he would jump through the cat flap and race to the front door, so that when the door opened, he would be sitting there, looking up at them. Even Amy felt some anxiety if she came home before Harry and couldn't see Mykonos on the terrace. Would this be the day that he had vanished? She would breathe a sigh of relief when she opened the front door and found Mykonos sitting there attentively. She'd then chastise herself for having worried about him. *He's only a cat, Amy. He's a cat.*

Chapter 6
The Snip

By late November Mykonos was ready to be neutered – 'the snip' – as Amy would call it.

Charlotte's mythical tale of the pedigree Bengal that started to mark out its territory by peeing all over the house had been preying on Amy's mind for the last couple of months and she was keen for Mykonos to have 'the snip' as soon as possible.

Harry had called the local vet's practice and had been told that they recommended neutering at five months old, so Mykonos had been booked in for the third week of November. Harry told Patricia that he would arrive at the office late that morning and that he would need to leave at four so he could collect Mykonos from the vet.

Harry was conflicted. Instinctively, he felt like having Mykonos neutered was the cruellest thing that one male could do to another male. It was emasculating and he worried that it would change Mykonos' personality. He loved Mykonos exactly the way he was. And yet despite this, he understood that Mykonos' physicality and personality were already changing and that on a rational basis, it was the right thing to do. Mykonos' legs had grown long and gangly, his coat was fuller, his paws were huge, and his long and once slender tail looked even more like a fox's brush. He no longer moved like a Japanese Ninja. Instead, when he walked slowly, his movement was slinky, like a catwalk model, caressing doors and the legs of furniture and people as he glided past them. And when he got faster, he would break into a trot, with his dark brush pointing in the air behind him. Indeed, from behind he could easily have been mistaken for a fox.

Not only had his physicality changed, but his personality had started to evolve. Right from the start, for example, Mykonos would jump onto Harry's lap, curl up and sleep there, or roll onto his back and stretch out, waiting to have his tummy rubbed. Sometimes he would purr with contentment. Harry couldn't sit in front of a movie, or at the kitchen table, or work at his desk, without Mykonos jumping onto his lap and going to sleep. But now Mykonos would get bored after a few minutes on his lap, and would claw at his jumper, or pretend to bite his arm. It wasn't a real bite. It was only play fighting, but Harry got used to Mykonos clawing his hands and sinking his teeth ever so gently into his arm. Indeed, work colleagues who owned cats would look at Harry's hands and comment, "Got a kitten, have you?" gesturing at Harry's hands.

If this is how Mykonos is developing, thought Harry, he's going to be a very frustrated adult cat and the kindest thing we can do is remove the source of that frustration. But he continued to worry that neutering would cause some kind of material change to Mykonos' personality.

The appointed day arrived. Mykonos hadn't been fed the night before because he needed to have an empty stomach for the general anaesthetic. It was several months since Mykonos had experienced hunger and he was distressed without really understanding the connotations.

Harry had made the decision not to adopt some ruthless feeding regime and there were always kibbles in Mykonos' bowl so he could snack whenever he liked. Harry didn't want Mykonos to experience hunger again. But on this particular day, Mykonos couldn't be fed, and it brought back some unpleasant feelings for him.

Harry took the kennel that was used to transport Mykonos from Greece to London out of the attic and put Mykonos in it. Mykonos was anxious. He had got comfortable in the apartment. He felt secure in the apartment. Where was he going? Would he ever come back? The anxiety was unbearable, and he broke into a distressed meow.

Harry carried the kennel into the street and walked towards the taxi rank on Sloane Square. Mykonos was cowering in the corner of the kennel and bleating loudly.

The taxi ride lasted fifteen minutes and by the time they reached the vet's practice, Mykonos was exhausting from bleating.

Harry sat in the surgery waiting room with the kennel between his legs. Mykonos watched nervously as dogs on leads skirted past them. Eventually they were summoned to see the vet. After reviewing the medical records in Mykonos' passport and examining a nervous but compliant Mykonos, the vet asked a few questions.

"Can he get outside?" asked the vet.

"Only on our roof terrace," answered Harry. "He doesn't have access to the garden or the street."

"Good," said the vet. "If you are thinking about letting him in the garden, there are some injections he needs to have to make sure that he doesn't catch anything. Any other cats in the garden?"

"I don't think so," replied Harry. "The garden runs behind our building, but it looks like it is totally secure," he continued. "I was going to take him into the garden when he's a bit bigger."

"Well, you'll need to bring him back in a couple of weeks so I can check his stitches, and we can give him his injections then, but don't let him in the garden for the time being," ordered the vet.

"Okay," replied Harry.

"And if he is going to be in the garden, you will need to worm him a couple of times a year. He had it done before he left...er, Greece, so he should be fine for now. Anyway, the good news is that he's fit and healthy. Nice coat. Does he groom himself a lot?" asked the vet.

"Yes, constantly," replied Harry.

"Teeth look fine," said the vet, pulling back Mykonos' cheeks to reveal his gums and a set of perfectly sharp canines. "Leave him with us and I'll be operating on him this afternoon. He should be ready to collect at around five. The nurse will call you once he comes around," explained the vet, putting Mykonos back into the kennel. "He'll be woozy mind," said the vet, "so don't let him on that roof terrace and make sure he has food and plenty of water."

"Okay. Thank you," replied Harry, and with that, he left Mykonos with the vet and went to work, where he waited anxiously for the call to say that all was well.

Mykonos had loved his last eight weeks in the apartment and his small heart sank at the thought of not going back. He felt his kennel being lifted and he was taken downstairs to a dark room. Through the bars of the kennel he could see two other cats in similar cages who would meow intermittently. He was hungry and he was scared. Eventually a hand reached into the kennel and placed a small rag over his nose. He resisted for a moment and then felt drowsy. The liquid on the rag was a sedative. He was aware of having been removed from his kennel and then there was a sharp stabbing pain as a needle administered the anaesthetic, and then nothing.

Sometime later he awoke. He tried to stand up, but his mouth was dry, and he felt wobbly, so he sat down. He felt sore around his groin and when he investigated with his tongue, he found a small area of skin that had no fur. He licked it. There was something strange in his skin. It was the stitches. He saw a woman looking into his kennel. He could hear other cats meowing.

It was around three thirty when Harry's mobile rang. He answered immediately.

"Harry Parkman."

"Mr Parkman?" a woman asked.

"Yes, that's me," answered Harry.

"It's Sandra from Fulham Vets," she explained.

"Hello," said Harry.

"Just wanted to let you know that everything went well with Mykonos. He's awake and you can pick him up any time after four thirty. We close at six," said Sandra.

"Thank you. That's great news," replied Harry.

Harry was bathed in relief and overcome with joy. He knew it was a simple procedure, but he'd read horrible stories on the internet about how things could and did go wrong, so he was happy to know that his boy was okay. He left the office early, texting Amy to say that Mykonos was fine and that he was on his way to collect him from the vet.

By the time Harry reached the vet, Mykonos was standing and much steadier on his feet. It was Mykonos' turn to be overcome with joy when he heard Harry's voice and then saw Harry's face pressed up against the bars of the kennel.

"Time to go home, Mykonossi," said Harry, lifting the kennel.

Once home and released from the kennel, Mykonos rolled onto his back on the hall carpet, revelling in the sheer delight of being back in his territory and the place he loved. After a dinner of tuna and salmon, he cleaned himself, grooming every inch of his body. When he got to his crotch, he tugged at those annoying stitches. It hurt when he pulled them, so he stopped, but they were a source of irritation for several days.

That night, Mykonos climbed gingerly onto the bed, conscious of the soreness in his groin, and sat on top of Harry, gently pummelling Harry's chest for several minutes.

"He's giving you a massage," said Amy. "Must have learnt that from Maria. She's so bonkers, she gives him massages."

"No, I've read about this," replied Harry. "When a kitten is born, it's blind, so this is how it finds its mother's teat. By working its paws along her body. So cute."

"You mean he thinks you're his mother and he's looking for your nipples?" asked an incredulous Amy.

"No, it means his feelings for me conjure up memories from when he was a kitten and how he felt about his mother, I guess," said Harry.

"He loves you," quipped Amy. "I don't think he'll be massaging me."

Mykonos stopped massaging Harry and curled up in his armpit. Of course he had no concept of what he had been through that day. The trauma of the visit to the vet was soon forgotten and he had no inkling of the instincts and urges he would never know as a result of having had 'the snip'. He wouldn't know how it would feel to be driven to despair by a searing feline libido and the scent of a female in the air was ready to mate. But he did know how it felt to be lonely, and 'the snip' wouldn't provide relief from the craving he felt for the company of his own kind. His loneliness increased as the weeks passed. Yes, he felt safe and secure, and his stomach was full. But he was a cat who needed to love, and to be loved by more than just Harry and Maria.

Chapter 7
Fall from the Catwalk

In the silence of night, Mykonos would typically leave the bedroom at around two-thirty in the morning and explore the first floor terraces along the full length of the street before returning to the bedroom before sunrise to wake Harry and Amy up by scratching their feet.

Amy would respond by shoving him off the bed with her feet, whilst shouting, "Fuck off, Mykonos. Jesus Christ!" She'd then reach for her phone, elbow Harry and exclaim, "It's half past bloody five!"

Harry had become so accustomed to this routine that when he felt those tiny claws scratching at his feet, his auto-pilot kicked in and he got out of bed, ejected Mykonos from the bedroom, closed the door behind him, and slipped back into bed without pausing for breath. Mykonos would then sit on the other side of the door and alternate between banging his paws on the door and bleating. When he was smaller, Harry would open the door and let him back in, but eventually Harry learnt that if they ignored him, he would soon stop banging and bleating, and they would get a couple of hours precious sleep before the alarm rang in the morning.

For those few hours every night when Mykonos would explore the neighbours' terraces, he would utilise his highly evolved night vision to jump from balustrade to window box to garden chair as he traversed this first floor high line. His earlier encounter with Agro Attwood hadn't made much of an impression on him, but his second encounter with her would. It was three in the morning when Mykonos passed her French windows as he walked along the ledge on top of the balustrade outside her drawing room. It was dark inside Agnes' apartment and Mykonos could not see Agnes through the reflective glass that her husband had installed to protect them from prying neighbours. Agnes had got out of bed to make sure that she had locked the French doors after a dinner party that she had thrown that evening. As she lay in bed, listening to Charlie snoring, she remembered that some of the guests had stepped out onto the balcony for a cigarette and she was certain that she hadn't locked the French doors after they came back in. She got out of bed and on reaching the French doors (that had, indeed, been left open), she could see the shadow of an animal walking along the ledge above the balustrade. Mykonos was unaware that he was being watched from the other side of the glass. Without any warning, Agnes jumped out of the shadows and through open the French doors. She rushed at him, shouting, "Bugger off!"

Mykonos jumped back and slipped off the ledge. As he fell, one paw clung for a second to the guttering below, but then slipped and he dropped like a dead weight into the well of the basement, narrowly missing the pointed railings and landing awkwardly on the bottom of the cement steps. He had manged to right himself as he fell so that he could land on all fours, but the drop didn't give him time to prepare for the impact, and when he did hit the ground, it wasn't an even surface. He found himself straddling two steps and then bouncing down onto the floor of the basement. Ironically, if he had fallen twice the distance, he would have had more time to prepare to hit the ground. But he hadn't, and the impact was brutal.

Mykonos lay still on the cold cement floor for a couple of minutes. He was in shock, and he was in pain. His eyes moved from side to side as he surveyed the surroundings. He could see that he was at the bottom of some steps that appeared to lead up to the street. Eventually he pulled himself up. His knees and one shoulder had taken the brunt of the impact.

Despite the excruciating pain, he slowly climbed the steps to the street and limped along the pavement until he reached the entrance to the building where he thought he lived. He looked up and recognised his terrace, but there was no way of climbing up to it, so he huddled under a parked car opposite the front door. He was cold and he was shaking.

Amy was up first that morning. She had an eight o'clock breakfast with a potential client at the brasserie on Sloane Square.

"Good luck," shouted Harry from the shower, as Amy sped out of the bedroom.

"Thanks!" she replied.

As Amy exited the apartment, she couldn't see Mykonos, which was unusual at that time of the morning. Normally he would be hanging around the hall outside the bedroom door. But she didn't think much of it.

As she left the front door of the building, Mykonos could see her feet coming down the steps to the pavement and he meowed and pulled himself onto the kerb. But a passing car drowned the sound of his feint meow and Amy didn't see him. He retreated back under the vehicle for shelter.

Twenty minutes later Harry grabbed his coat and ran out of the bedroom and down the hall towards the front door. He didn't make breakfast at home and would grab something on his way into the office. Harry paused opposite the drawing room and shouted, "Mykonos!" Harry too thought it odd that Mykonos wasn't hanging around the bedroom. Normally he would have watched Harry shower and then crouched on the bed while Harry got dressed. Harry stepped into the kitchen. He always left Mykonos a small amount of kibbles, so he had something to eat during the night. Normally they were finished. This morning they hadn't been touched. Harry looked at his watch. It was ten past eight and he had a conference call at nine. He couldn't be late. Maria didn't come on Thursdays, and he didn't want to go to work without having located Mykonos. He went out onto the terrace, rattled his keys and shook a bag of treats. Normally Mykonos would appear within a few seconds. Mykonos had heard the sounds from below, at street level. He managed a faint meow and climbed back onto the kerb from under the car. His timing was good. A moment later the driver got into the car, and it pulled away.

Harry locked the apartment door and went downstairs and out of the main door of the building. He looked left and right, up and down the street, but could see nothing. And then he heard Mykonos exhale one desperate meow. Harry looked down and saw Mykonos cowering on the kerb, just a few feet directly in front of him. Mykonos didn't move but he was shaking. Harry picked him up and Mykonos' claws clung to Harry's coat as if his life depended on it. Harry carried him inside and up the stairs. He let them back into the apartment and then put Mykonos on the hall floor.

Mykonos was still in shock, but the shock was subsiding, and he was overcome with relief to be in a safe place. Tentatively, he stretched his back and tried to walk to his food bowl in the kitchen.

He found that he could walk but his body ached, especially around his right hip bone, which had taken the brunt of the impact when he fell onto the cement steps. Harry watched Mykonos limp to the food bowl and start to eat. Harry was relieved to see that Mykonos could walk and that he was eating. He rang Amy to see if she could come home and take Mykonos straight to the vet, but Amy didn't pick up. So he called Patricia and asked her to move his nine o'clock conference call, citing 'personal reasons'. This didn't go down well with his boss and eyebrows were raised at the office.

Harry called the vet's practice and was told that he should bring Mykonos to the surgery right away. Harry put Mykonos into his carrying kennel and jumped in a cab. Mykonos was subdued and crouched in the corner of the kennel. After the trauma of his fall, his escape from the basement and several hours under the car, he was now being taken from his safe place. Tired, and still in some pain, he didn't have the energy to express his displeasure. So he crouched in the kennel and quietly awaited his fate. Harry talked to him throughout the short cab ride and Mykonos was re-assured by the sound of Harry's voice.

Once inside the vet's surgery, Harry lifted Mykonos out of his kennel and placed him on a table. The vet felt Mykonos' jaw and examined his teeth.

"Well, the good news," said the vet, "is that his jaw isn't fractured, and he hasn't damaged his teeth. You said he ate something when you brought him in?"

"Yes," replied Harry, "he went to his bowl and ate a few kibbles."

"Which is why I thought his jaw would be okay," continued the vet. "It would have been very painful for him to eat if it was fractured."

The vet continued his examination and Mykonos flinched and yelped when the vet felt around his hip bone.

"He's definitely had a bit of a knock. You think he fell from the first floor?" asked the vet.

"Yes, I found him on the street. There's no way down from the first floor to the street, so I guess he fell," explained Harry.

"Well, I don't think he has a fracture, but I think we should do some x-rays to be on the safe side. Do you have insurance?" asked the vet.

"Yes, I do," replied Harry.

"Just bring the details when you collect him and give them to Sandra. She'll register the claim," explained the vet.

"Thank you. What time should I collect him?" asked Harry.

"Sandra will give you a call, but he should be ready any time after two this afternoon."

Harry left Mykonos at the vet's and took a cab to the office. After frantically flicking through e-mails on his iPhone, he called Amy and this time she picked up.

"Hi there."

"It's me," said Harry.

"I know. What's up?" she asked.

"I found Mykonos in the street this morning," he continued.

"How did he get down there?" she asked.

"No idea," he replied.

"Is he okay?" she asked.

"I think he's in shock," replied Harry. "He's limping a bit but seems to be okay. I've just left him with the vet. They want to do some x-rays to be on the safe side."

"I thought it was odd that he wasn't hanging around the bedroom door this morning," said Amy.

"Anyway, I missed my nine o'clock conference call," fretted Harry.

"But wasn't that with your Chinese clients?" she asked.

"Yes, not ideal. Just saw the emails. Went down like a fish milkshake," said Harry.

"Fine if you're a cat?" retorted Amy.

"True, but sadly the client is not a cat and was less than amused. Anyway, I've got a mare of a day and won't be able to collect Mykonos later. I don't suppose you can get him?" he asked.

"What time? I'm sloping off early to meet Charlotte at Pilates at three," she responded.

"The vet's open until five thirty. Can you get there by then?" asked Harry.

"Well we were going to have a cheeky spritzer after Pilates," replied Amy.

"I'm sure Charlotte will understand, Amy. Somebody's got to collect him," Harry insisted.

"Okay, okay. Text me the address and I'll get him," said Amy.

"Will do, and I've asked Patricia to email you his insurance details for the vet," continued Harry.

"Got to go. Just text me the address," interjected Amy.

"Don't go! Listen! As soon as you get home, lock the cat flap so he can't get onto the terrace. It's important he can't get out," urged Harry.

"Got it. Will do. Got to go," said Amy, ending the call.

Sandra, the vet's receptionist, left a message for Harry at around three o'clock to say that Mykonos was ready to collect and that he didn't have any fractures.

Amy had time for one spritzer with Charlotte and made it to the vet's by five thirty.

Mykonos had endure x-rays and a further examination. The vet had popped a pain killer down his throat (he had been too exhausted to resist) and as a result, the pain was much reduced. He had curled up in the corner of his kennel at around two o'clock and lay there still until he heard Amy's voice just before five-thirty, at which point he moved to the front of the kennel to see if it was her. As somebody lifted the kennel and gave it to Amy, he hoped that this would be the start of his journey back to the safety of his home.

Once inside the apartment, Amy released Mykonos from the kennel and gave him some wet food and fresh water. She locked the cat flap and sealed it with tape whilst he ate. He was very hungry.

Despite her general antipathy towards Mykonos, Amy spent several minutes stroking him and rubbing his tummy, after which he curled up on his favourite armchair and went to sleep.

The cat flap had given Mykonos access to his first floor catwalk and a unique vantage point that ran the length of Sloane Gardens. His window on the world was now well and truly closed, but it wouldn't be long before a new one opened.

Chapter 8
Window to the Garden

It was a lonely, drawn out winter for Mykonos. Harry and Amy disappeared to Thailand for two weeks over Christmas and New Year. Maria was paid to come in almost every day to feed and play with him. She left extra food for him for the couple of days when she couldn't visit. Mykonos would spend many hours sitting on the piano, looking down onto the street.

The birds in the trees outside tormented him, so close and yet so far from his grasp. He had nothing to hunt, and he had no companionship.

Occasionally he would push the cat flap to see if it would open, but it would not. He could tell from the temperature of the windows that it was cold outside. At night, he would sleep close to the radiator in Harry and Amy's bedroom, because it was especially cosy and warm, and because the bedroom smelled of Harry. And from daybreak he would sleep by the front door, waiting for Harry to come home.

Even though Harry and Amy were not going to be in London for Christmas, Amy still wanted to have a Christmas tree in the drawing room, and she prided herself on her decorative skills when it came to dressing the tree. She had ordered a tree that was over three metres tall, and which would showcase the ceiling height in the apartment. When it was delivered, two men struggled to carry the tree up the stairs and into the apartment. It was wrapped in netting to keep the branches vertical against the trunk, so that it was easier to manoeuvre into place.

Mykonos darted around the drawing room, watching the men secure the tree in its stand. He was excited. The tree was just asking to be climbed, and the plastic netting that was wrapped around its branches made it a six-month-old kitten's adventure playground. As the men stepped back and felt in their pockets for a scalpel to remove the netting and release the branches, Mykonos shot out from under the sofa and scaled the netting to the top of the tree.

"Mykonos, get down from there now!" exclaimed Amy. The two men laughed.

Mykonos was not coming down. He was at the highest point in the apartment, and it afforded him a unique view of his territory. This was the most fun he'd had in weeks. Amy shook the tree, but to no avail. The two men suggested that they start to release the netting so that the branches would spring free and that this might encourage Mykonos to come down. They were in a hurry to get the job done because their truck was double parked on the street below.

So the men ripped through the plastic netting and the branches were released, revealing a resplendent, perfectly shaped Christmas tree.

Amy stepped back to admire it. "It's an absolute gem," she purred.

Mykonos continued to hold court at the top of the tree, and he wasn't going to be moved. Amy gave the two men a ten-pound note for their trouble, and they left her to work out how she was going to coax Mykonos down.

Whilst Amy unpacked the Christmas decorations that she had carefully selected at Peter Jones department store, Mykonos looked on. Eventually she resorted to using a bag of treats to lure him down and what became obvious to Amy, as Mykonos descended through the branches, was that the Christmas tree was going to be a climbing frame for the kitten. *This is going to be a nightmare,* she thought. And she was right.

Amy's Christmas tree was an important seasonal expression of her good taste and flair for design. It was strategically placed in front of the double French doors and therefore visible from the street for neighbours to admire. This year's creation was a heady mix of gold and white bows, with sprigs of plastic mistletoe that she had bought in a Cologne market a few years back, all encased in a lattice of white fairy lights. The star for the top of the tree was created from glistening diamante. She had made it herself.

Harry had been keen to decorate the tree with Amy, but he was stuck in the office, and, in truth, this was something that she liked to do on her own. Every bow, every sprig of mistletoe, every ornament, every light had to be perfectly placed to create the desired effect. This was a labour of love. Only she knew how the tree was going to look and only she could perfectly place every single element.

Mykonos, however, had a different idea. Whilst Amy dressed the tree, he would jump into the foliage, shoot up the trunk and dislodge a decoration, before jumping out again. Amy wanted to lock him out of the drawing room, but she couldn't catch him, and she couldn't lure him out of the room with treats. He was having too much fun. And so he'd sprint across the floor, down the back of the sofa and then behind the piano, hiding in all the places where she couldn't reach him. Eventually she did manage to lure Mykonos out of the drawing room by using more treats. Having locked him out, she completed the decorations without interruption.

That night Harry came home to find the double doors to the drawing room firmly closed and Mykonos pushing against them in vain.

"I'm home!" cried Harry.

Amy appeared from the bedroom.

"What's going on?" he asked, gesturing to the closed doors.

"Don't ask," said Amy. "The trees up and it looks beautiful…"

"Fantastic!" exclaimed Harry. "Can I see?"

"The problem is Mykonos," replied Amy.

"What problem?" asked Harry.

"He was up the tree like a rat up a drainpipe and keeps pulling the bloody decorations off," explained Amy.

Harry laughed and picked up Mykonos.

"It's not funny," protested Amy.

"Show me the tree. I'll hold Mykonos," said Harry.

Amy opened the door and Harry admired the tree, resplendent in the bay window. It really was a triumph.

Mykonos struggled to get out of Harry's arms. Eventually Harry let him go and Mykonos disappeared into the tree and re-appeared close to the top.

"What shall we do?" asked Amy. "I don't want to keep the doors closed, but he's a nightmare."

Amy spent the following two weeks collecting decorations from the floor and re-hanging them on the Christmas tree. She was pleased to see the back of Mykonos by the time they jetted off to Thailand.

Whilst in Thailand, Harry sent Maria messages on a daily basis to make sure that all was well at home and Maria would respond with daily updates on Mykonos and attach pictures to re-assure Harry that Mykonos was fine. Harry would share these pictures with Amy, and it wasn't long before Amy got irritated by the Mykonos updates.

"Honestly, Harry, I think you care more about Mykonos that you do about me," complained Amy whilst she peeled a mango at breakfast one morning.

"That's ridiculous!" retorted Harry. "I love you."

Harry was enjoying their holiday and it had rekindled some of the passion that had been missing from their relationship during the last year. Nevertheless, the frequency with which Amy complained that Harry cared more about Mykonos than he did about her, and the lengths to which Harry went to comfort Amy eventually took its toll on their relationship. Harry tired of reassuring Amy and, ironically, she ran the risk of making her complaint a self-fulfilling prophesy.

For the rest of the holiday, Harry messaged Maria when Amy wouldn't notice, and didn't share any more photos of Mykonos with Amy.

By the end of their two weeks in Thailand, Harry couldn't wait to get home. When their cab from the airport pulled up in Sloane Gardens, Harry jumped out and sprinted up the stairs to open the front door, and there was Mykonos, waiting for him. Mykonos was overwhelmed with joy as Harry picked him up and held him close to his chest. Mykonos rubbed his face against Harry's and purred loudly. He knew Harry would come back.

Amy was left downstairs to pay the driver and get the suitcases out of the cab. She rang the door buzzer from the street repeatedly and Harry went back downstairs to get the suitcases.

"Sorry," he said, carrying the suitcases upstairs. "I didn't mean to leave you with the cases."

"I know," said Amy, "you couldn't wait to see Mykonos. It's fine. How is he?"

"He was very pleased to see me," replied Harry.

It had been twenty-eight degrees Celsius in Thailand and it was just two degrees in London. Harry didn't much feel the cold and was pretty nonchalant when it came to dressing warmly. He never bothered with a scarf or gloves.

And so shortly after returning from Thailand, Harry fell sick and developed a severe chest infection. It might have been caused by the sudden change in temperature, but Harry had never got sick like this before, and he had never had a lung infection. One of Harry's oldest friends from his time at Oxford, Claude Hunter, was now the chest consultant at the local Chelsea and Westminster Hospital. Claude examined Harry and concluded that the chest infection may well have been the culmination of Harry's body fully adjusting to Mykonos. Once Harry shook off the chest infection he found that he no longer had the slightest allergic reaction to cats. Mykonos could snuggle up to his face at night and Harry's eyes didn't water and his nose didn't run. Claude theorised that the adjustment to Mykonos might have temporarily weakened Harry's lungs, hence the chest infection. This had been the final stage of a recalibration that resulted in Harry shedding his cat allergy.

Later in January Mykonos had injections that became an annual event, and which protected him from diseases that he might pick up in the garden. In February, Harry decided to take him into the communal gardens for the first time. Mykonos had continued to grow, and it was as much a source of relief as it was pride, that he was clearly going to be a good sized cat. Harry had known next to nothing about cats, and he had wondered whether Mykonos' illness and poor nutrition as a small kitten might have impeded his growth in some way. This was evidently not the case.

Mykonos was now just over eight months old. Having surveyed the communal gardens several times to ensure that there was no means of escape,

Harry decided to take the risk of releasing him into the garden. He had tried to get Mykonos to wear a collar and name tag, but Mykonos had gone crazy every time Harry had tried to place the collar around his head, pulling away whilst pushing his nails into Harry's hands. Eventually Harry gave up on the idea. It meant giving Mykonos the run of the garden was that bit riskier – because if he did go missing, anybody who found him would not be able to identify his owner from his collar. But Harry had registered Mykonos' microchip on various websites, which meant that he could be identified by a vet in the unlikely event that he managed to escape from the garden and was taken to a vet.

Harry opened the front door of his apartment. Mykonos went straight out of the door onto the landing, but contrary to Harry's expectations, he was hesitant about going down the stairs. Eventually he followed Harry, sniffing every nook and cranny as they made their way to the ground floor, and then to the door at the rear of the building. Harry unlocked the door and walked across the narrow metal walkway that bridged the well of the basement below in order to get access to the garden. Mykonos proceeded with caution, looking up at Harry for re-assurance. He didn't like the metal bridge. It was a meshed structure and his paws felt unsteady on it. He could see through it to the basement below and instinctively it felt unsafe. So he moved across it very slowly.

Once across the metal bridge and in the garden, Mykonos didn't bolt off as Harry had expected. Instead, he sat upright on the gravel terrace at the rear of the building, sniffing the air and surveying the scene. He hadn't seen this much space since he was a kitten in the wasteland. He looked left and right. The garden was long and stretched out as far as the eye could see in both directions. Whilst it ran the full length of the terrace – eighty metres or so – it was only six metres deep. In front of Mykonos was the four-metre high wall which ran the entire length of the back of the garden. Mykonos stepped from the gravel terrace onto the grass lawn, which felt moist and spongy under his paws. He could hear noises coming from the street behind the wall. The sound of a car engine and a dog barking. For a moment Mykonos was conflicted. Should he find a safe corner to hide in, or should he explore? He looked up at Harry, who looked down at him. Mykonos' gaze told Harry that he was nervous, so Harry walked ahead of him on the lawn. Mykonos concluded that he didn't need a corner to hide in and that it was safe for him to explore the garden. And so explore he did. He travelled the full length of the back wall, moving through the shrubs that lined it, every now and then glancing back to make sure that Harry was not out of sight. This was his new territory, with so many new smells to process and tree trunks to scratch. Whilst Harry thought Mykonos was scurrying randomly back and forth, Mykonos was actually mapping and memorising the layout of the garden. Every now and then he would stop and crouch down to observe birds gliding between the tall trees above him. When some of the birds settled on the back wall, Mykonos' mouth trembled with excitement and his fox's brush of a tail moved from left to right and back again in a sweeping motion behind him. He was intoxicated by the possibility that he might actually catch one of those flying creatures. And then the birds disappeared from the trees above him, Mykonos resumed his forensic exploration of the garden. His nose and his ears were in overdrive.

After about an hour, Harry carried Mykonos back into the house. Mykonos wasn't much pleased, but he didn't resist, and that night he slept through until Amy's alarm went at seven thirty. Even then he remained curled up on the duvet. His sojourn in the garden had exercised his body and his mind. He had slept all the better for it. And as a result, so did Harry and Amy.

Over the coming month, Mykonos spent many hours each week in the garden. Maria would take him downstairs when she arrived in the morning, and he would race ahead of her and sit impatiently at the back door waiting for her to open it. Sometimes he would survey the garden from the security of the window ledge at the rear of the ground floor apartment. Other times he would dash across the lawn and disappear into the shrubs that lined the garden wall. It was now Spring, so the weather was getting warmer, the days were getting longer, and Mykonos was getting less inclined to return to the apartment. Sometimes Maria needed thirty minutes to locate him and coax him back into the building.

Although there were around twenty terraced houses along this side of the street, only eight or nine of these had back doors that gave them direct access to the garden. During the winter the garden was always empty. Even in the summer it was unusual to see any neighbours outside. Dogs were strictly prohibited, so all in all, it seemed like a safe place for a cat to roam.

By early May the sun was getting higher in the sky and the flowers in the garden had started to bloom. Mykonos would sit on the lawn with the sun on his back. It felt warm and soothing, and reminded him of when he was a kitten. He was now eleven months old and still growing at a rate of knots.

Harry and Amy had started to leave him outside for most of the day if the forecast was dry, but they would always bring him in before sunset. Harry didn't want Mykonos roaming the garden at night. He was convinced that Mykonos looked so much like a fox from behind, with his huge tail, that somebody might mistake him for a city fox and shoot him. Of course, this was ridiculous. Nobody possessed a rifle in Sloane Gardens. But in any event, Mykonos' dark coat would make it almost impossible to find him in the garden and retrieve him once it was dark.

One Saturday in mid-May, Harry had put Mykonos in the garden at around eleven in the morning and then went to bring him in at around two because he and Amy were going to friends and wouldn't be back until later that evening. It was the warmest day of the year thus far and Mykonos was basking in the early summer sun. Daffodils had appeared in the lawn, buds were on the trees and the air was full of insects buzzing. Mykonos leapt in the air and snapped his jaw, hoping to catch one. He was in cat heaven and really not in the mood to return to the apartment.

Harry and Amy were running late, and Harry was in a rush to retrieve Mykonos from the garden. Having located Mykonos, Harry kneeled down and reached out to him. Mykonos thought Harry was going to stroke him on the head or scratch him under his cheek, but instead Harry whisked Mykonos up into his arms and carried him upside down, cradled like a baby, across the metal bridge and back into the building. Mykonos was unhappy and began to struggle. He wanted to get out of Harry's arms. By now they were at the bottom of the stairs inside and Harry refused to release him. So out of sheer frustration, Mykonos lashed out with one paw, and two nails caught Harry's left ear lobe. Mykonos' claws were as sharp as a razor, and they sliced though Harry's ear lobe like a knife through butter. Harry was in shock, but he didn't let go of Mykonos. When Mykonos had been a kitten, Harry regularly got scratched on his hands and wrists. But up until now, Mykonos had never lashed out deliberately. Harry was kind of aware that Mykonos' claws had connected with his ear, but it had all happened so quickly. He felt no pain and he was more concerned about getting Mykonos up the stairs and into the apartment. It was only as they got through the front door that he felt liquid trickling down his neck. He pushed the front door shut behind him with his foot and dropped Mykonos to the floor. Mykonos, now resigned to being inside, sauntered into the kitchen to use his litter tray. Meanwhile, Harry ran two fingers along his cheek and then looked at them. They were covered in blood. At that moment, Amy came out of the bedroom and into the hall.

"Come on. You need to change. We've got to leave in twenty minutes. What's the matter?" she asked.

"Mykonos scratched me," said Harry.

Amy walked quickly down the hallway.

"There's blood on your shirt!" exclaimed Amy. She took a closer look. "Yuk! There's blood coming from your ear!"

"Can you get me a towel of something?" asked Harry.

"Okay, okay, but don't look at it. Don't look at it!" she shouted. "And try not to drip blood on the carpet!"

A moment later she returned with a towel and started to dab his ear.

"It's horrid," observed Amy. "You need to go to A&E."

Harry stepped into the guest cloakroom, turned the light on and leaned into the mirror. He had never been that squeamish about blood, but he was nevertheless shocked to see most of the skin that had been his left earlobe now hanging from a small thread of flesh. The sight of this dangling, almost detached earlobe was not pleasant. And blood continued to run freely from it, dripping onto Harry's shoulder and onto the floor. His ear was still numb with pain, but the sensation was starting to come back.

Amy appeared behind him in the bathroom. "Oh my God! I told you not to look at it!"

"Not good," said Harry, taking the towel and pressing it gently to his ear.

"I've got keys, come on, we need to jump in a cab and get you to the Chelsea and Westminster. Go and get a cab, I'll lock up," insisted Amy.

Harry ran downstairs and onto the street, pressing the towel to his ear, which was now very painful. Amy followed and within a minute they were in a cab and on their way to Chelsea and Westminster Hospital.

Harry and Amy presented themselves to the receptionist in A&E at the hospital. She started to enter his details onto the computer whist he removed the blood soaked towel for a moment to reveal his mutilated ear to the receptionist.

"Take a seat for a moment," said the receptionist. "I'm sure a nurse will assess you right away."

Harry and Amy sat down.

"They can sow it back on nowadays, can't they, even if it comes off?" rambled Amy.

"Oh God, I hope it doesn't come off," replied Harry.

A young man in a white coat appeared through double doors at one end of the emergency room. "Harry Parkman?" he asked, reading from his clipboard.

"Here," replied Harry, standing up.

Harry and Amy followed the young man into a small room.

"I'm Doctor Nelson. What's happened?"

Harry removed the towel. The doctor winced.

"Ooh!" said the doctor. "How did it happen?"

"Our cat..."

"Your cat!" said Amy, cutting across Harry.

"My cat clawed my ear. He was playing. He didn't mean to do it," explained Harry.

"So the cat's claw went through your ear lobe?" asked the doctor.

"Sliced right through," replied Harry.

"I can see. It's a nasty laceration," said the doctor. "Does it hurt?" he asked, examining the ear lobe more closely.

"It didn't at first," replied Harry, "but it does now."

"I'm going to use a syringe to douse the wound with an antiseptic. It's going to sting a bit but there will be less pain afterwards," explained the doctor.

Harry could feel the cold liquid around his ear and running down the side of his neck.

"Ears bleed a lot, I'm afraid," said the doctor. "How are you with injections?" he enquired.

"Fine," replied Harry. "Just do whatever has to be done. I don't want to lose my ear lobe."

"Okay," said the doctor. "I'm going to have to numb your ear and then you'll need three or four stitches."

"Okay," said Harry.

Amy turned away as the doctor presented the syringe and injected Harry's ear with the anaesthetic. She then turned back slowly, watching through the corner of her eye, as the doctor prepared the needle and thread. Harry noticed that the young doctor's hands were shaking as he started to stitch the torn ear lobe back onto his ear. Slowly, the doctor pulled one stitch through and then started on the next one.

"I'm only using three stitches," said the doctor. "I think it's more likely to heal if there aren't too many."

"I'm not going to lose the ear lobe then?" asked Harry, tentatively.

"No, I don't think so," replied the doctor. "There aren't that many capillaries at the extremities of the ear and sometimes they don't heal well, but I think this will." He finished the last stitch and then put some tape across the wound.

"I'm going to prescribe some anti-biotics for you and please do make sure you take them. Cats are highly infectious and it's important that your ear doesn't get infected," the doctor added.

"How long before the stitches can come out?" asked Harry.

"Make an appointment to see your GP in a week's time and they'll remove them and check that it's healing up nicely," replied the doctor.

"Thank you very much, doctor," said Harry.

"Yes, thank you," chipped in Amy.

They took a cab back home to the apartment. Harry opened the door but couldn't see Mykonos.

"That's odd," remarked Harry.

"What?" asked Amy, heading towards the bedroom.

"Where's Mykonos?"

"I locked him in the guest cloakroom," replied Amy.

"Why?" asked Harry.

"To teach him a lesson, of course," she retorted.

"He won't understand," said Harry. "He won't know what he's done wrong."

Amy rolled her eyes as Harry released Mykonos from the cloakroom. As he opened the door, Mykonos shot out like a bullet and ran around the apartment. The cloakroom was pitch dark and he'd been scratching the door and meowing for almost two hours, desperate to get out.

Harry picked Mykonos up and cradled him in his arms as he walked around the apartment.

Mykonos nuzzled Harry's armpit and purred. He had no idea why he had been locked in the cloakroom and he was oblivious to the injury he had caused.

Later that evening, Harry got the nail clippers they had bought for Mykonos but never used, and wrapped Mykonos' torso and hind legs in a towel, so he couldn't use his feet to scratch or push back. He sat Mykonos on his lap and proceeded to cut his nails. It took him a while to work out exactly how to get a nail to present itself, but once he got the hang of it, it didn't take long. Mykonos, for his part, was reasonably compliant. He wined and wriggled a bit every now and then, but once he realised that the strange metal object snapping at his paws wasn't going to cause him any pain, he was prepared to let Harry do whatever it was that Harry was doing. It was only when he stretched out and placed his paws on the top of his scratching post later that evening, that he discovered that the sharpness of his claws had gone. Mykonos was confused. His claws were the most important weapon in his armoury. Something had gone awry. Nevertheless, Harry didn't bother to cut them very often, and once they grew back, Mykonos would spend many a day sharpening them at his leisure.

Harry's ear healed so quickly that when he went to have the stitches removed a week later, the skin had actually grown over the thread. As a result, the skin had to be cut in order to remove the stitches. Harry's ear lobe had been saved, and all that remained was a faint scar that was only visible in the brightest sunlight.

Chapter 9
Summer Time

As the days got longer, and Mykonos spent most of his time outside, Harry made sure that there was always a bowl of water by the back door in case Mykonos got thirsty. For his part, Mykonos had got to know every inch of the garden and now felt totally safe in it.

Mornings were spent hunting in the shade of the trees and shrubs that ran along the garden wall, where he'd sometimes catch a beetle or a spider. In the afternoons, when the sun gradually disappeared behind the building, he would sprint across the lawn, chasing birds that were never quite within his grasp. And as dusk approached, he would dance on his hind legs, snapping at the swarm of insects that buzzed in the air above him.

Most of all, however, Mykonos enjoyed sitting on the window ledge by the back door, surveying his territory and enjoying the warm breeze. Even though his coat had become much thicker, and he had acclimatised to the British weather, there was something about the light and the heat that reminded Mykonos of where he'd come from. It made him feel good.

In July, a young Italian couple, Stefano and Sofia Pignataro, moved into the basement apartment of the building. Their apartment was what was known as 'lower ground' level, which was an acronym for basement. It had a small patio at the rear, in the well of the building, with an iron ladder attached to the patio wall which they could climb to access the garden. This couple had an enormous, grey and white, long haired tom cat called Puccini. They would leave their bedroom window open, so Puccini could roam around the small basement patio. And to their surprise, Puccini was able to pull himself up the ladder, rung by rung, until he reached the garden.

Puccini's arrival transformed Mykonos' life. He first became aware of Puccini the day after the Pignataro's moved into their apartment. He was sitting in his favourite spot on the window ledge at the rear of the ground floor apartment, surveying the garden, when he heard the window opening in the basement. He looked down into the patio below and to his surprise, out popped what he immediately knew to be a cat. Not that he really understood the exact difference between a cat, dog or human, but he knew from the way Puccini looked and moved that this was his species, and he longed for contact with his own kind. Puccini was just as surprised to look up and see Mykonos staring down from the ledge above him. Mykonos then proceeded to jump off his window ledge and pace up and down the iron railings that ran around the edge of the well to prevent people from falling into the basement. Mykonos howled at Puccini and Puccini howled back from the basement patio below.

As the days grew longer Harry and Amy had got into the habit of leaving Mykonos in the garden until just before it got dark, which was almost nine o'clock at this time of year.

On this particular evening, Harry was late home from work and so it was Amy who went down to the garden to bring Mykonos indoors.

Amy was armed with a bag of treats in her pocket. She opened the back door and called out his name. Sometimes Mykonos would be keen to come up to the apartment and required little encouragement. On other days, however, he needed plenty of encouragement, and the treats were her way of luring him through the back door and up the stairs to their apartment.

On this particular evening, Amy found Mykonos staring down through the railings into the well of the basement whilst making a loud howling sound. She then heard a similar sound echoing from below, and when she looked down, she saw Puccini. At that moment, Puccini started to pull himself up the ladder until he reached the top, where he jumped triumphantly through the railings and into the garden. The two cats started to circle each other, howling intermittently, and standing on their hind legs trying to make themselves appear taller than the other cat. Mykonos was big for a one-year-old, but Puccini was nearly three years old and fully grown. He was long haired, with white and grey patches. With all that fur, Puccini looked almost twice the size of Mykonos.

"Mykonos!" shouted Amy, trying to distract him. Mykonos ignored her. He was fixated with Puccini and the two cats continued to circle each other.

A man's head then appeared out of the basement window below. It was Stefano. He shouted up to Amy, "Is there a big grey and white cat up there?" Stefano spoke with a strong Italian accent.

"Yes, he climbed up the ladder!" Amy shouted back. "He's here with my cat. They seem to be sizing each other up."

"I'll come up!" shouted Stefano.

By the time Stefano had made it up the internal stairs from the basement and out of the back door, Mykonos and Puccini's howls had got quieter and their noses had come close to touching a couple of times.

Stefano stretched his arm out towards Amy and shook her hand. "Hiya, I'm Stefano," he said, introducing himself. He was a handsome man in his mid-twenties.

"Hi, I'm Amy. *We* live on the first floor," she said, pointing up to their kitchen window above. "Your cat is huge. He looks like he could eat ours for breakfast. I assume he is a he?"

"Don't worry about him," explained Stefano. "He is blind in one eye. He won't do anything."

"Oh, poor thing," replied Amy.

"What is yours called?" asked Stefano.

"Mykonos," replied Amy. "We, well my partner rescued him when we were on holiday in Mykonos."

"Ah yes, my girlfriend, Sofia, she rescued Puccini," explained Stefano.

Amy thought she might bond with Stefano as two long suffering partners of kitten rescuers.

"Is the garden safe for the cats?" asked Stefano.

"Puccini. Good name," replied Amy. "Absolutely," she continued, "the garden is safe. Dogs aren't allowed and the wall goes to the very end, so they can't get out."

Mykonos and Puccini were, by now, having a good sniff of each other. Mykonos thought Puccini smelt familiar and smelt good. But at that moment Stefano scooped Puccini into his arms and carried him towards the back door.

"He can climb up the ladder," said Stefano, "but I don't know if he will be able to get back down, so I'll take him."

"I saw him climb the ladder," replied Amy. "I couldn't believe it. I didn't know cats could do that."

"Neither did I until just now. Anyway, I'm glad he has a friend in the garden, but I need to put him indoors as we are going out. Nice to meet you," said Stefano, disappearing inside.

"Nice to meet you too," replied Amy.

Mykonos followed Stefano and Puccini indoors and Amy followed, locking the back door behind her.

Having got Mykonos inside, Amy had to get him up the stairs, but instead Mykonos followed Stefano and Puccini downstairs to the front door of the basement apartment. Stefano went inside with Puccini and quickly closed the front door behind him, leaving Mykonos to pace up and down frantically outside. He knew Puccini was on the other side of that door and similarly, Puccini was pacing up and down on the other side. Mykonos was agitated and frustrated. This bromance had ended scarcely before it had begun. But he needn't have worried. They would spend most of that summer together in the garden.

After several minutes Mykonos became reconciled to not getting into the basement apartment and Amy was able to tempt him back upstairs using the treats. She had just got him into their apartment when Harry arrived home from work. Mykonos raced to Harry as he came through the front door and Harry dropped his bag onto the floor and scooped Mykonos up into his arms.

"Hello darling, how was your day?" asked Amy.

"It was fine, thanks," replied Harry. "Sorry I'm so late, how was yours?"

"Problems in the paint effects department, but fine other than that," replied Amy.

"Took me ages to get Mykonos in. He has a new friend in the garden," she continued.

"What kind of friend?" Harry enquired.

"Huge, fluffy, grey and white Italian tom cat kind of friend," explained Amy.

"That's exciting," said Harry. "Italian?"

"Yes, I met the owner. Stefano," Amy continued. "Must have moved into the basement with his girlfriend. The cat's called Puccini."

"Ah, yes. I think I've seen her. Slim and pretty. Long dark hair," said Harry.

Amy bristled. "She sounds lovely. Anyway, Puccini can climb the bloody ladder from the basement into the garden. Which is how he just met Mykonos."

"And they are alright with each other?" asked Harry.

"Apparently so," replied Amy. "Lots of wailing followed by bottom sniffing. That kind of stuff. Anyway, Stefano took Puccini back inside and Mykonos was glued to their front door in the basement. Couldn't get him to move. Lots more wailing, but I finally got him to come upstairs using treats."

"Why didn't you just carry him up?" asked Harry.

"I'm afraid to pick him up when he's agitated like that," Amy replied. "I don't want to lose an ear…"

"That was an accident," Harry interjected.

"I know, I know. Anyway, he was a bit stoked up and I didn't want to take the risk," explained Amy.

And so that summer, Mykonos and Puccini would spend many an hour in the garden together. They were an unlikely pair of toms. Mykonos was remarkably un-territorial about the garden. His desperate need for company far outweighed any feline instincts he had to jealously guard his patch. He was also aware of Puccini's disability, and he sensed that Puccini posed no physical threat.

The two cats would often sneak up on each other, crouching low and wiggling their bottoms as if they were stalking their prey, before pouncing on the other. Mykonos would typically sneak up and pounce from Puccini's blind side. Occasionally there was a skirmish when Puccini tried to mount Mykonos and Mykonos did not much appreciate it. However, when push came to shove, Mykonos could easily see Puccini off, despite Puccini's advantage in size, and Mykonos took great pleasure in occasionally reminding Puccini that he could put him in a corner if he wanted to. Puccini would respond by showing his teeth and hissing for a moment, but this was little more than posturing, and for the most part they happily shared the garden and chased, flies, wasps, birds and each other from pillar to post. They were the best of friends, but when it came to exploration of their territory, Puccini was by far the bolder of the two.

For example, the houses that backed onto the garden had sash windows that were often left open in the summer. Mykonos was curious enough to climb onto a ground floor windowsill and poke his head through the window to see what was inside. But he was cautious by nature and ultimately, his cautious nature outweighed his feline curiosity. He played it safe.

Puccini, on the other hand, was much more driven by his feline curiosity and would regularly climb through an open window and into a neighbour's apartment. Once inside the neighbour's apartments, Puccini would start to explore, room by room. He was a bad influence on Mykonos, who would occasionally follow him through a window. But Mykonos did this tentatively and nervously. It would only be a matter of seconds before he turned around and jumped out of the window and back into the garden.

It was around nine o'clock one Friday evening in July when Harry went into the garden to retrieve Mykonos. He was late home from work and Amy had put

Mykonos outside at around six before she went out for dinner with some girlfriends. Harry shook his keys as he stepped into the garden and Mykonos appeared from some shrubs and came running across the lawn towards him and brushed up against his legs. Harry noticed Stefano and Sofia at the far end of the garden. They looked as though they were peering into one of the houses. As he approached them, he could see that Sofia was tearful. Mykonos followed Harry.

"Hi there," said Harry, greeting them.

"Hi," replied Stefano. "You have to excuse us. Sofia is very upset. We cannot find Puccini."

"I have been looking for him for two hours," explained Sofia. "He is gone."

"Well he must be somewhere," replied Harry. "I'm sure we'll find him. Maybe he's gone into one of the ground floor apartments? I've had to pull Mykonos out of a couple of open windows myself."

"But now it is getting dark. How will we find him?" Sofia despaired.

Harry looked down at Mykonos, who was looking up at Harry.

"Mykonos," said Harry, "where's Puccini? Where's Puccini?"

Mykonos ran around in a circle. He understood some of what Harry was saying, including Puccini's name which had certain intonations.

So if Harry said, "Do you want to go outside?" Mykonos would run to the front door. (He almost always wanted to go outside).

Mykonos understood that something was wrong, and he sensed that Puccini was missing. He ran in circles around Harry's feet whilst looking up at him.

"Listen," said Harry, "I need to take Mykonos inside, but I'll come back down to help you look for Puccini."

A few minutes later Harry joined Stefano and Sofia as they worked their way along that side of the street, buzzing the entry systems for the ground floor apartments. It was a summer Friday, however, in a wealthy neighbourhood, so most people had left town for the weekend. Those who did answer the door said that they would search their apartments. Later that evening Stefano printed a flyer with a picture of Puccini on it, contact details, and the offer of a reward for the recovery of their beloved cat. Harry felt so sorry for them. He imagined how he would feel if Mykonos had gone missing. He'd be devastated.

The next day Harry and Amy debated whether it would be safe to leave Mykonos in the garden.

"Of course it will be," said Amy. "Puccini's probably hidden himself under somebody's bed and they've gone away for the weekend. He'll re-appear sooner or later."

"But what if he's been taken? Kidnapped. There are some crazy people out there," Harry fretted.

"Just put him outside," said Amy. "We'll meet Ben and Clarissa at Chelsea Farmers Market for lunch, and we'll be back by three."

And so Harry took Mykonos into the garden. Mykonos had been leaping up at the front door, trying to reach the latch, which was a sure indication that he was desperate to go outside. Harry escorted him downstairs, and he shot through the back door and into the sunshine. Harry figured that if something terrible had happened in the garden, Mykonos would have sensed it and wouldn't have been so keen to go outside.

Once outside, Mykonos sniffed around the lawn and the shrubs along the garden wall. He couldn't pick up Puccini's scent. So he waited at the top of the metal ladder that Puccini climbed to get into the garden, hoping to see his friend appear at the basement window below. Beneath him he could see bowls of food and water that Sofia had left out overnight in the hope that Puccini would return.

After around half an hour of waiting at the top of the ladder, Mykonos sensed that Puccini wasn't going to jump out of the window of the basement apartment below. Mykonos sighed and then yawned. He decided to check out the birds that were nesting at the top of a huge climbing rose tree that covered the wall opposite the back of Agro Atwood's home.

Agnes and Charlie Atwood had a ground and first floor duplex, and their kitchen on the ground floor had a door that opened onto the garden. Agnes had nurtured this rose tree for many years, and it was a source of great pride and satisfaction that the tree had become the nesting ground for a variety of robins and tits. When she stood at her kitchen sink she had a wonderful view of the climbing rose in full bloom, as well as the nesting birds' comings and goings. The regular sightings of Puccini and Mykonos staking out the rose tree was, therefore, a source of considerable irritation to Agnes.

"Those bloody cats are menaces," she said to her husband through gritted teeth.

"They can't get up to the nests. Not even close. They just sit there on the lawn, gawping up at the birds. I don't know what you're worried about," replied Charlie.

"They shouldn't be allowed in the garden," protested Agnes. "Dogs aren't. So why are cats?"

"Well you can't really stop cats, can you?" suggested Charlie.

"And what if a chick falls out of the nest?" continued Agnes.

"The crows will get it before those two muppets. Have you seen them? Those moggies couldn't catch a cold. It's the crows you've got to worry about. They're vicious," replied Charlie.

Agnes was not so sure.

Meanwhile, Harry and Amy walked home along the Kings Road from lunch and bought an ice cream on the way.

Amy was feeling buoyed by lunch. Ben and Clarissa had just got engaged and Harry seemed remarkably entertained by two hours of wedding conversation. And he didn't mention Mykonos once. He didn't even reach for his phone to show them a picture or three of Mykonos. *Things are looking up*, she thought.

When they got home, Amy went upstairs, and Harry went into the garden to check on Mykonos. As he stepped out of the back door, he saw Agnes chasing Mykonos down the garden with a broom.

"What the hell do you think you're doing?" shouted Harry, as Mykonos sped past him and through the back door into the house. He ran towards Agnes and shouted, "Don't you dare go near my cat again!"

"So the cats are yours, are they?" asked Agnes.

"This one is," said Harry. "The other one has gone missing. I don't suppose you know anything about that?" he asked, pointedly.

"I have no idea what you're talking about, you silly little poof," replied Agnes.

This remark confounded Harry momentarily but he thought she might have drawn this conclusion because he had never reacted to her flirty looks when they had passed each other on the street. She must have been at least forty years older than him.

"Just keep your cats away from *MY* rose tree," commanded Agnes. "The birds nest there every year and I don't want your cats disturbing them," she continued.

"I only have one cat," repeated Harry, "and I can't stop him from hanging around the rose tree, which, by the way, is not *YOUR* rose tree, it's all of our rose tree, because it's in *OUR* garden! And don't you ever, ever go near my cat, do you understand?"

Harry was trembling with anger. How dare she threaten his boy?

There are cat people and there are bird people, and emotions run high when their worlds collide.

Agnes beat a retreat and proceeded to tell Charlie that the nasty neighbour from twenty-nine had threatened her. Harry took Mykonos upstairs and then went back downstairs to have a word with Stefano. He told Stefano that he had caught Agro Attwood chasing Mykonos with a broom and that she was very angry about the cats hanging around the rose tree where the birds were nesting. He wondered whether Stefano should ask Agnes if she knew anything about Puccini's disappearance.

Stefano did not get to speak to Agnes, but he did have a lengthy conversation with her husband, Charlie.

It transpired that Charlie was an animal lover. He owned a dog for many years and that dog was his pride and joy. He would let if have the run of the garden (even though dogs were not allowed). Charlie claimed that he started to receive anonymous letters demanding that he stop putting his dog in the garden and one day his dog was found dead in the bushes opposite his building. An autopsy revealed that the dog had been poisoned. It was a strange anecdote which Stefano re-told to Harry. They concluded that there had probably never been a dog or a poisoning, and that Charlie's story was simply a veiled threat and a ploy to make them less inclined to leave their cats in the garden.

Puccini didn't re-appear, and Sofia was unable to go to work that week because she was so upset about his disappearance. Flyers with Puccini's photo and their phone number were now pinned to every tree in the neighbourhood. As a precaution, Harry asked Maria to check the garden regularly when she was at his apartment to make sure that Mykonos was okay. He didn't want to force Mykonos to stay indoors. But he was afraid to leave him outside.

And then five days after Puccini had vanished, there was a miracle. A woman phoned Stefano to say that she had found Puccini in her apartment. She had been on holiday since the previous Friday afternoon and had returned that day to find a flyer in their letterbox and Puccini in their guest bedroom. Despite six days without food or water, Puccini was in remarkably good shape. In fact he had needed to lose some weight. The experience undoubtedly had a lasting impact on his confidence though, and when Stefano and Sophia eventually allowed him to go back into the garden several weeks later, Puccini didn't venture through an open window ever again.

Chapter 10
The Russians

It was late July before Stefano and Sofia allowed Puccini to go back into the garden. Until then, Puccini was confined to the basement flat.

Mykonos knew Puccini was there. He could see his friend staring up at him from the window below, whilst he sat patiently at the top of the metal ladder, waiting for them to be reunited in the garden. When, eventually, Puccini was allowed to go back into the garden, the two tom cats chased each other around and around, until they were totally exhausted, at which point they would rub noses for a moment, catch their breath, and then chase each other around and around again.

As a result of all that exercise, Mykonos slept very well at night. He would settle in the 'V' of Harry's leg, just below his crotch, and, much to Harry and Amy's relief, sleep through to six or seven in the morning. When Mykonos did wake up, he would go to the kitchen to do his mess, have a drink, snack on some kibbles, and then come back to bed without Harry or Amy being any the wiser. He had become remarkably civilised, and Harry appreciated not getting the early morning wake-up call (aka the scratching of his feet).

It felt like normal service had been resumed and even Amy admitted to Charlotte, albeit begrudgingly, that Mykonos was a bit of character and generally nice to have around. She hated the fact that he had shredded two of her armchairs, however this had given her the excuse to do a bit of remodelling of the drawing room at Harry's expense, and she had recovered the armchairs in velvet because she had figured out that Mykonos did not scratch velvet. Of course, changing some of the fabrics on the furnishings meant that Amy had an excuse to change the roman blinds in the drawing room as well. And so forth…

Harry and Amy had loved the island of Mykonos and decided to return there for a week's holiday in early that September. They both agreed that Mykonos the kitten had prevented them from exploring quite as much as they would have liked on their previous visit. It felt like unfinished business, and they were keen to go back.

Harry's friends joked about him returning from Mykonos with a second kitten. Harry replied, *"Just take me out and shoot me if we come home with another one."* Of course he adored Mykonos (the cat), but Mykonos had disrupted their lives in a way that he hadn't envisaged. He hadn't turned out to be the aloof, independent, low maintenance caricature of a cat that he'd been led to expect.

Mykonos was a loving and attentive pet who was very much the proxy child in Harry's life. Harry felt bad about leaving him for too long on his own, so when he and Amy went back to Mykonos (the island) for a week, Harry paid Maria to spend a few hours every day with Mykonos (the cat).

Mykonos had learnt over the last year that the packing of suitcases was not a good thing. Indeed, the sight of a suitcase made him terribly anxious. A small suitcase indicated that Harry would be going away but that he would be back soon. Two big suitcases signalled that they would both be gone, and for longer. Mykonos had also learnt from experience that they did always return, and this was some comfort. As a result, their absences had become less traumatic for him over time, because they had always returned. Nevertheless, when Mykonos saw the big suitcases open on the bed and being filled with clothes, he climbed into one of the suitcases and he refused to move. It was his way of saying *'please don't go'* or *'take me with you'*, and it made Harry feel all the more guilty about leaving him.

On this occasion, Mykonos expressed his displeasure by leaving a neat little poo in Amy's half-packed suitcase, which she had left unattended. He carefully covered the poo by moving a blouse over it with his paw. Amy didn't spot his 'present' when she returned to finish her packing. She only discovered the poo, placed neatly between her carefully folded blouses, when she opened her case in the hotel room. She was furious.

Harry and Amy had a relaxing week in Mykonos. Maria sent Harry photos of Mykonos (the cat) whilst they were away, and when they returned home, Mykonos was euphoric to see them. It had been a long, tedious week for him and many an hour was spent by the front door, hoping it would open and that there would be Harry.

When they did return home, Mykonos spent the first night curled up on the bed close to Harry and let out a series of high pitched sighs of contentment.

The next morning, Harry and Amy both left the apartment for work at the same time. As they came down the stairs, they ran into a tall, slim and rather beautiful young woman who introduced herself as Olga Dudin, the new tenant in the top floor of the building. Olga had an Eastern European accent and spoke broken English. She explained that she had moved into the top floor, that she was from Moscow, and that she travelled a lot. She asked them whether they had any children, (to which Amy answered 'not yet') and explained that she had a five-year-old son, Dimitri, and that her maid, who she had brought from Moscow, lived with them. Harry and Amy were most welcoming and said that if she needed anything, Olga shouldn't hesitate to ask.

As Harry and Amy made their way down the street to Sloane Square tube station, Amy said that she was certain that she recognised the woman.

"What did she say her name was?" asked Amy.

"Olga," said Harry. "Olga Dudin, or something like that."

"Well, she's rather slender and gorgeous, don't you think?" posited Amy. "And did you see that Fendi handbag?"

"Yes, very attractive," responded Harry nonchalantly. "Can't say I noticed the handbag."

In fact Harry had thought Olga to be absolutely gorgeous and totally charming, but he certainly wasn't going to share that sentiment with Amy.

Amy googled Olga on her phone as they walked into the station.

"Found her!" said Amy, frantically tapping the keyboard of her phone. "She's a super model. I knew I recognised her. Look!" said Amy, waving her phone in Harry's face.

"How do you know it's her?" asked Harry, squinting to see the photos.

"It's her!" insisted Amy. "Olga Dudin, earnt four million dollars last year, the face of D&G. We have a celebrity neighbour!"

Harry and Amy went in different directions once inside the station. Amy called Charlotte as soon as she got out of the tube at South Kensington to tell her about their new super model neighbour. Harry asked Patricia, his assistant, if she knew who Olga Dudin was, and of course Patricia did.

"Russian chick, right? Used to be a Victoria Secrets' model, now does D&G and that bank, was married to some football player but got divorced," said Patricia.

"How come you know all of this, and I had never heard of her?" asked Harry.

"I guess we're on different social media," replied Patricia.

"I'm not on social media," said Harry.

"Exactly," replied Patricia. "You've got that conference call with Shanghai in a minute. Don't want to miss it. The dial-in numbers are in your calendar."

That evening, when Harry got home, Amy was in a heightened state of excitement and couldn't wait to tell Harry the news.

"Guess what," said Amy, as Harry closed the front door behind him.

"By the look on your face, this will have something to do with our new neighbour," speculated Harry, as he threw his bag on the hall floor. Mykonos had shot out of the bedroom and sped down the hall when he heard the front door opening. He rubbed against Harry's leg and then sat in front of him, looking up attentively.

"Hello boy," said Harry, leaning down to tousle his head. "I'm going to get changed and then I'm going to brush you."

"Olga has a cat," continued Amy. "Isn't that great news?"

"How so?" asked Harry.

"Her cat can play with Mykonos. What a great ice-breaker," explained Amy.

"Let's hope her cat gets on with Mykonos and Puccini," said Harry. "Do we know the sex of this cat?"

"Yes, it's a male. Niki. He's beautiful. Some kind of pedigree Persian blue something," Amy elaborated.

"So you've seen him then?" enquired Harry.

"Yes," said Amy, "Olga's maid came down and asked me to show her how to use the entry system. So I went upstairs. The little boy is super cute and speaks good English. Better than Olga and the maid. And I saw the cat. Niki."

"Well it will be nice for Mykonos to have another cat in the garden, so long as they all get on," said Harry.

"Dimitri – the boy – says that Niki has never been outside, and they probably won't take him in the garden. Apparently he never left their apartment in Moscow, and he is afraid of going outside," explained Amy.

"Oh," said Harry, "that's sad."

"Exactly," said Amy. "Which is why I suggested I take Mykonos upstairs to meet Niki. They can have a play date."

Harry didn't like the idea. "You want to take Mykonos into another cat's home. A cat that's never been outside its apartment. That's presumably had no contact with another cat?"

"Why not? It will be a play date. Anyway, Dimitri loved the idea and the maid, who, by the way, looks more like a bodyguard, said she would ask Olga," continued Amy.

Harry was concerned. "Dimitri is a five-year-old child. Of course he loved the idea. I just don't think it's a good idea to throw cats together like that."

"We'll be careful," said Amy, "and Charlotte will be there to help keep an eye on things."

"Oh, I get it," said Harry. "I see what you're doing. You're using Mykonos to get chummy with our celebrity neighbour." Harry looked down at Mykonos. "They're using you, mate!"

"And why not? Everybody LOVES Mykonos, although I'm not sure what Olga will make of him. Niki is BEAUTIFUL. One of those very expensive pedigree cats. And Mykonos is…"

"A moggy?" interjected Harry.

"No," continued Amy. "He looks like a little tiger, he is lovely looking, but he's not exactly your pedigree, designer cat."

A week later Amy had secured the invitation to take Mykonos on a play date with Niki. Olga had invited Amy for cocktails at six and was happy for her to bring her friend Charlotte.

Mykonos was in the habit of going up the stairs to the higher floors anyway because Maria would give him the run of the stairwell if it was raining, and she couldn't put him in the garden. In fact, Mykonos had already picked up the scent of the new cat from outside Olga's apartment.

Harry had noticed how Mykonos had become obsessed with visiting the top floor since Olga had moved into the building. He would shoot up the stairs and pace around the landing outside Olga's front door. He knew there was a cat on the other side of that door, so when it came to the night of the playdate, he needed little encouragement to climb the stairs with Amy and Charlotte and enter Olga's apartment with them.

Amy and Charlotte had debated what to wear for cocktails with a super model. Amy had told Charlotte that Olga always looked immaculate when she stepped out of the front door, but after much debate they agreed that she (Olga) would probably be in jeans, a t-shirt, and maybe designer sneakers for cocktails with the neighbours, and that they needed to try very hard not to look like they were trying too hard.

Charlotte couldn't believe how easily Mykonos followed her and Amy up the stairs.

"He's like a bloody dog, isn't he?" remarked Charlotte.

"He is," agreed Amy. "I didn't think cats were like this at all."

"I don't think they normally are," said Charlotte, looking down at Mykonos, who followed them up the stairs trotting like a pit pony on the heels of their designer sneakers.

They reached Olga's front door and rang the bell. There were trainers and shoes lined up on the landing outside the apartment. Mykonos was agitated and stood up against the front door as if he was trying to push it open. When Olga opened the door, Mykonos stepped back. Amy and Charlotte breathed a sigh of relief. Olga was in jeans and a sweatshirt. Her feet were bare, and her hair was up in a grip. She was indeed tall, slender and breathtakingly beautiful.

"Hello," she said, "please come in."

"Olga, this is my friend Charlotte," said Amy.

"So pleased to meet you Charlotte," said Olga, "please come in. I will leave the door open, and we will see if your cat comes in. Do you mind removing your shoes?"

Amy and Charlotte looked down at the white, deep pile carpet. "No, of course not," they chorused. *Thank goodness we didn't wear heels,* they both thought.

Meanwhile, downstairs, Harry had arrived home. He'd agreed to cook Amy and Charlotte spaghetti bolognaise whilst they had cocktails with Olga, so he started to prepare dinner in the kitchen. Harry couldn't really cook, but spaghetti bolognaise was his signature dish. He used pancetta and red wine to give it a rich, intense flavour. This one recipe pretty well represented the full extent of his culinary repertoire. Whilst Harry pan-fried his pancetta with some chopped onion, the play date upstairs was about to start.

A somewhat apprehensive Mykonos had ventured from the landing into the hallway of Olga's apartment, following Amy and Charlotte, who had gone inside. He sniffed the white carpet beneath his feet and picked up the scent of Niki. He moved forward tentatively, crouching low, his belly rubbing along the luxurious pile.

Mykonos recognised that the layout of the apartment was similar to his own. Once inside the hall, he looked through the open doors into the drawing room on his left. Amy and Charlotte had completely forgotten about him. They were seated on a leather couch and Olga was pouring white wine into glasses perched on a sideboard. (Charlotte had initially asked for a gin and tonic, but Olga only had wine.) Dimitri, Olga's son, was playing with Niki on the other side of the room. And then the moment came when Niki saw Mykonos and Mykonos saw Niki.

Amy and Charlotte were too fixated on Olga and the excellent Chablis to notice that the two cats had had a visceral reaction each other. Mykonos froze, crouching low with his tail swaying from side to side. Niki also crouched low and backed himself into the far corner of the room, as far away from Mykonos as possible.

Niki was four years old and hadn't been in the presence of another cat since he was a small kitten. The sight of Mykonos in his space made him deeply anxious. With his rear now wedged into the corner of the room, he hissed and pulled back his lips to show Mykonos his teeth. Mykonos was not deterred and moved slowly towards him. His body position was still low, and he was making quiet, groaning noises. He could see that Niki was scared, but all he wanted to do was rub noses. It had worked with Puccini. He thought it would work with Niki. And so ever so slowly, Mykonos edged commando style across the room towards Niki.

The tension in the room became palpable, with Mykonos groaning and Niki hissing. The conversation between the three women stopped rather suddenly.

"Maybe this is not good idea," said Olga getting up from an armchair. "Dimitri, go to your room."

As Dimitri left, Amy and Charlotte got up from the sofa and put down their glasses.

Amy was concerned. "I think I better take Mykonos home," she said.

Mykonos had now got within a metre of Niki. His tail was swishing aggressively from side to side and his eyes were fixed on Niki. Suddenly Mykonos felt a pair of hands grab him from behind and lift him in the air. He didn't know who it was, and he panicked. Fighting to release himself, he bit Amy in the face, and then on the arm and the hand as she dropped him to the floor.

"Bloody hell!" screamed Charlotte. "He's bitten you, he's bloody bitten you!"

Mykonos ran into Olga's kitchen. Amy stood rigid in the drawing room, frozen with shock. She could feel warm blood running down her chin. She looked down and could see that her t-shirt was drenched red and that there were droplets of blood on the white carpet below.

In sheer panic, Amy ran out of Olga's apartment and down two flights of stairs, leaving blood smeared along the wooden handrail. She felt no pain because of the adrenalin rush, but her hand was also bleeding profusely. The front door of her apartment had been left ajar. She ran through the front door and into the kitchen, where Harry was standing at the stove. Amy stood there, looking at him. Harry saw the blood on her face, and all over her t-shirt. He could also see specks of blood on the hall floor behind her.

"What's happened?" asked Harry. "Where's Mykonos?"

"He bit me," replied Amy, holding back the tears.

"Shit!" said Harry. "I knew it was a bad idea. Where is he?"

"I don't know!" screamed Amy.

"Take this," he said, handing her a tea towel, "and see if you can stop the bleeding. I'll get Mykonos and then I'll take you to A&E."

Upstairs, Mykonos was cowering in the corner of Olga's kitchen whilst Charlotte tried to help Olga remove blood stains from the white carpet.

"Don't worry, don't worry," said Olga, "my maid will clean the carpet. Please go and help your friend. She needs you."

At that moment Harry appeared in the hallway. He was holding Mykonos' travel kennel.

"Olga, I'm so sorry," he said, surveying the scene. "Of course we'll pay for the carpet to be cleaned."

"Please, it is not a problem. My maid will clean. How is Amy?" replied Olga.

"Mykonos attacked her," Charlotte interjected.

"It was not his fault," said Olga. "He was very stressed."

"Where is he?" asked Harry.

"In the kitchen," gestured Olga.

Harry entered the kitchen. Mykonos was trembling. He knew something bad had happened. He couldn't remember exactly what he had done, but he knew it was bad. He looked up at Harry. Harry put the kennel on the kitchen floor.

Downstairs, Amy sobbed with disbelief when she looked at herself in the bathroom mirror and saw her mutilated top lip and the full extent of the injuries to her hand and her arm. She used towels as tourniquets for her hand and her arm, and she pressed a face sponge up against her face. No longer numb with shock, she was in considerable pain. And she was angry.

Amy raced back up the stairs and into Olga's apartment. Charlotte was on her hands and knees, helping to clean the carpet. She glanced up and saw Amy going into the kitchen, where Harry was trying to coax Mykonos into his kennel. Amy leant down and grabbed Mykonos by the scruff of the neck, carrying him out of the apartment, followed closely by Harry and Charlotte. Once outside, Amy threw Mykonos down the stairs. He went high into the air and landed by the elevator on the half-landing some twenty feet below. It was a soft landing on all four paws. Mykonos looked up at Amy for a moment and then ran down the remaining stairs and back into his own apartment.

"It's not his fault!" Harry shouted at Amy.

"He attacked me!" she replied, bursting into tears again. "He'll have to go."

"It's not his fault!" repeated Harry.

"Go, on, take the side of your precious cat," blurted Amy, through the tears.

"I think you should go to hospital, love," Charlotte interjected.

"Yes, I know. Will you come with me, Charlotte?" asked Amy.

"I'll come with you," insisted Harry.

"No, it's okay," replied Amy. "Clearly your cat is way more important than me. I hope you'll be happy together."

Nevertheless, Harry insisted on taking Amy to the hospital. Charlotte came with them. Nobody spoke in the taxi on the way to Chelsea and Westminster Hospital, and they only had to wait a few minutes after arriving at A&E before they were seen. The bites in Amy's hand and arm were deep, and her arm had already started to swell. The doctors explained that she would need to stay at the hospital overnight so that they could give her antibiotics intravenously. They also put four stitches in her lip. She asked whether there would be a scar on her lip, and they said that there might be a small one. A friend of a friend of Charlotte's knew the consultant plastic surgeon at the hospital. He was on duty and Charlotte pulled in a favour and asked him to see Amy. The plastic surgeon told Amy that regular stitches would most likely leave a scar and that as she was staying overnight, he would redo the stitches the next day.

Amy was traumatised by the prospect of having the smallest of scars and barely slept overnight. She was angry and she was anxious. Angry with Harry for bringing Mykonos into their life, angry with Mykonos for biting her, angry with herself for having taken him upstairs to Olga's apartment, and anxious that she would be scarred for life. The next day, she had fifteen micro-stitches in her lip. As a result, there was no visible scar once the lip had healed. Her arm had continued to balloon overnight as the infection worsened and she spent a further week in hospital so it could be treated before she was allowed home.

Whilst Amy was in hospital, Harry would spend each night in bed with Mykonos curled up asleep on the duvet between his legs. Sometimes Mykonos would stand on his chest and massage it before preening himself and then curling up to go to sleep.

Harry explained to Maria how Amy had ended up in hospital and asked Maria to be careful when she picked Mykonos up or put her face close to his, but Maria was not in the least bit concerned. She trusted Mykonos and told Harry that Amy should never have taken Mykonos into the neighbour's apartment. Of course Harry agreed with her.

"You're going to keep him, aren't you?" asked Maria. "If you don't want to keep him, I'll take him," she continued, "but I think you should keep him. He loves you."

Harry re-assured Maria that he had no intention of giving up Mykonos. He was certain that this was a one-off feral moment of madness triggered by the ridiculous 'play date' in Olga's apartment, but how could he convince Amy?

Patricia, his assistant, who was never shy when it came to asking the killer question, asked Harry whether, if he had to choose between Mykonos and Amy, would he choose his cat or his girlfriend? Harry laughed the question off.

"Come on, Harry," said a persistent Patricia, "you've got to choose. Mykonos or Amy? Who's is it going to be? She's not going to stay in the apartment with that cat."

"That's ridiculous," insisted Harry. "There won't need to be a choice. Amy will come home, and Mykonos is staying."

Chapter 11
Another Long Winter

When Amy returned home from hospital, there was no talk of sending Mykonos away. She'd had a week in hospital to reflect on what had happened, and deep down she knew that it had been foolish to take Mykonos into another cat's home. She'd used the pretext of the play date to secure a social engagement with Olga and the whole thing had backfired.

Or had it? On Amy's second day in hospital, Harry delivered a bouquet of flowers from Olga, accompanied by a nice hand written note. And on her fifth day in hospital, Harry delivered an envelope from Olga which contained invitations for Amy and Charlotte to attend London Fashion Week's opening party that September. It almost made the whole unfortunate incident of the cat, the mutilated lip, and the deep-tissue infection worthwhile.

Amy was relieved to get home after a week in hospital. When the front door opened, Mykonos came to greet her and rubbed his torso against her legs. He then looked up at her as if to say *'sorry'*. She leant down to stroke him, as if to tell him everything was okay. She was nervous about having him in the bedroom for the first couple of nights but once he had spent a night on the bed, she realised that this had been some kind of aberration. Her mother, an ardent cat lover, had pointed out that cats aren't fully domesticated. They still have that feral instinct. It's why homeless cats survive on the streets when a stray dog would most likely starve. "You just have to keep an eye on when the ears go back and they show their teeth, darling." It was her advice to Amy.

And so the summer drew to an end and Mykonos slipped back into his usual weekday routine. He would sit on the piano watching the comings and goings in the street below. He would spend an inordinate amount of time grooming himself. And he would get a few hours in the garden in the morning when Maria came to clean. Most of all, though, he would spend many hours sleeping by the front door, waiting for Harry and Amy to come home from work. Because when Harry and Amy came home, that's when the magic started.

Firstly, there was the magic of light. When Harry or Amy came home and it was getting dark indoors, the lights came on. He didn't understand why. But he knew that when they came through the door, the lights would come on.

And then there was the magic of the water that would flow from the silver apertures in some of the rooms. The water never flowed when he was on his own, but Harry and Amy had the ability to make the water flow. Mykonos would jump up onto the work surface by the kitchen sink and put his head under the silver aperture. This was the signal for Harry or Amy to make the water flow. He had no interest in drinking from a water bowl when he could drink from a water fountain. He loved the sight and sound of running water, and even when he didn't want to drink, he would still fixate on it for as long as the tap was left on.

And then there were all the magical smells of Harry and Amy. Unfamiliar smells on their clothes and their shoes that told him something about where they had been that day. And the familiar smells of Harry's sweat and the gym kits thrown on the floor of the dressing room that would drive Mykonos into a frenzy. The only other smell to have that effect was the smell of olives. The smell of the anchovies and brine that the olives had been doused in drove Mykonos crazy. He would race around the apartment after having inhaled the heady mix of olives and anchovies in brine.

During the evenings Mykonos would curl up and sleep on Harry's lap whilst Harry replied to emails that he'd received from the US after London had closed. And when Harry went to bed, he would follow shortly afterwards.

Mykonos lived for the weekends, or what he knew to be the days when Harry and Amy didn't leave early and come home late. In the Autumn, Mykonos could still spend much of the day in the garden. But as winter approached and it was sometimes too rainy or just too cold for him to go outside for long, Harry produced a stick with string attached to the end of it, and a feather attached to the end of the string. Mykonos didn't quite understand what the stick was, and why the feather suddenly came to life, but it provided him with many hours of exercise, as Harry flicked the feather from side to side and dragged it around the apartment. Mykonos would chase the feather as if his life depended on it. When he eventually caught it, he'd hold the feather, or the string attached to it tightly in his mouth. Harry would then place the stick on the floor and Mykonos would triumphantly drag the stick around the apartment behind him.

Mykonos was not the only inhabitant of the building to be lonely. Olga's son, Dimitri, would spend many a week without his mother when she was travelling for a photo shoot or a fashion show. Olga's Russian maid come bodyguard, Zoya, would look after Dimitri – taking and fetching him from school, cooking for him, and generally chaperoning for him. And Dimitri did have Niki for companionship, but he was under strict instructions not to allow Niki out of the apartment (let alone into the garden).

Sometimes after school or at the weekend, Dimitri would take a small football into the garden and kick it around on his own.

It wasn't long before Dimitri found himself in the garden at the same time as Mykonos. He had been in his bedroom when Mykonos had bitten Amy, so he hadn't seen the full horror of that attack, but his mother had warned him to be careful around Mykonos. Indeed, the word had spread throughout the building and along that end of the street that Mykonos was unpredictable and had attacked his owner, which was somewhat unfair, given the circumstances, but that's how reputations are formed. In any event, Dimitri was not afraid of Mykonos and when Mykonos started to chase and intercept his football, Dimitri was happy to kick the ball around and have Mykonos snapping at his heels. Sometimes Mykonos was successful and managed to take the ball from Dimitri. Other times, Dimitri would simply kick the ball down the garden and then watch Mykonos chase after it and retrieve it. Despite the size of the ball, Mykonos would push it along the grass and deposit it back at Dimitri's feet. Dimitri was impressed by Mykonos' ball skills and Mykonos never tired of chasing the ball up and down the garden. But as Autumn drew to a close and the weather deteriorated, Dimitri spent less time in the garden, and so did Mykonos.

Maria would still take Mykonos downstairs to the back door and give him the option of going outside, even if it was raining. After poking his head outside and sniffing the cold air, Mykonos would usually follow her back upstairs to the apartment. He yearned for those long summer days, stretched out on the lawn with the sun beating on his back and Puccini by his side.

As Christmas approached, Amy decided to take the risk of having another Christmas tree. Mykonos was now eighteen months old, five kilos in weight (and still growing), and Amy figured that he was probably too big now to crawl between the branches and climb the tree. She was right.

This year's tree was the biggest and the best ever. It was a triumph. Amy had learnt that, provided there were no decorations that Mykonos could reach from the floor or from adjacent furniture, her Christmas decorations were safe. This, of course, was hugely frustrating for Mykonos.

Harry and Amy went to Thailand for two weeks over Christmas and New Year. It was the one time of the year for Harry when the constant flow of work emails almost dried up and he could get a real break. He loved Thailand because the weather had always been good at that time of year, the food and service were excellent, and the remote corner of Phuket where they stayed was a quiet and relaxing haven.

Harry felt guilty about leaving Mykonos for so long, but it had been a tough year at work for his firm, he had been under a huge amount of sustained pressure, and he needed the break. Maria could come in most days to check on Mykonos, and Harry arranged for Matt, the caretaker living in the basement of the building next door, to pop in and feed Mykonos on the days that Maria couldn't visit. Harry would text Maria and Matt on the pretext that he wanted to make sure that Mykonos was fine, but what he really wanted to do was make sure that they had been to the apartment.

On New Year's Day Matt sent Harry a picture of his right hand which clearly had bite marks on it (in fact the perfect arch of Mykonos' bite). The message from Matt said that when he had gone to feed Mykonos, the cat had slipped out of the front door as soon as he had opened it, and when he grabbed Mykonos and tried to pick him up to bring him in, Mykonos had bitten his hand. Harry was mortified. Matt replied not to worry, that he would get some antibiotics, and that he had managed to get Mykonos back into the apartment.

Truth be told, this was probably the worst two weeks of Mykonos' adult life. Harry and Amy had been away before, and they had always come home. Mykonos didn't have an exact concept of how long these absences had lasted. Sometimes it felt like no time at all. Other times it felt much longer. But they did always come back. So he would sleep by the door in the hope that he would hear the key turning in the lock, the door would open, and it would be Harry. This time, however, it felt longer, and doubts began to play on his mind. Would Harry ever come back? Although this pattern of Harry and Amy going away had happened repeatedly over the years, Mykonos' loneliness during their absences was becoming more intense.

It was snowing on 3 January, when Harry and Amy arrived back in London. They were tanned and relaxed. It had been the perfect break. But from the moment they boarded their plane in Bangkok, Harry could not wait to get home and see Mykonos. As the taxi sped into town, the sense of expectation was heightened, and when they finally arrived outside their house, Harry raced upstairs, leaving the suitcases downstairs in the hall, and opened the front door. And there was Mykonos. He had been asleep by the front door and the sound of the key turning in the lock had woken him. He looked up. It was Harry.

"Hello boy," said Harry.

Mykonos was overcome with joy. He rolled onto his back and stretched out. Harry kneeled down and rubbed his fluffy tummy. He then sat on the floor as Mykonos circled him, rubbing up against him, and meowing loudly, as if to say, *'Where the hell have you been?'*

Amy had been downstairs collecting the post and appeared at the door with a sack full of Christmas cards.

"Hello Mykonos," she said, leaning down to stroke him. "How is he?" she asked Harry.

"Seems fine," replied Harry, "but very pleased to see us."

"Well, at least it's nice and warm in here," said Amy. "Are you going to bring the suitcases up?"

"In a minute," said Harry, as he picked Mykonos up and cradled him in his arms.

Once the suitcases were in the bedroom, Harry started to unpack whilst Amy sat on the bed, opening Christmas cards. She gave Harry a running commentary on who had sent which card and whether the card was tasteful or tacky. Every now and then she would interrupt his unpacking to show him a card that was of special interest.

"Look at Seamus and Juanita's card. It's a lovely picture of their twins dressed as Santa's elves," gushed Amy, shoving the card in front of Harry's face so he could admire the one-year-old twins.

"Wonderful," replied Harry, with a hint of sarcasm in his voice. "We should put Mykonos on our Christmas card next year. Under the mistletoe. Or in front of the tree. He'd be great."

"Don't be ridiculous," replied Amy. "Oh look, the Rouses have got all four children skiing in Switzerland. Lovely," gushed Amy.

Meanwhile, Mykonos was jumping in and out of Harry's suitcase, as Harry removed clothes and placed them in his wash basket. Harry stopped momentarily to admire the Rouse children skiing in Switzerland.

It felt to Amy as if all of their friends were now married and sending Christmas cards that featured their families. She knew that if she pressured Harry into marriage, it would probably have the opposite effect to that intended. But they had had a wonderful time together in Thailand and it was just crazy that they weren't engaged by now and planning their own wedding. She was in urgent need of some strategising with Charlotte over a glass or two of red wine.

Chapter 12
Never Say Never

It wasn't long before Spring arrived and the daffodils pushed through the lawn in the communal gardens. Mykonos and Puccini were reunited and leapt from flowerbed to plant trough to windowsill like a pair of spring lambs. Sometimes Dimitri would join them and kick a ball around. Puccini would disappear down the metal step ladder into the basement when Dimitri appeared, but Mykonos would chase the ball around Dimitri's feet and down the garden when Dimitri gave it a good kick.

Olga had told Amy that she was taking a villa in Mykonos for the month of August and that some of her supermodel friends would be joining her on the island. Harry and Amy had been thinking of going back to Mykonos that summer with Charlotte and her husband, Ed. The opportunity to mingle with Olga's set gave Amy and Charlotte an added incentive to make this happen.

Charlotte's husband, Ed Lazard, wasn't especially keen to holiday on what he perceived to be a party island. Partying was not exactly Ed's scene.

Ed had been born into a banking dynasty and was a gentleman of independent means. After graduating from Cambridge, he spent a few years in the family bank before taking a year out to find himself in Goa, after which he trained as a landscape gardener.

Charlotte had met Ed at Henley Regatta shortly before he went to Goa, and although she hadn't thought of herself as somebody who would marry a landscape gardener, Ed was well connected, and they wouldn't exactly be lying awake at night worrying about money. She had come to the conclusion that he was quite a catch. And what's more, she liked him.

The news that Olga would be in Mykonos (the island) for all of August crystalised Charlotte and Amy's plan to go there for a summer holiday. Amy booked two rooms at the Helias Ambassador Hotel. She and Harry had liked the hotel very much and it was within walking distance of the glamorous beach club, Namos, which Olga had declared to be her favourite beach club in the world.

Harry faced the usual jibes at work when colleagues discovered that he was holidaying in Mykonos yet again.

"Will you be returning with another cat then, Harry?" they taunted.

"Take me out and shoot me if I do!" he replied.

A few months later, Harry, Amy, Charlotte, and Ed set off for their ten days holiday in Mykonos. Despite Ed's preconceptions about Mykonos as a party island, he and Charlotte were enraptured by the turquoise sea, the whitewashed houses, the dry heat and the warm breeze. Days were spent exploring the island or lounging around at the ludicrously expensive Namos beach club where Amy and Charlotte people watched, whilst Harry and Ed quietly compared notes on the numerous, perfectly shaped, bikini clad women who caught their attention. They agreed that of all the beautiful women on the beach, Olga was the most stunning. What Harry didn't share with Ed was that not only did he find Olga incredibly sexy, he'd also discovered that she was clever, interesting and funny.

Panos, the beach club manager, had allocated Harry and Amy sun loungers in the third row (of five) on their first holiday two years earlier, with a look that said, 'You're lucky to have a sun lounger at all.' This year a nod from Olga had got them promoted to the second row. A significant though discreet wad of cash from Ed resulted in a further promotion to the front row the following day (and just a stones-throw away from the D Squared twins and their entourage). Amy felt that they had finally arrived. She and Charlotte would arrive at the beach at around noon most days to secure their positions. Olga and the supermodel set would get to the beach at around three in the afternoon and take a late lunch in the restaurant.

In the evenings, Harry, Amy, Charlotte and Ed would weave their way around the narrow, whitewashed streets of Mykonos Town, stopping every now and then for Amy and Charlotte to explore a sunglasses shop or a fashion boutique. There were plenty of cats hanging around on street corners or sitting on the porches of small shops and houses. Harry tried to avert his gaze. He didn't like seeing some of these skinny and mange-ridden cats, and when he did look at them, Ed would joke, "Step away from the cat, Harry."

And so it came to the last day of their holiday in Mykonos and the two couples were in a very long line at the island's small and slightly chaotic airport waiting to check bags in for their flight back to London. And then it happened.

As Harry pushed his baggage trolly forward, there, right in front of him, was a small black and white kitten trying to eat a piece of croissant that somebody had discarded on the floor.

The kitten sat up and looked at Harry.

It was small and malnourished, with tiny, dainty white paws, a white belly and perfectly shaped black mask on its white face. Harry knelt down by the kitten and stroked it. The kitten sat elegantly, like a sphynx, with its paws together, and stared into Harry's eyes.

Ed turned to Amy.

"Ames, you better watch out!" he exclaimed, gesturing towards Harry.

"Don't worry," said Amy, "there is no frickin' way we we're getting another cat."

"Well, if he's going to rescue that kitten," chipped in Charlotte, "he's got an hour in which to do it."

They pushed their bags forward towards the check-in counter as the line shortened, but Harry stayed with the kitten.

"Come on, Harry!" shouted Ed. "Step away from the kitten."

"One minute!" Harry shouted back at them.

The kitten rubbed up against Harry's arm as he stroked it and continued to look into Harry's eyes. Harry took out his phone and took photos of the kitten. He then pushed his suitcase forward and re-joined Amy, Ed, and Charlotte.

"You had us worried there for a moment," joked Charlotte.

"It's actually a very cute kitten," said Ed.

"It is, isn't it," said Harry. "Sad to see it living off crumbs dropped on the floor."

"It looks like Zorro, with that black mask on its white face," observed Charlotte.

"You're all mad," said Amy, as they finally reached the check-in desk.

Once through security and in the airport's antiquated departure area, Harry rummaged through the contacts in his phone. He was sure that he still had the mobile number for the vet's nurse. *What was her name?* he thought, *come on, you have got to remember it.*

Harry scrolled through his contacts and spotted '*Cristina Mykonos*'. That was her daughter. He remembered that he had emailed Cristina to organise the collection of Mykonos. He continued to scroll through his contacts and there it was. '*Lyra Mykonos*'.

By now their flight had been called and passengers were queuing to get onto the busses that would take them out to the aircraft. As they stood in line for the bus, Harry sent Lyra a message. It said, '*Lyra, I hope you are well. We have been in Mykonos. I'm so sorry we didn't come to see you. There is a kitten in the airport that I want to rescue. I have attached a picture. Please see if you can find it. I can't do anything now. We are getting on our flight back to London. If you can look after the kitten for me, I will send money tomorrow for its food and for the vet. I promise I will come back for it. Many thanks, Harry Parkman*'. He attached a photo of the kitten and, as they climbed the steps to the aircraft door, he sent the message.

Harry could scarcely believe that he had done this. As they shuffled along the aisle of the plane to their seats, he reflected on why he had been uncharacteristically compulsive for a second time.

'*Why did he have the need to rescue these kittens? Why did he feel a sudden connection with this kitten? Lyra would probably not get the message and it would come to nothing anyway*'.

Amy could see that Harry was preoccupied. "Work?" she asked.

"Something which couldn't wait," Harry replied.

Half an hour later, as their plane climbed out of Mykonos airport, Harry thought about Mykonos at home, and how he couldn't wait to see the little fella. Four hours and several beers and vodka tonics later, the two couples arrived back in London. Once the wheels hit the runway, Harry turned on his phone, and by the time the plane was turning onto its stand, he had a signal and text messages had started to load up; Patricia asking him whether he would be happy to get in at eight the next morning for an early call with the Singapore team, his mother asking whether he and Amy would like to come for lunch with his brother's family the following Sunday. But no message from Lyra.

As they walked through the airport towards border control, Harry flicked through the latest batch of emails on his phone, and there it was. An email from Christina. He opened it quickly and found it contained a picture of Lyra holding a small and startled kitten close to her face. The kitten was the one from Mykonos airport. Christina's message said, *'Dear Mr Parkman, we have the kitten. My mother says it is a girl. She is safe with us. Please let us know what arrangements you are making. Best regards, Christina'*.

Harry was elated and skipped all the way to the baggage belt. "It's a girl!" he said to himself. "A girl!"

"Good news?" asked Amy.

"Er, yes, actually," replied Harry. "A new client I've been wooing has given us a project."

"Great," said Amy. "Who is it?"

"Top secret," replied Harry.

"Don't be silly," said Amy, "you can tell me."

Harry's momentary elation turned into apprehension. How was he going to break the news to Amy?

In the cab home from the airport Harry thought of Mykonos sitting by the front door waiting for them to come home and how he would look when the door opened. His thoughts then moved on to how happy Mykonos would be to have a companion.

When the taxi finally pulled up outside the building he could barely wait to sprint up the stairs and open the apartment door.

Mykonos had indeed spent much of the ten days they'd been away sitting by the front door, waiting for Harry to return. And as the key turned in the lock, he stood up, stretched, and looked up to see who it would be. It was Harry! Mykonos believed Harry would come back, and there he was. Harry leaned down and scooped Mykonos up into his arms, and Mykonos let out a meow and rubbed the side of his chin on Harry's face.

Harry went back downstairs to get the suitcases. A few minutes later, they unpacked the suitcases, leaving Mykonos to roll around in the piles of dirty washing on the bedroom floor, intoxicated by the smell of Harry's body odour.

Whilst Amy opened a pile of mail which Maria had left in the kitchen, Harry sent Christina a message asking for her mother's bank details so he could send money for the vet's fees and to cover all of the expenses for the new kitten. Of course, this time he already knew about the whole process of microchipping, vaccinations and the pet passport. His message also asked Christina to reassure her mother that he would arrange for the new kitten to be collected in three or four weeks' time.

The next morning Harry arrived early at the office for his Singapore conference call, after which he briefed Patricia on the new kitten and asked her to see if she could contact Panos at Aegean Animal Transport to make the arrangements for collecting her.

"Struth!" exclaimed Patricia, on hearing the news. "How did you persuade Amy to have another one?"

"She doesn't know yet," replied Harry. "I'm going to tell her tonight. If she calls, don't mention it."

"Okay, I won't, but she's not going to be happy," said Patricia.

"She'll be fine when she realises that Mykonos will be much happier if he has a companion, and we won't have to worry about him so much," explained Harry.

"Like she gives a damn!" quipped Patricia. "And how do you know that these cats are going to get on anyway?" she continued. "They might hate each other. Mykonos might eat the kitten for breakfast."

This was something Harry hadn't fully considered, and when he did Google the subject of introducing a kitten to an adult cat, he was surprised to find that it might be fraught with difficulties. Nevertheless, the articles he read said that introducing a kitten had a better chance of succeeding than introducing a second adult cat. Harry learnt that this was because a kitten's body language is different to an adult cats, and generally less threatening. And the fact that Mykonos was a boy, and the kitten was a girl was also helpful when introducing a second cat into the household.

Christina had replied to Harry's email that afternoon and she provided him with her mother's bank details and a breakdown of the vet's costs. She also asked what the kitten was going to be called, because the vet needed to put her name in the pet passport. Harry thought about what name he could give her and then decided to let Amy choose a name, in the hope that this might help her warm to the idea.

That evening Amy had cooked dinner by the time Harry got home from the office. Mykonos was crouched over a bowl of his favourite tuna and salmon in jelly on the kitchen floor and barely looked up at Harry as he came through the front door. Normal service had been resumed. Amy was adding the finishing touches to her stir-fry and there were plates and cutlery on the table.

They sat down to eat and, as usual, Harry moved Mykonos' bowl onto the kitchen table so he could dine with them.

Amy told Harry about her day and then Harry took the plunge and broached the subject of the new kitten.

"Don't you sometimes think about how lonely he must be?" asked Harry, gesturing to Mykonos.

"Don't be silly," replied Amy, "he's got us, and Maria, and Puccini, and we're always having people over. He must be the most socialised cat in the world."

"But what about the days when Maria doesn't come, and all those weeks that we're away?" asked Harry.

"He's safe, he's warm, he's always got plenty of food," replied Amy. "He won the cat lottery, that one," she continued, tilting her head towards Mykonos.

"But what if he had a friend? A companion?" asked Harry.

"Where are you going with this?" enquired Amy. "This isn't about that kitten at the airport is it? Please tell me it's not about the kitten at the airport."

Harry pulled his phone out of his pocket, looked sheepishly at Amy and then showed her the photo of Lyra with the kitten.

"Who's that?" she asked.

"It's Lyra, the vet's assistant in Mykonos," he replied hesitantly.

Amy peered at the photo. "Is she holding the kitten from the airport?"

"Yes," he replied.

"Why is that woman holding the kitten from the airport, Harry?" asked an increasingly alarmed Amy.

"Because..." Harry hesitated. "Because I asked her to rescue her from the airport. Because I said that I, that we would bring her to London," explained Harry.

"You didn't!" exclaimed Amy, in total disbelief.

"I did," he replied. "I know I should have asked you, but it was such a rush at the airport, so I sent Lyra a photo of the kitten from my phone and by the time we had got back to London, she'd been to the airport and rescued her."

"Can't we just pay her to look after the kitten?" asked Amy. "Use the money you'll save by not bringing the kitten to London and give it to whatever she's called?"

"Lyra," he interjected.

"Yeah, whatever." Amy was dumbfounded.

"Patricia's tried to get hold of the guy who got Mykonos to London, but he went out of business. To be honest, it will be much cheaper for me to organise the paperwork and collect her myself, now I know what's involved," continued Harry.

"When?" asked Amy, still trying get her head around the possibility that there would be a second cat in the apartment.

"In around four weeks," replied Harry. "The kitten is a girl. They think she's seven or eight weeks old. She needs to be twelve weeks to bring into the country, and she needs to have her rabies jab three weeks before she can be moved, just like it was with Mykonos."

"Right!" said Amy. "Well I guess that's it, isn't it? A done deal."

Harry took her hand across the table. "It will be fine. We won't have to worry about Mykonos being on his own."

"I don't worry about him being on his own," Amy interjected, pulling her hand away from his.

"Okay. Well once you've got one cat, how much extra work can a second cat be?" Harry posited.

"I don't know," replied Amy, "but I can tell you now, I'm not sleeping with two cats on the bed. I just won't."

"That's fine," replied Harry. "Mykonos won't want to sleep with us because he'll have her to curl up with. We'll lock them out of the bedroom."

"You promise?" asked Amy.

"I promise," replied Harry. "The bedroom door will be closed at night, and we will have the bed to ourselves."

"Good," said Amy, trying to console herself in the knowledge that at least she would be able to reclaim the bedroom.

"She needs a name," explained Harry, "for her pet passport. I thought you might like to choose a name."

"Well, how about *'stupid impulse'* or *'moment of madness'*? Yes, let's call her *'moment of madness'*," said Amy sarcastically.

Amy grabbed a jacket and stomped out of the front door, slamming it behind her. She was furious.

Harry was confused by Amy's volatility. One minute she seemed happy to have excluded the cats from the bedroom, the next minute she was so angry that she had stormed out. But he knew he should have consulted her before making the decision to rescue a second kitten.

For Amy, Harry's unilateral decision to acquire a second kitten provided further evidence of his inability to embrace what it meant to be a proper couple. The cats symbolised his failure to commit to her.

Mykonos, who had finished his tuna and mackerel by now, and who'd been sitting on the kitchen table cleaning himself, climbed onto Harry's lap and made himself comfortable. Harry stroked Mykonos and Mykonos rolled onto his back to expose his furry tummy, which Harry rubbed as Mykonos purred.

An hour later, Amy had not returned home. Harry reflected further. *What was he to do about Amy? He should have told her before he arranged for the new kitten to be rescued, but it all happened so quickly. Or maybe he did just decide to do it and now he didn't want to deal with her reaction. She'd get used to the idea and they, well he, wouldn't need to worry about leaving Mykonos on his own so much because Mykonos would have a friend. It would all work out fine. Amy would be fine.*

Before going to bed, Harry emailed Christina to say that the kitten's name was Athena. She couldn't be Mykonos, so she would be the Greek goddess of wisdom and capital of Greece. Christina e-mailed back to say that her mother thought this was a great name and that they would microchip Athena that week and give her the rabies injection. They asked when somebody would be coming to collect her.

Patricia started to make arrangements for Harry to bring Athena back to London. Harry had a number of business trips planned over the next five weeks and he was going to the wedding of Amy's cousin in the last weekend of September. Amy would kill him if he didn't go to that weeding. So Harry asked Lyra is she would look after Athena until the first weekend in October and of course Lyra said that she would.

Patricia had to break the news to Harry that the only direct flight to Mykonos on the first Saturday in October was at six in the morning from Gatwick airport. Despite the early start on that Saturday morning, Harry still wouldn't be able to complete the round trip from Mykonos Island to Athens and then back to London on the same day. He would have to stay overnight in Mykonos, leaving early Sunday morning with Athena on the first flight to Athens. Harry would have to take Athena in the cabin on that short flight, and once at Athens airport, he would need to deliver Athena to Aegean Airlines cargo handlers who would put her in the hold for the flight to London. Harry would travel back to London on the same aircraft as Athena and then collect her from the Animal Reception Centre at Heathrow. Patricia worked out that the entire venture would costs no more than twelve hundred Euros and Harry could complete it that weekend.

In the meantime, Athena was getting used to living in Christina's bedroom. Whilst Mykonos had enjoyed the security of that small, comfortable room after his traumatic escape from the wasteland, Athena had been born in an abandoned aircraft hangar at the airport and had successfully scavenged food from the floor of the airport terminal after losing her mother and siblings when five weeks' old. She was used to space, and she could fend for herself. She had been undernourished, but she wasn't sick, and after a few days of premium kitten food, she was in remarkably good health.

Athena was a clever kitten who had adapted to living in a crowded and chaotic airport terminal. Indeed, Christina wrote to Harry to say that whilst Mykonos would always be '*the best*' in Lyra's eyes, her mother had, nevertheless, conceded that Athena was '*much smarter*' than Mykonos. He had been their gorgeous boy. She was their clever and inscrutable girl. Athena didn't want to be confined to Christina's bedroom and she was not frightened by the noise of dogs barking downstairs. Having lived literally under the feet of thousands of tourists and luggage trollies for several weeks, she had learnt to fearlessly navigate crowded spaces. She was a clever, inscrutable and fearless girl.

Christina's bedroom felt very small to Athena, and whilst she did not miss that feeling of perpetual hunger, she did miss the space of the airport and the stimulation of her senses. There was a world out there that she wanted to explore, and which she didn't fear.

Chapter 13
Next Stop Mykonos

Before travelling to Mykonos, Harry had to go to the US on an extended business trip, leaving Amy to contemplate the arrival of the new kitten. Charlotte took Amy to the local tapas bar for a bottle or two of red wine and a good talking to whilst Harry was away.

"I mean, how long have you been living together?" asked Charlotte.

"Over two years," replied Amy.

"And has he ever mentioned marriage?" asked Charlotte, pointedly.

"No," replied Amy.

"And has he ever mentioned children?" continued Charlotte.

"Oh God, no," Amy conceded.

"So two cats and no ring," observed Charlotte. "Clearly, he's got some kind of commitment-phobia."

"I don't know," said Amy. "He's just very laid back and not all that romantic."

"Well, give him an ultimatum. Tell him that you want to get married and you want to have children, and if he doesn't want the same things, well then maybe it's time to go your separate ways," Charlotte postulated.

"I know, I know," said Amy, "but he would make such a good father. You should see him with Mykonos…"

"Mykonos is a cat!" exclaimed Charlotte.

"I know, I know. You're right," Amy conceded.

Amy resolved to broach the subject with Harry as soon as he returned from the States, however Harry's return from the States was followed by two unexpectedly passionate nights during which Mykonos was excluded from the bedroom. Given their physical reconnection, Amy decided to put the ultimatum conversation off until after Harry had been to Greece to collect Athena.

Whilst travelling in the US, Harry utilised interminable delays in crowded airports to do some research into how one introduces a new kitten to the family cat. The online consensus seemed to be that you should keep the kitten in a room on its own and not introduce it to the adult cat for a few days. Some websites suggested wiping a cloth on the kitten to pick up its scent and then smearing the scent around the home so that the adult cat would start to get used to the kitten's smell before actually meeting it. The sites said that after a couple of days, you could then introduce the kitten to the adult cat by placing the kitten in its kennel or pen and allowing the adult cat to see it. For the next couple of days, the kitten would remain in the pen so the adult cat could see it but not attack it. Eventually you could release the kitten into the room with the adult cat and keep a careful eye on them.

It sounded like a lengthy process, and all of this made Harry nervous. *'What if Mykonos didn't take to Athena? Or even worse, what if Mykonos killed Athena?* This was too terrible to contemplate. *Mykonos was lonely – he wasn't the territorial type. Everything would be fine,* Harry re-assured himself.

The following Saturday, Harry had a minicab collect him at four in the morning and take him to Gatwick airport. As he sat bleary eyed in the cab, feeling like death, he reflected on how on earth he had ended up making a day trip to Mykonos to collect a kitten that he had known for less than a minute. Harry didn't much like early mornings, and he knew that he needed to be up before sun rise again the next day because Lyra was bringing Athena to Mykonos airport at six to hand her over. "What was I thinking?" he asked himself.

Harry had taken the kennel that was originally used to bring Mykonos back to London. He was carrying this as cabin luggage and inside the kennel was a smaller pet carrier that he would have to use to take Athena with him in the cabin for the short flight from Mykonos to Athens airport. That pet carrier needed to fit under the seat in front of him for the flight to Athens, whereas Athena needed to be in a proper cargo kennel for the journey in the hold to London. He put clean underwear, a t-shirt and his toiletries bag in the kennel as well. Basically everything he needed was packed into this Russia doll construction, with the kennel housing the pet carrier, housing a shopping bag housing his toiletry kit.

Once through security at the airport, Harry bought some breakfast and ate it at the gate. It was five fifteen in the morning, the airport was deserted, and it was still pitch dark outside. Eventually EasyJet started to board the flight. There was just a handful of passengers making the end of season trip to Mykonos, so the plane was almost empty. Once in the air, a cheerful cabin crew member announced, "There are only seventeen of you on our flight this morning, so we expect to know every single one of you by name by the time we get to Mykonos!" *No way,* thought Harry, as he stretched out over three seats. They were far too perky for that time of the morning. He slept for most of the four-hour flight.

Despite being early October, it was a warm and sunny day when the plane touched down in Mykonos. Harry prayed that during his one night on the island he wouldn't encounter a sick kitten. He was part joking, part serious. He didn't want to be confronted with another animal that needed rescuing. He took a taxi to a low budget hotel on the edge of the town and after calling Amy and having a shower, he walked into the port to get some dinner.

Mykonos Town in early October was very different to the Mykonos he knew from his summer holidays. The port's narrow, winding passageways that one could barely weave ones way through in August were almost empty. The small number of tourists were mainly Chinese. He had an early dinner at one of his favourite tavernas, where the waiter explained to him that Mykonos was a popular 'out of season' destination for Chinese honeymooners. As Harry wandered back to his hotel after dinner, he thought it somewhat incongruous to see these ever so young Chinese honeymooning couples dressed in their winter coats, exploring the whitewashed passageways of Mykonos.

Whilst eating his dinner, Harry thought about Athena, and how he would feel when he saw her the next morning. There had never been any question of leaving Mykonos (the kitten) for dead at the end of their first holiday on the island. Mykonos had lived with them for over a week, after all. But he didn't really know Athena, other than that she had come to him in the airport and that she was cute and looked like she was wearing a black mask.

Once back in his hotel room, he set his alarm for four thirty in the morning. The hotel had arranged a car to take him to the airport.

The next morning Harry was woken up abruptly by the sound of the alarm. He had a quick shower and waited outside the hotel for his taxi. It was dark outside and there was a chill in the air. He was hungry and he was tired. The taxi ride took less than ten minutes. It was still dark when he got to the small, run down domestic terminal at the rear of the main airport building. It was deserted other than for two young women at a check-in counter and the diminutive figure of Lyra standing on her own, with a small pet kennel by her feet.

Inside the kennel was a confused Athena. She had never felt like Christina's bedroom was likely to be her future home. And even though she had wanted to escape from it, she was anxious when she was put into the kennel and found herself back at the airport. Athena knew very well where she was, and she was confused. Was she was being returned to the airport? And would she need to fend for herself like she had done before?

Harry walked towards Lyra and gave her a hug. She was crying.

"Lyra, thank you so much for looking after Athena," he said. "Are you okay?"

"I am okay," she replied, "just sad, goodbye is sad, but she will have a better life in the UK." Lyra knew that Athena would be leaving Greece for a better life with Harry, but she had grown very fond of Athena over the last five weeks, and there was something tragically symbolic about the need for Athena to travel to another country because she would most likely die if she stayed in the country where she was born. Times had continued to be tough in Greece, and cats were viewed as little more than vermin on the island.

"We will take good care of her," said Harry, giving Lyra a reassuring hug.

Lyra handed Harry a large envelope. "These are her documents. Pet passport, certificate from the vet, you know."

"Thank you," said Harry, taking them.

"If you open your kennel, I will put her in," said Lyra.

"Oh, yes," replied Harry. "She needs to go in the smaller carrier on the flight to Athens, and then I'll put her in the big kennel when we get to Athens airport," explained Harry, taking the small, collapsible carrier from inside the bigger kennel.

Lyra reached into her own kennel and lifted Athena out of it. Athena clung to Lyra's blouse and didn't want to let go. Of course she didn't remember Harry and Harry didn't much remember her. Lyra managed to remove Athena's claws from her blouse, and she forced Athena into the small carrier. Harry quickly zipped it shut so she couldn't get out.

"She hasn't eaten this morning, has she?" asked Harry.

"No, nothing since last night," confirmed Lyra. "I must go," she said, tearfully.

"Lyra, did I send enough money?" asked Harry. "Can I give you something to say thank you?"

"No, Harry. You're a good man. I do not need more money. You're a good man. I must go." And with that Lyra turned around and walked out of the terminal.

Athena could see Lyra walk away through the mesh window of the carrier. She then felt Harry lift the carrier into the air and she had the opportunity to study his face whilst he looked at her. She could also smell Harry. His pheromones were like nothing she had ever smelled before, and she liked them. Her instincts told her that she wasn't going to be left at the airport, and despite her intense dislike of being confined in such a small space, she sat down in the carrier and reconciled herself to being imprisoned there for the time being.

Harry wanted to feel the same connection with Athena that he had with Mykonos, but he wasn't feeling it. He loved Athena's mask, and the slightly sinister look of her slightly too close together yellow eyes peering out from the black mask, but she had turned into an oddly proportioned kitten and nothing like the small, elegant creature he had found in the airport terminal five weeks earlier. She was rather stocky, but with gangly limbs. And most disconcertingly, she had a large, pink bottom. Harry had never been aware of Mykonos' bottom. Mykonos was generally considered to have 'medium' length hair, but he was long haired compared to Athena. And from behind Mykonos looked like he was wearing a furry pair of chaps. Nobody had even seen Mykonos' bottom. Athena, however, was short haired, and her bottom was therefore fully visible. Harry thought her tail looked like a thin black snake, however Mykonos' tail hadn't become bushy until he was a good five or six months old, so maybe all was not lost with Athena, and her tail would fill out, he thought. He certainly hoped so. He concluded that his reaction to Athena was akin to some kind of ridiculous parental anxiety, probably brought on by tiredness and the horribly early hour. He knew that this was his kitten and that he would need to love her, but it was just so easy and instant and natural with Mykonos.

Harry presented himself and Athena at the check-in counter and the agent looked at Athena's paperwork and then gave Harry his boarding pass. The sun was rising as Harry made his way into the tiny departure area. By now there were around a dozen passengers waiting to board the small plane for the thirty-minute flight to Athens.

A woman asked the passengers gathered in the departure area to get onto a coach that would take them out to the aircraft. Athena had been quiet up until now but once the coach started moving, Athena started wining and she wined almost continuously from this point until she was released from the small carrier at Athens airport. The interior of the plane was cramped. There were two seats on either side of a narrow aisle and Athena's carrier barely fitted under one of them. By now, she was distressed. She didn't like being in the small carrier and she couldn't see where she was from under the seat. Harry tried to placate her by rubbing his finger on the outside of the mesh panels. But she continued to whine to the irritation of the passengers on the plane, and to Harry's embarrassment.

As soon as they were on the ground and inside the terminal at Athens airport, Harry transferred Athena into the bigger, solid kennel. She went into it without hesitation. Harry and Athena then had another good look at each other. Harry transferred his dirty clothes and toilet bag into the smaller, now empty carrier, and set off to find the Aegean Airlines information desk. Everything was going according to plan.

Patricia had given Harry detailed instructions for what he had to do when he got to Athens airport. They would have around two hours before their Aegean Airlines flight departed to London. Harry would have to take Athena to the cargo area which was around two miles from the main terminal. Aegean Airlines had sent an e-mail to Patricia giving Harry authority to use the airline's staff bus to get from the passenger terminal to the cargo area. The e-mail advised Harry to go to the Aegean Airlines information counter where he would be given a pass for the bus.

Once at the information counter, Harry presented the email from Aegean Airlines.

"What is this?" asked the man at the counter.

"Aegean is transporting my cat to London on the nine thirty flight this morning. I need to take her to the cargo area. It says here that you will give me a pass for the staff bus so I can take the bus to the cargo area," explained Harry.

"Why does it say this?" asked the man, staring at the e-mail.

"I don't know," said Harry, "but as you can see, they say that you will give me a pass to use the bus and I don't have much time to get my kitten to the cargo area."

"But this is impossible," said the man.

Harry was exacerbated. "Perhaps you could read the email and then explain what I need to do to get to the cargo area," said Harry.

The man started to go through the email and suddenly his face lit up. "Let me see the cat," he said.

Harry held up the kennel.

The man beamed. "She is Athena?"

"Yes," replied Harry. "Athena."

"What a lovely name. Athena. You chose a good name," he said. "I'll give you the pass. You need to go outside the terminal to bus stop F for foxtrot. That is where the staff bus goes from." And with that, Harry had his pass for the staff bus.

Athena sat calmly in the kennel whilst Harry carried her through the airport and onto the bus. She was relieved to not be in the small carrier, although she wasn't much pleased to be incarcerated in the kennel. She wasn't frightened. She was a brave cat, and she liked the smell of Harry. Her instincts told her that she was on a journey, and she sat calmly on the floor of the kennel. Harry had put some water in the bowl attached to the interior of the kennel, so she wasn't thirsty, but she was starting to get hungry. It would be another six hours before she would get something to eat.

The bus driver was friendly and said that he would tell Harry when they got to the cargo area. Once there, Harry entered a large warehouse and went to a counter where Athena's paperwork was checked, her kennel was weighed, and Harry handed over almost five hundred euros in cash. And like that, he left Athena, and took a bus back to the terminal. Athena could see Harry walking away. She was distressed. She liked him and she didn't know whether she would see him again. Soon she was on the back of a truck skirting around the edge of a runaway and back towards the terminal. She was loaded into the cargo hold and when the door shut, she was in complete darkness. She sat in the corner of her kennel, trembling.

Harry, meanwhile, was boarding the aircraft and thinking about his new kitten who was in the hold beneath him on her way to her new home in London. The engines roared as the plane sped down the runway and he thought about how scary that must have been for Athena. It was.

The four-hour flight seemed to take forever but when they finally arrived at Heathrow Airport, Harry knew exactly what he had to do to retrieve Athena. He had learnt the ropes when he had collected Mykonos two years previous.

Athena had curled up and slept for most of the flight. She was hungry and anxious when she was woken suddenly by the thud of the planes undercarriage hitting the tarmac on landing. Shortly afterwards the cargo hold was flooded with light and her kennel was lifted from the hold and put onto a truck. She was transferred from this truck to a van and taken to the Animal Reception Centre. There, a man and woman she had never seen before opened up the kennel door and encouraged her to come out of the kennel. She was apprehensive at first, but she could see them putting food into a bowl and she decided to take a chance. She stepped out of the kennel and onto a table surface. She sniffed the food. It smelled good. She sniffed it again to be sure and then crouched down and started to eat. The people were making noises and one of them examined Athena whilst she ate, whilst the other removed some of the excrement that had become attached to her fur. She felt safe.

The Aegean plane had arrived at a terminal that was in walking distance of the cargo area and the Animal Reception Centre. Harry went by foot to the cargo area to get the paperwork he would need to present at the Animal Reception Centre, and then onto the Animal Reception Area to collect Athena. After a short wait a nurse appeared carrying Athena in the kennel and handed her over.

"Everything's in order and she seems fine," said the nurse handing her kennel to Harry. "She's eaten a small amount of kitten food and drank some water."

"Thanks," said Harry, taking the kennel. Patricia had booked a mini cab to take them home and it was already waiting in the car park outside.

Chapter 14
Don't You Want Me Baby?

Harry sat in the back of the cab on his way home from the airport with Athena in the kennel next to him. He texted Amy to say that they were on their way but got no response. He spent most of the journey studying Athena and putting his fingers through the bars of the kennel so she could sniff them, and he would scratch the side of her head. She was happy to be reunited with him. She loved his smell and she felt safe. Her instincts told her that soon she'd be out of the kennel and that her long journey would be over.

Harry tried to understand why he didn't feel an immediate connection with Athena. He wanted to. He was determined to. He had made the commitment to Athena, and he hoped upon hope that Mykonos would like her and be grateful for the companionship.

It was after three o'clock in the afternoon by the time Harry and Athena got home. Harry placed Athena's kennel on the landing outside the front door of the apartment and let himself in. The door was double locked, which meant that Amy must have been out. Mykonos was waiting for Harry just inside the front door and Harry was careful not to let him out of the apartment and into the stairwell. Mykonos was very happy to see Harry. He rolled over onto his back and stretched whilst Harry rubbed his tummy. Outside on the landing, Athena surveyed her new surroundings through the bars of the kennel. She had already picked up Mykonos' scent from the carpet in the common parts. Inside, Harry locked Mykonos into the kitchen so he could bring Athena's kennel into the apartment without Mykonos seeing her.

Once Harry had put Athena's kennel in the guest bedroom, he got a bowl of water and a bowl of kitten food and placed these on the bedroom floor. He then took Mykonos downstairs and into the garden for an hour or so before it got dark. Mykonos was keen to go outside, having been locked into the apartment all day.

This meant that Harry and Athena were on their own. Harry returned to the guest bedroom and opened the kennel door. Athena shot out. She had been confined for over ten hours by now and was desperate to stretch the full length of her body.

The guest bedroom door was closed for the time being because Harry wanted her to become accustomed to this room before exploring the entire apartment. On the other hand though, he thought, if she explored the apartment whilst Mykonos was in the garden, this would be a good way of leaving her scent around the place.

It took Athena all of two minutes to get to her know the guest bedroom. She jumped excitedly onto the bed, and from the bed to the window ledge, and then to the top of the chest of drawers in three quick movements, like a ninja on speed. It was as if she had springs in her heels. She loved the room. It was warm and comfortable, with a cosy soft fleece on the bed, and a carpet that was perfect for scratching. She consumed a little of the kitten food, but she was way too excited to eat. She drank from the water bowl, before flicking it over so that water poured all over the carpet. Harry placed a small litter tray in the corner of the bedroom, which she used immediately.

What the hell? Thought Harry. The guest bedroom already felt too small for this energised kitten, so Harry decided to let her run around the apartment before he brought Mykonos in from the garden. After all, it would spare him the trouble of smearing her scent on the furniture.

And so Harry opened the guest bedroom door and Athena shot out and into the hallway. She had been used to living a feral life in open spaces. Her free spirit and sense of adventure had been suffocated by her confinement in Christina's room and the lengthy journey in the kennel to London. And so she raced around the apartment, mapping out the rooms and the furniture, pausing momentarily to take in the view from a window, or to test a fabric or floor covering for its 'scratch ability'. Every now and then she would return to Harry to rub her body along the side of his calves. After around thirty minutes of sprinting and jumping, Athena began to slow down.

Harry couldn't understand why he hadn't heard from Amy. Whilst Athena continued to explore every nook and cranny in the apartment, Harry visited their en-suite bathroom, which was accessed through a hidden door concealed in the wood panelling of the master bedroom wall. The hidden bathroom opened onto a dressing room, and when Harry entered the dressing room, he could see that the shelves and hanging space were not quite as full as usual.

His heart rate increased, and he could feel himself perspiring. It was at that moment he realised that Amy had moved out. The empty shelves and hanging rails said it all. There was a letter on his bedside table from Amy. She said that she felt that they needed some space apart and that she had moved out to give him the opportunity to reflect on whether he was prepared to make a long term commitment to her. She said that it felt as though he was more interested in the cats than he was in planning a future with her, that she wanted to have a family, and that he had shown no particular interest in having children.

In fact, Amy hadn't wanted to move out. Charlotte had persuaded her that the only way in which she would get a proposal of marriage out of Harry was to remove herself from his life and wait for Harry to fully comprehend what he had lost and pursue her on bended knees, wedding ring in hand.

Charlotte promised Amy that she would have her marriage proposal within two months if she left Harry, and had argued, quite convincingly, that nothing would change if she stayed. Amy had had second thoughts that morning, when Harry was on his way back from Mykonos, but Charlotte came to the apartment to stiffen her resolve and helped her pack. Their mutual friend, Hugo, an interior designer, would be travelling in South America for two months, and was happy for Amy to use his house in Notting Hill whilst he was away.

Harry was shocked that Amy had left him, but he was also confused. He thought he wanted to be with her. He certainly didn't want her to go. But he realised that he had been avoiding the marriage issue for some time, even though he had pretended otherwise. He respected her decision and concluded that she was right. He needed to reflect on why he hadn't been able to make that commitment to her.

In the meantime, the urgent took priority over the important. Harry had to get Athena back into her room and then get Mykonos in from the garden. Harry scooped Athena up and carried her back into the guest bedroom. She didn't want to be confined there but she had no choice. Harry then brought Mykonos up from the garden. Mykonos walked through the front door of the apartment and into the hall, where he stopped. He sniffed the carpet and sniffed the air and glanced into the drawing room and the kitchen.

He was certain that he could smell a cat. Another cat had been there whilst he was in the garden and might still be there, he thought. Mykonos trotted around the apartment, with Harry following close behind. Harry could tell from the way in which Mykonos searched the apartment from room to room, that he knew there had been a visitor. And then something happened that the websites Harry had scrutinised so methodically didn't anticipate. Athena started meowing from her room. Athena's meow sounded more like a cross between a mouse squeaking and a pig squealing. It was an odd, high pitched noise. Mykonos ran to the guest bedroom door and stood outside. He looked back at Harry and then meowed and whimpered in response. Mykonos was beyond excited. There was a cat in the guest bedroom, and he wanted to see it. He wanted to meet it.

Harry looked on, confused. The websites hadn't told him what to do when the cats started meowing at each other, and they certainly hadn't told him what to do when, unexpectedly, Athena's paw appeared from under the door. The apartment was in an old Victorian building and the floors did slope in some places. As a result, there was a small gap between the carpet and the bottom of one end of the guest bedroom door. Even as a kitten, Mykonos' big paws wouldn't have been able to slide through that gap, however Athena's paws were small and very dainty. Dainty enough to slide under the door.

When Athena's paw appeared, Mykonos jumped back in surprise. But as the paw moved backwards and forwards, he edged towards it and then touched it with his paw, at which point Athena quickly retracted hers. Mykonos tried to press his nose against the gap under the door. He continued his whimpering and Athena's squeaky meow continued in response.

Harry decided to put Athena in her kennel and allow Mykonos into the guest room, so they could at least see each other. He managed to slide through a slightly open door into the guest bedroom, holding Mykonos back with his foot. Once inside, it wasn't easy getting Athena back into the kennel, but eventually Harry managed to grab her and stuff her inside.

Athena was distraught at being incarcerated again. Harry opened the bedroom door and Mykonos cautiously walked into the bedroom, crouched low, edging his way towards the kennel. Athena could see Mykonos approaching. She went from beyond distraught to beyond excited. It was a cat. She hadn't seen a cat since she became separated from her mother and her siblings. She could see that it was a big cat, but she had no understanding of the nuances of an adult cat's body language or the territorial issues that might ensue. She just wanted to play. Nevertheless, she sensed from Mykonos' body language that he was nervous, maybe even frightened of her. And so she had absolutely no fear of him, even though he could have quite easily killed her if he'd wanted to.

Cats are partially colour blind, and the yellow hue of Athena's slightly too close together eyes, recessed in that black fur mask, were difficult for Mykonos to make out. It was almost as if she had no eyes at all in the front of her head. From more than a couple of metres away, she looked to him like some kind of kitten zombie. Mykonos crawled forward, his tummy rubbing along the carpet, until he was a metre or so away from Athena's kennel. He was whimpering and looked up every now and then at Harry for reassurance.

It was at that moment that Harry made the potentially reckless decision to dispense with all of the advice he'd read online from the cat experts. Once Mykonos saw Athena's paw appear from under the bedroom door, the genie was out of the bottle. And Mykonos showed no signs of aggression towards the kitten – more a mixture of excitement and fear. So Harry took the risk of opening the kennel door, and without a second's hesitation, Athena jumped out of the kennel as if she had springs in her heels. She faced the big adult cat head on, and then something totally unexpected happened. Mykonos took fright and ran out of the bedroom, down the hall and into the drawing room, with Athena chasing not far behind him. Mykonos positioned himself on the top of the back of an armchair looking down on her. Athena circled around the armchair. Her kitten moves were not those of an adult cat, and Mykonos felt confused rather than confronted by her body language. The impenetrable pale eyes in the black mask frightened the hell out of him, and when Athena jumped up onto the back of the armchair where he was perching, Mykonos leapt to the floor and ran back down the hall to the main bedroom. Athena gave chase close behind him.

This was the most fun Athena had ever had. She had never known such happiness. She wasn't hungry or thirsty. She had plenty of space, she felt safe, and there was a playmate of her own species.

Eventually Athena caught up with Mykonos on Harry's king size bed and launched herself at him. There was a brief tussle on the bed before Mykonos ran back to the drawing room with Athena in hot pursuit.

How ironic, thought Harry, that having been anxious for weeks about whether Mykonos would kill the kitten that had invaded his territory, Mykonos was absolutely petrified of her, and she was ruling the roost. After another tussle in the drawing room, Mykonos and Athena both paused for breath.

By now Mykonos had been able to establish at close quarters that Athena really did have eyes and that she was not a zombie kitten. He had also gathered from a brief encounter on the sofa that he did have the advantage over her in terms of weight and strength, and that this was simply a game as far as she was concerned. Before Mykonos had fully got his breath back, Athena went on the attack again and launched herself into the air, landing on top of him in a ninja move, before running out of the drawing room. This time, he pursued her and after a rolling around on the bed, they stopped again to pause for breath. Harry couldn't believe his luck. They appeared to be playing. Mykonos had accepted Athena into his home.

Eventually both cats collapsed in the kitchen. They were exhausted. Harry attempted to feed them separately, because Athena had to have kitten food, and this was too fatty for an adult cat to eat. Harry soon realised, however, that this was easier said than done. He tried to keep them apart, but Mykonos and Athena ended up sharing both the adult food and the kitten food. It was something that never changed. From this day forward they always shared their food, switching bowls at regular intervals. Food would never be a source of conflict.

Harry's thoughts turned to Amy. He needed to get advice from somebody he trusted and who wasn't part of his and Amy's set of married or soon to be married friends. He settled into an armchair whilst the cats rested and preened themselves and decided to call one of his oldest friends from Oxford, Robert Dibble. Robert had missed most of his lectures and tutorials at Oxford because he was too busy socialising in London. Despite scraping a third class degree, his flamboyant personality and sharp eye for spotting the next big thing had enabled Robert to carve out a successful career as a contemporary art dealer.

Harry phoned Robert and announced that Amy had left him.

"How do you feel about her going, love?" asked Robert.

"I'm shocked," said Harry.

"Shocked?" asked Robert. "Shocked because you thought you were going to marry her and you can't imagine life without her, or shocked because she's actually walked out on you and the flat is going to feel empty?"

"Honestly, I don't know," replied Harry.

"Well, the fact that you don't know is probably why she's left you," Robert speculated.

"So you think I've made a terrible mistake?" asked Harry. "I should never have got another cat," he continued. "What was I thinking?"

"Listen, love," said Robert, "I like Amy, and every relationship is different, so I'm not judging your relationship…"

"However," interjected Harry.

"However," continued Robert, "you've been together for three years, right, and if you're not feeling like you want to track her down and sweep her off her feet and beg her to marry you, and you're more interested in collecting cats, well…maybe it had run its course?"

"I don't know if I want to marry her," replied Harry. "That's the problem."

"Listen, love," Robert continued, "she's left because she's given up waiting for you to know, and because you love Mykonos more that you love her."

"She did say that I paid more attention to Mykonos," said Harry. "And then I announced that we'd got a new kitten. That was the last straw. I can see that."

"Well, there you go," said Robert. "And how *is* the new kitten?"

"She's okay," Harry answered. "I don't feel the connection with Athena that I felt with Mykonos. She has a large, pink bottom and her eyes are a bit too close together. She scares the shit out of Mykonos."

"I'm not surprised, based on that description. You're not exactly selling her. Can't you send her back?" asked Robert.

"Send her back! Absolutely not!" replied Harry. "Anyway, she'll be great company for Mykonos, and they seem to have bonded already."

"Harry, I never thought I'd see the day that you'd have two cats and no girlfriend. You're like the bloody spinster of the parish," Robert quipped.

"Thanks," replied Harry.

"Let's have a drink after work tomorrow. Come to me. I've got some of that petrol station champagne somebody re-gifted me to get rid of," announced Robert, and with that he hung up.

Harry took a hot bath and then climbed into bed. He had an early start the next morning, and he was exhausted from the weekend's dramas. To Harry's surprise, both Mykonos and Athena climbed onto the bed and went to sleep with him. As usual, Harry was lying on his back with his legs splayed, like a pair of scissors. Mykonos curled up on the duvet roughly between Harry's thighs, with Athena also curled up between his legs, just below Mykonos. The three of them went to sleep.

At around four in the morning Athena started to scratch Harry's bare feet, which were sticking out of the end of the duvet cover. Harry was annoyed. He had been through the whole early-morning-feet-scratching thing with Mykonos, who hadn't grown out of it until he was around eight months old. He didn't want to go through this all over again with Athena. So he got up and carried Athena out of the bedroom, gently depositing her on the sofa in the drawing room.

Mykonos followed them. Harry quickly returned to the bedroom and closed the door behind him. He stretched out in the bed, unencumbered by cats, and fell into a deep sleep.

Mykonos and Athena were not in the mood to go back to sleep. They raced around the apartment, chasing each other until around half past five in the morning, when an exhausted Mykonos then decided that he wanted to join Harry in bed, and started to meow outside the bedroom door. Mykonos was a great communicator. His loud meowing expressed his heartfelt desire to go back into the bedroom and woke Harry up. Harry climbed out of bed, frustrated that his sleep had been interrupted for the second time. He opened the door and let Mykonos back into the bedroom. Athena followed. Harry climbed into bed and looked at the time on his phone. He could probably eke out one more hour's sleep before he had to get up. The cats resumed their positions between Harry's legs and after a few minutes all three fell asleep.

Harry's alarm went at six thirty and he had shaved, showered, and was out of the apartment by seven. He ran into Olga on the stairwell. She looked like she was going for an early morning run, her slender figure adorned in a skin-tight running suit.

"Amy has left you, right?" enquired Olga.

"Er, yes, she has left me," replied Harry. "I don't know if she will be coming back," he added.

"You did not ask her to marry you, then?" continued Olga.

"Er, no, I did not," replied Harry awkwardly.

"I'm sorry it did not work out, Harry, but I could see that you were not in love with her," observed Olga.

"Listen, I really need to get to work," Harry interjected. "Nice to see you, Olga. Let's chat another time," he muttered, as he bounded down the stairs and out of the front door.

"If you would like to talk, call me!" Olga shouted after him.

Harry wasn't accustomed to Olga's directness. That, and her striking good looks, made him feel uncharacteristically nervous when he was in her presence. He kicked himself for not having been more charming when he ran into her, but he was late for work, and he didn't really want to talk to Olga about his breakup with Amy.

Harry took the subway to work and as he sat there in the half empty carriage, he thought about Mykonos and Athena at home alone together for the first time.

He hoped that everything would be okay. He was sure that everything would be okay. They seemed to be getting on well and, if anything, Mykonos was intimidated by Athena. But he'd read so many horror stories on the internet about what happened when an adult cat didn't accept a new cat into the home, that he still worried that things might go terribly wrong. He sent Maria a text to remind her that Mykonos could go into the garden, but Athena needed to stay in the apartment until she had had her injections. He then focused on the workday ahead.

Chapter 15
Mother Maria

Once Harry had gone to work, Athena wasted no time in starting to explore the nooks and crannies in the apartment. There was the narrow passageway between the back of the sofa and the radiator behind it in the drawing room. There was the inside of the grand piano and underneath the commode in the bedroom. It was her adventure playground and she loved it.

Because of her size, Athena was able to get under or behind furniture that Mykonos was no longer able to because he had grown too big. She, on the other hand, was a small and overly curious kitten who took great pleasure in squeezing herself into impossibly tight spaces, leaving Mykonos to watch in awe. Even as an adult cat, Athena would manage to squeeze herself into impossibly tight spaces.

Athena's presence in the apartment was transformational for Mykonos. Not only was he no longer alone, but he was totally captivated by her. The way she sprinted around the apartment and fearlessly jumped from kitchen chair to work surface to floor to couch. The way she pounced on him link a crazy ninja with springs in her heels and then ran off. The way that she curled up next to him when the two of them collapsed, exhausted on an armchair in the drawing room after several minutes of sprinting around the home.

All of this was totally beguiling for a cat who had spent the best part of two years on his own.

For Athena, this was the first time she had felt properly safe in her short life. She had been hungry for the first eight weeks and although the hunger ended when she was rescued by Lyra, Christina's bedroom had been like a prison for a kitten who lived feral at the airport and was used to open spaces. Her instincts now told her that her journey was over, and this was home. It was spacious, it was comfortable, and it also had huge windows in every room that provided her with fascinating views of a world outside that she so wanted to explore.

In the kitchen, there were two shiny water bowls and two shiny food bowls which Mykonos and Athena shared.

There were also the two litter trays behind the kitchen door. Harry had assumed the two cats wouldn't want to share one litter tray, and that each would want its own, personal facility. But Mykonos and Athena shared one litter tray from the outset and Harry dispensed with the second litter tray after a couple of days.

At around nine-thirty that morning, and after more than two hours on their own, Athena heard the front door open and was confronted with Maria. Mykonos immediately walked up to Maria and circled around her legs, rubbing up against them. Maria knelt down and gave Mykonos and stroke and a cuddle. Athena, who initially kept her distance, was re-assured by the intimacy between Mykonos and Maria, and slowly walked towards Maria. Maria extended her hand and Athena sniffed it. It smelled of Mykonos. Maria then stroked Athena, who rolled onto her back and stretched out, allowing Maria to rub her white underbelly. This was Athena's signature position – on her back, stretched out, getting her tummy rubbed by somebody she trusted.

Mykonos sat by the front door meowing and looking up at the latch. He had observed over time that when somebody touched the latch, the door magically opened. So he leapt up against the door in a hopeless attempt to open it. Having failed to get his paw on this magical latch, he then sat in the hall with his gaze alternating between Maria and the latch. He'd make eye contact with Maria, then tilt his head towards the latch, and then tilt it back towards Maria. He had become an adept communicator and Maria knew exactly what his big green eyes were saying.

Maria opened the front door and let him into the hall, closing the door behind her so Athena couldn't get out. She walked downstairs with Mykonos following close behind and let him into the garden. She then went back upstairs to play with Athena before she began cleaning. Harry had not told Maria that Amy had moved out, but Maria realised something was amiss once she discovered that most of Amy's clothes had gone from the walk-in closet. She hoped Harry was okay, but for her part, she wasn't disappointed.

Athena wanted to go wherever Mykonos had gone, and she followed Maria around the apartment, venting her displeasure by making a squeaky noise. Even when Athena grew into an adult cat, she squeaked more than meowed, and was less inclined to make eye contact than Mykonos. In any event, if she had wanted to communicate through her eyes, it would have been difficult. Once her pupils were dilated, her eyes blended into her black mask, and it wasn't that easy to see them. Indeed, Harry found her almost impossible to photograph because she often looked as though she had no eyes.

Whilst Athena preferred to communicate by squeaking her frustration or discontent, she purred uncontrollably when she was happy. Mykonos would purr when he had settled on Harry's lap and had rolled onto his back for a tummy rub. But Athena purred so much that the tip of her pink tongue would be visible poking out of her mouth. You could see the pink tip of her tongue trembling as she purred with pleasure.

Maria started to vacuum the drawing room. Athena had not seen or heard a vacuum cleaner before. She sought refuge in the guest bedroom and from the window of the guest bedroom she could see the garden below. She marvelled at the verdant green lawn that stretched into the distance. She knew all at once that she wanted to be in the garden.

As Athena surveyed the outdoor space, she spotted Mykonos in the shrubs growing along the back wall. She stood up on her back legs and placed her paws on the window to get a better view. There was another cat with Mykonos. She could see Puccini. Athena was beyond excited. She had to get into the garden. She desperately wanted to explore this world outside and she went to tell Maria.

By now, Maria had stopped hoovering and had started dusting. Whilst Maria flicked the duster around the ornaments in the drawing room, Athena furiously encircled Maria's ankles, squeaking her frustration. Maria had absolutely no idea why Athena was squeaking but she put the duster down and spent a couple of minutes playing with the kitten before resuming the cleaning. Athena returned to the window ledge in the guest bedroom and waited there patiently until Maria eventually retrieved Mykonos from the garden and brought him upstairs. She hadn't needed to use treats today to lure him inside. Once she had got him safely into the apartment, Maria grabbed her coat and quickly shut the front door behind her. She was late, as usual.

Athena greeted Mykonos with a ninja move, running at him and then jumping over him. She then leapt onto the back of an armchair and from there trampolined from a footstall onto the butler's tray. It was as if she had springs in her paws. Mykonos chased Athena around the flat for a good fifteen minutes, until he was exhausted and collapsed on Harry's bed. Athena could see that Mykonos wasn't going to play anymore, so she jumped onto the bed and curled up next to him. Mykonos was preening himself. He had a beautiful, shiny coat because he spent several hours a day grooming. Then, for the first time, he leaned across Athena and, very gently, he started to preen her. She didn't resist. For Mykonos, it was a gesture of affection and protection. He was so grateful that she had come into his life. For Athena, it signaled his affection and protection, and whilst she was indifferent with regard to his protection, she did so crave his affection. Mykonos carefully preened her face, behind her ears, and along the top of her head – the places her own tongue couldn't reach – but then she stretched out and he continued to clean her body. He was over two years old and she was only fifteen weeks old. She was too young to instinctively return the favor.

Meanwhile, Harry was having a stressful day at work. He couldn't stop thinking about Amy. Should he send her a message and, if so, what should the message say? He also couldn't stop thinking about Mykonos and Athena, who he'd left on their own together for the first time. He'd messaged Maria to make sure everything was fine, and Maria had sent a message back to say the cats were okay. He didn't want to get home to find that Mykonos had killed the kitten. How he regretted having read so many of those horror stories on the internet.

On top of all of this, Harry was increasingly worried about work. His employer was an American owned firm, and its New York headquarters had announced sweeping redundancies in the US following the loss of some key clients. Rumors were rife that there would be redundancies in the London office as well. Harry had every reason to assume that he was secure. He was leading some key assignments in Europe and Asia, he'd been with the firm for six years, he'd been promoted to partner, and his appraisals had been excellent. In theory he was well positioned, and yet he didn't feel secure. He'd come to the conclusion that this would be a good time to be seen to be getting in early, leaving late and staying close to his boss.

Harry had agreed to go to his friend, Robert Dibble, that evening for drinks and a quick supper. A doctor friend of theirs, Claude Hunter, was going to join them. Harry should have gone directly to Robert's from the office, however he decided to take a detour and go home first to make sure that Mykonos and Athena were okay. Harry attempted to slip away from work unnoticed at six thirty, however one of his colleagues, Gavin Thomas, made a point of shouting, '*Half-*

day, Parkman?' across the open plan offices. Harry ignored Gavin's thinly veiled political maneuver to draw attention to Harry's departure and pretended that he hadn't heard. The uncertainty about redundancies had brought out the worst in Harry's colleagues. Gavin had been promoted to partner at roughly the same time as Harry. Their peer group in London numbered around twenty, and it was clear that some of them would lose their jobs.

Harry was back at his apartment by seven fifteen. He opened the front door with trepidation, fearful of what he might find. He needn't have worried. He was greeted by two cats staring up at him. Mykonos' eyes were bright and longing. He was so happy to see Harry at home. Athena's stare was harder to make out but seemed quizzical. Harry breathed a sigh of relief. They were both well. He threw his jacket on a chair and kneeled on the floor. Mykonos rubbed his cheek on Harry's face. Athena rolled onto her back and waited for her tummy to be rubbed.

Harry fed them, putting kitten wet food in one bowl for Athena, and adult wet food in another bowl for Mykonos. He tried to keep them from eating each other's food, and initially each ate what it was given. Harry looked at his watch. He didn't have much time. He waited for a minute longer to make sure that they were eating their own food and then left the cats in the kitchen whilst he changed into jeans and a polo shirt. When he returned to the kitchen, Mykonos and Athena had once again swapped bowls. This became their routine whenever they were fed. Harry knew that Athena needed to eat some of the kitten food to get the nutrients she needed, especially for developing her bones, and he knew that kitten food was way too fatty for Mykonos. But what could he do about it? If they were sharing their food, it probably wouldn't impede Athena's development. And all that fat probably wouldn't harm Mykonos' liver if it was only for a few months.

Mykonos jumped onto the work surface by the sink and Harry turned the tap on so he could drink whilst Athena looked on. He then put fresh water in their water bowls, cleared the poos from the litter tray that they had decided to share, and closed the front door behind him. As he jumped into a cab on Sloane Square, he breathed a sigh of relief. They were happy. They were well. They got on. This was going to be easier than he thought.

Chapter 16
Love Me, Love My Cats

Whilst Harry spent the ten-minute cab ride checking his emails on his way to Robert's house in South Kensington, Mykonos and Athena licked clean the contents of their food bowls.

Athena couldn't quite leap directly from the floor up onto the kitchen work surface, so she hopped from the floor onto a chair, from the chair onto the kitchen table, and from the table it was a short jump onto the work top. She then sauntered along the work top until she reached the sink. She sat by the sink for a few moments staring up the barrel of the kitchen tap, trying to figure out why it wouldn't spurt water. Eventually she got bored and jumped back down onto the kitchen floor and headed down the hall towards the bedroom.

Meanwhile, Mykonos curled up on Harry's bed and went to sleep. This was his routine when he had a full stomach, and he was left alone for what he assumed would be long enough for a good cat nap. Athena had a different idea. She jumped onto the bed and started to nudge him with her paws. He opened one eye and looked up at her. He was exhausted from the day's antics and really needed to rest. He buried his face deep into his bushy tail and pretended that she wasn't there.

Athena was not going to be deterred. She jumped over Mykonos and landed on all fours, next to his head. She then bit his neck and jumped backwards as he tried to push her away with his paw. The bating continued until he stood up, stretched, and ran after her. They chased each other around the apartment for another hour before collapsing on the bed and curling up together. Mykonos was relieved. He had finally worn her out. They preened themselves for a few minutes before they went to sleep, her head resting on his furry chest.

Meanwhile in South Kensington, Harry, Robert and Claude were on their second bottle of wine. Robert and Claude were trying to help Harry resolve his feelings about Amy.

"The thing is, I just knew I wanted to marry Lizzy from the first time I laid eyes on her," said Claude. "I never had any doubts. I couldn't believe my luck. I spent most of our engagement worrying that she might change her mind."

"That's all well and lovely for you, darling, but I don't know many chaps who are a hundred percent certain that they want to get married. Most of the chaps I know just seem to fall into marriage. It's all about timing," Robert postulated. "They marry whoever happens to come along at that moment when they're ready to take the plunge."

Robert refilled their glasses. He was an attentive host.

"Harry, how did you feel when you realised Amy had moved out?" asked Claude.

"Mixed emotions, if I'm honest," replied Harry. "I liked getting my home back."

"Ouch!" interjected Claude.

"I know. I feel bad saying it," confessed Harry.

"Liked getting your home back or life back, love?" asked Robert.

"Good question," replied Harry. He paused for a moment. "Probably both."

"Better to be honest with yourself, if that's how you feel," observed Robert.

"I think it's because I felt the pressure from her, you know, to have the apartment the way she wanted it. And I definitely felt pressure to propose to her. It was like every time we went out for dinner she was waiting for me to produce the ring," explained Harry.

"I know exactly what you mean," replied Robert. "I was dating this super-hot Guatemalan guy and I'd bought him a few things, you know, t-shirts from Dolce and Gabbana, a bracelet from Links, and the next thing you know he's expecting a bloody trinket every time I see him."

Harry and Claude were confused. The comparison was not really valid, but it was a well-intentioned effort by Robert to empathise with Harry's situation.

"Sounds like a rather 'transactional' relationship, Rob, if you don't mind me saying," Harry quipped.

"Too bloody right," replied Robert. "I found out some months later that he'd lost his amateur status."

"In which case, you had a lucky escape," Harry concluded.

"Too bloody right," concurred Robert.

"Anyway," interjected Claude, "getting back to you, Harry, I don't think you'll know how you feel for at least a few weeks."

"I just need some space to find out how I feel," said Harry.

"But you need to say something to Amy. You need to speak to her," Claude continued. "Maybe have dinner with her?"

"That's all well and good, love," Robert interjected, "but she wants Harry to marry her, and if he's not going to marry her, he needs to be careful not to send her confusing messages. He'll be torturing her and torturing himself."

"But maybe he *will* want to marry her when he realises how much he misses her?" suggested Claude.

"You are bloody joking, aren't you," replied Robert. "Why are married straights so desperate for everybody else to be in the same boat?"

Harry laughed. "It does feel like that, Claude."

"I just want you to be sure you don't regret having let Amy go," replied Claude. "Four years is a long time to be with somebody…"

"And not marry them!" Robert interjected.

"Lizzy heard from Charlotte that the second cat was the final straw. Charlotte said they're proxy children and that there was no hope for Amy," said Claude, putting his hands in the air. "Don't shoot the messenger," he continued. "Just telling you what they're saying."

"Don't worry Claude. I know what Charlotte thinks and I can guess what they're saying," said Harry, wincing. "Charlotte likes to dish out advice but anybody with half a brain would politely listen and then do exactly the opposite of whatever Charlotte recommended. Unfortunately Amy hasn't worked that out yet."

Claude nodded in agreement. "I know," he continued. "Charlotte's a moronic social climber. Too many weekends spent hanging around *Lord and Lady Much-Crapping*."

"Well said!" Robert interjected.

"But doesn't that make Amy a moronic social climber as well?" asked Harry.

"No, of course not," replied Claude. "Charlotte manipulates Amy. Anyway, I just thought you should know that Charlotte's telling everyone that if you had to choose between Mykonos and Amy, you'd choose Mykonos."

"Sensible choice if you ask me," quipped Robert.

"Amy and I didn't split up because of the cats, Claude," insisted Harry. "We split up because things weren't right. The cats brought that into focus. And, yes, if I'm honest, there's a bit of me that's excited about being single, and free, and able to date different woman."

"Well, there you have it!" exclaimed Robert.

"I hadn't realised that things had got that bad," confessed Claude.

"Not bad, Claude. Just not good. And I want good. I want to be excited," explained Harry. "I want to feel like I feel when I run into our neighbour, Olga."

"Olga, the super model?" asked Robert.

"Yes, Olga, the super model," replied Harry.

"Even I feel horny looking at Olga!" exclaimed Robert.

"Yes, she's hot, but she's also smart, and really interesting. And, yes, I know she's out of my league," continued Harry, "but I like the way I feel when I chat to her."

"Don't undersell yourself, love. You're no pig in a poke. Go for it!" exalted Robert.

"I'm just using her as an example," said Harry. "Don't get it into your heads that I think I'm going to land Olga."

"Does Olga like cats?" asked a bemused Claude.

"As it happens, she does," replied Harry. "She's very fond of Mykonos."

"When he's not biting somebody's face off!" interjected Robert, as he raised his wine glass. "A toast to Mykonos. Lovely chap when he's not biting your face off."

"Mykonos!" they chorused, clinking their glasses in the air.

That evening Harry arrived home at around midnight. As he opened the front door of his apartment, Mykonos and Athena shot out of the door, into the hallway and up the stairs. They'd had a good sleep, recharged their batteries and were ready to play. Harry was too tired to herd them back indoors. He assumed they'd be safe in the communal stairwell at that time of night, so he showered and cleaned his teeth before returning to the front door with a bag of treats. It was amazing how a couple of shakes of a packet of treats had the two of them back inside in a moment. He locked the front door, put more food in their bowls, sifted through their litter tray and collapsed into bed.

Mykonos and Athena joined him. Harry found their presence comforting. His anxiety about his work and what to do about Amy melted away as he drifted off into a deep sleep.

Chapter 17
In Sickness and in Health

As the weeks passed, it was clear to Harry that Mykonos was losing weight. He looked thinner and he seemed to be tired most of the time. Instead of leaping up at the front door and meowing loudly, whilst giving Harry that *'let me into the garden'* look, he skulked around the apartment or spent hours on end sitting under the large ottoman in the drawing room. Maria was also worried about Mykonos and sent Harry messages saying she thought he had cancer.

In contrast, Athena was growing in all directions. She had been a small, malnourished kitten when Harry found her in the airport (or when she found Harry, as he would put it). But several months of proper food and care had seen her grow exponentially. Her torso wasn't very long, and she was stout, with a barrel shaped body and almost no neck.

Athena had boundless energy and she longed to go outside and cavort in the garden. She was beyond frustrated at having to watch Mykonos and Puccini from the window of the guest bedroom. Harry could feel her frustration, but he had had to wait until she was old enough to have the injections that would enable him to let her outside. That time had now arrived, and he arranged to take both Mykonos and Athena to the vet the following Saturday morning. He had to do it on a Saturday because he couldn't take time off work, given the changes that were afoot. It would have been a bad move to arrive in the office late, or to leave early.

And so the following Saturday morning, Harry put Mykonos in the large kennel that had been used to transport both of them in the hold from Athens to London. Athena would go to the vet in the smaller pet carrier that he had used when he took her in the cabin for the short flight from Mykonos Island to Athens. Mykonos raised no objections when Harry pushed him into the kennel and locked the door. He was far too tired to resist. In contrast, Athena squealed and wriggled like a piglet in an attempt to not be put in the smaller pet carrier. Confined spaces were her nightmare and she continued to squeal her displeasure throughout the cab journey to the vet's practice.

Sandra, the receptionist, remembered Harry and Mykonos.

"Hello Mr Parkman, hello Mykonos, and this must be Athena," said Sandra, kneeling down to take a good look at the new addition. "She's a stocky little thing, isn't she?"

"Yes, she is rather," replied Harry.

"The vet is ready for you, so go on through," said Sandra, "but you don't want to have them both in there at the same time, getting all worked up, do you? Why don't we do Athena first, and you can leave Mykonos with me whilst you're in there."

"Right," replied Harry.

"Do you have Athena's pet passport?" asked Sandra.

"Yes, it's here," replied Harry, fumbling around in his coat pocket.

"Lovely," said Sandra. "Just give it to the vet. Do go through."

The door to the vet's consulting room was open and Harry went in, carrying Athena. Athena had stopped squealing. She was now anxious, and she sat still. This was the first time that she had left her home for over a month. She didn't want to go on another journey. She was blissfully happy where she was. And now she had been separated from Mykonos. *Why was she being taken into this room on her own? Would Harry leave her there with this stranger?*

"Hello there," said the vet. "This is…"

"Athena," replied Harry, handing over her passport.

The vet thumbed through the passport. "Ah, yes," he mumbled, "another kitten from Greece. Well let's get her out and take a look at her."

Harry unzipped Athena's carrier and put his hand in to stroke her. She hesitated for a moment. She hated being confined in the kennel but wondered whether she'd be safer staying inside than venture out. The vet made the decision for her, gently tipping the kennel at one end so she slid out. The vet stroked Athena and then gently picked her up. Athena didn't resist. In this respect, she was the most compliant and social of cats. Very occasionally she might hiss, but she never scratched, and she never bit.

"Stocky, isn't she?" commented the vet, taking a good look at her.

"Yes, stocky does seem to the best way to describe her. I think she looks stocky because she doesn't have much of a neck?" explained Harry.

"Well she seems to be in good fettle," said the vet, pulling her lips back to check her teeth. "How was she when you found her?" he asked.

"Thin, but not ill," replied Harry.

"I can see she was wormed and de-liced just over a month ago," said the vet, reading the pet passport.

"Yes, I just want her to have the same vaccinations that you give my other cat so she can go in the garden with him," said Harry.

"Right you are," said the vet, looking at Mykonos' records. "Still in the same place? My notes say the garden is enclosed, so no chance of them having contact with other cats?"

"There's one other cat in the garden, but he's had all his vaccinations," replied Harry.

"Okay, in which case she can have the same as Mykonos," the vet confirmed. He weighed Athena and then called a nurse in to assist him. The injection was administered so quickly in the loose skin on the back of Athena's neck that she barely had time to flinch.

"Do you want her to have kittens?" asked the vet, as he placed Athena back in the carrier.

"Oh God, no!" exclaimed Harry at the thought of more cats. "I mean, Mykonos was neutered, and I assumed she would be as well."

"Well you should book her in to be done in a couple of weeks. Is the other cat in the garden a male?" asked the vet.

"Yes, he is," replied Harry.

"In which case I wouldn't take any chances and I would get her done before she's six months old," said the vet. "Do you want to pop her outside and bring, er, Mykonos in?"

Harry left Athena with the receptionist and took Mykonos into the consulting room.

"Looking at my notes, he can turn a bit nasty, can't he?" probed the vet.

"He's fine at home," replied Harry defensively, "but he did get a bit anxious last time I brought him in. He doesn't like injections."

"And what seems to be the problem?" asked the vet, taking a closer look at Mykonos.

"He's lost weight over the last couple of weeks and doesn't seem to be himself," replied Harry.

"How does he get on with the kitten?" asked the vet.

"They got on from day one," replied Harry. "They sleep together, he cleans her, it sounds corny, but they really seem to love each other."

"That's lucky. It doesn't always turn out like that," observed the vet. "Let's try to get him out and we'll weigh him. It's about time for his annual injections," said the vet, glancing at his computer screen, "so we'll do those whilst he's here."

Harry managed to tip Mykonos out of the kennel and onto the tabletop. Mykonos crouched low and whimpered. Harry stroked him and lifted him onto the scales.

"He weighs more than he did a year ago," said the vet, "but he looks thin, and he should be a kilo heavier for a cat with his frame."

"What do you think it is?" asked Harry.

"I assume the kitten is very active?" asked the vet.

"Yes, she is," replied Harry. "Very."

"It could be worms, I suppose. Is he eating more than usual?" asked the vet.

"No, not really, but he is eating some of the kitten food. I can't stop him from doing that. I don't think he's eating more. He's just tired all the time," explained Harry.

"If he's trying to keep up with the kitten, I suspect the problem is that he's running a marathon every day," the vet postulated. "That would tire him out and might explain why he's losing weight. I'd like to do some blood test to be on the safe side. Can you put him back on the table? Thanks."

Harry lifted Mykonos back onto the table and as the vet reached down to touch him, Mykonos jumped off the table and scampered to the corner of the room. He sat with his back to the wall and as Harry and the vet approached him, he started to hiss and show his teeth.

"We're going to have to sedate him before we can take some blood samples. And we need to give him his vaccinations. I'm afraid we're not going to have time today," the vet explained.

"In which case, let me see if I can get him back into his kennel," suggested Harry.

Harry knelt down on the floor and pushed the kennel towards Mykonos, holding the kennel door open.

"Come on boy," he said gently. He pushed the kennel up to Mykonos and Mykonos climbed inside. It was a safe place. He knew the other man couldn't get him when he was inside the kennel.

Harry breathed a sigh of relief and closed the kennel door.

"Well done," said the vet. "Now, can you bring him back on Monday?"

"What time do you open?" asked Harry.

"You can drop him off any time from eight thirty and we close at six, so you'll need to collect him by then," replied the vet.

"I have to be at the office by eight thirty on Monday, I'm afraid," said Harry.

"What about Tuesday?" asked the vet.

"Yes, that should work," replied Harry.

"In fact, I think we had a dog booked in for an exploratory on Tuesday that's sadly passed away. If you can bring both back on Tuesday," continued the vet, "we can neuter…sorry, what's she called?"

"Athena," replied Harry.

"That's it," said the vet. "Bring them back at eight thirty Tuesday morning and we'll get them sorted. We'll worm them both to be on the safe side. Now, she's going to have a general anaesthetic, so don't let her eat anything after ten o'clock on Monday night. All clear?"

"Okay," confirmed Harry. "And she'll have her vaccinations as well?"

"Absolutely," confirmed the vet. "We'll get everything done for both of them. Tell Sandra on the way out to book them in and we'll see you on Tuesday."

"Thank you," said Harry, picking up Mykonos' kennel.

"Bye for now," said the vet, as Harry exited the consulting room.

Mykonos and Athena were both silent on the way home in the taxi. Harry carried the kennels upstairs and released them both in the kitchen. The cats were euphoric to be home. Athena stretched out on the hall carpet and rolled onto her back. Harry stroked her tummy. She hadn't wanted to go on another journey, and she was so relieved to be back in her home. Mykonos had become accustomed to the occasional excursion to the vet, so he didn't have that fear that he would never see his home again. But visiting the vet's surgery had never been a pleasant experience and the very smell of the place evoked a sense of anxiety and trepidation. It was, after all, where he had been neutered almost two years ago.

Harry spent twelve hours at the office on Monday. The atmosphere was becoming increasingly toxic as colleagues vied for position and the fear of job losses pervaded the whole firm. It was far from ideal, but Harry knew that he wouldn't be in until gone nine on Tuesday and he put a note in his calendar to say that he needed to leave at five-thirty that day so he could collect the cats from the vet before they closed.

Mykonos and Athena were both hungry in the early hours of Tuesday morning because Harry had not left them any kibbles when he went to be bed. He couldn't because Athena wasn't allowed to eat before her operation. As a result, they were both quite fractious and woke him up at around five. Harry did some work before putting them in their carriers and dropping them off at the vet shortly before eight-thirty.

Initially, Mykonos and Athena were placed in the cattery that occupied the basement of the vet's practice. They sat nervously in their kennels and listened to the anxious meowing of several other cats that were also awaiting their fate. Athena was the third procedure to be undertaken in the operating theatre that morning. When it was her turn, the vet removed her from her kennel and placed her on the operating table. She looked around. The room was bright and there was a strange smell. She felt cold and she was shaking a little. The nurse stroked her reassuringly and then there was a small pain in the scruff of her neck which made her jump, and soon after she felt drowsy. She wasn't aware of the mask going over her face or the shaving of a small patch of fur on her inner thigh. She drifted off and when she regained consciousness, she felt drowsy for a couple of hours. It was only then that she became aware of the small wound in her inner thigh. She licked the wound and sniffed the stitches. She tried to remove the stitches with her teeth, but it hurt when she pulled on them, so she left them alone. She was confused. They didn't belong to her, but she couldn't get rid of them. She lay still. There was a little pain but not much. The painkillers she'd been given were doing their job. Every now and then she'd meow quietly to see if Mykonos was still there, and Mykonos would meow back.

Mykonos had been aware that Athena had been taken away in her kennel from that room in the basement. He could see her kennel being carried out and he had pressed his face against the bars of his kennel door and meowed loudly. It had been traumatic to see her being taken away by a stranger. When she was returned to the basement sometime later he could see her through the bars of his kennel. She was lying on the floor of her carrier, still and silent. He meowed to get her attention, but she did not move or acknowledge his cries. His meows became hysterical when he got no response from Athena. But eventually she let out one of her quiet, squeaky meows and he was overcome with relief. He could hear that she was weak, and he did not know why, but at least she was responding. He crouched low in his kennel and waited anxiously.

Why were they there? And where was Harry? Mykonos had this sense that something bad had happened to him last time he was in this room, but he couldn't remember what exactly. The door of the cattery opened every now and then and at one point a nurse came in and checked that Athena was fully conscious. After filling Athena's water container, she picked up Mykonos' kennel and carried him into the surgery. The vet tipped the kennel on one end and although Mykonos pressed his paws into the floor of the kennel, he couldn't stop himself from sliding out. And then before he knew it, the vet threw a blanket over him, and everything went dark. Mykonos then felt a heavy weight leaning down on him. He fought to escape and screamed out as he wriggled his body backwards, but he couldn't move. And then he felt a stinging sensation in the back of the neck as the vet plunged the needle into him through the blanket. Adrenalin was pumping through Mykonos' body, and he screamed even louder. And then the stinging stopped, and everything was still. The vet didn't move, and Mykonos didn't move. He started to feel lightheaded and his legs started to feel tired. Slowly, the vet released him and removed the blanket. The light seemed harsh to Mykonos. Worse than when Harry pulled the curtains back in the morning. His vision was blurry, and he felt sleepy. He was lying on his side. He was conscious that the nurse was stroking him, and he could feel something happening around the front of his neck. What he didn't realise was that the vet had shaved a small strip underneath his throat to remove his thick hair. The pink skin underneath was laid bare and after cleaning it, the vet took a series of blood samples. The whole procedure was over in a few minutes. The vet laid Mykonos on the floor of his kennel and secured the kennel door. The nurse then returned him to the cattery in the basement.

Athena was fully conscious by now and pulling on her stitches again with her teeth to see if she could remove them. She desisted once she realised that the pain was much worse when she tugged on the loose thread. Once she had fully regained consciousness, she realised that Mykonos was no longer in the room. She had called out to him but got no reply. When the nurse returned with Mykonos in his kennel and place it next to hers, she called out to him again, but there was no response. In fact Mykonos was conscious enough to hear her but, not sufficiently conscious to answer back. He was also conscious enough to know that he needed to defecate, but not sufficiently conscious to control his bowels. He soiled the floor of the kennel, and his tail and thighs became covered in a wet faeces.

It was half an hour before Mykonos got his voice back. He responded to Athena's squeaking with a melancholic meow. It was Athena's turn to be bathed in relief. Shortly after that he was able to stand up and stretch his body.

A few minutes later Mykonos realised that a patch of fur was missing from around his neck. He couldn't see it, but he could feel the skin with his paw. The sensation of his paw and slightly extended claw running along the bare skin was strange at first. It didn't hurt, but he was distressed to find this bare patch, and even more distressed when he realised that his thighs and his tail were soiled.

The vet's receptionist called Harry at four o'clock to say that he could collect Mykonos and Athena whenever he was ready and reassured Harry that they were both fine and that the procedures had been successful. She told Harry that they recommended putting Athena in a room on her own if possible that night to discourage her from being too active. They didn't want her to rip one of her stitches open through over exertion. Harry left the office at a quarter to five and reached the surgery by five thirty. Both kennels had been placed in the vet's reception area and both cats sat patiently, peering through the bars of their kennel, hoping upon hope that Harry would come to rescue them and that they would be going home.

Mykonos was euphoric when he heard Harry's voice and then saw him through the grill at the front of the kennel.

"Hello, I've come to collect Mykonos and Athena," said Harry, gesturing to the kennels.

"Hello Mr Parkman," said Sandra, the receptionist. "I just need your credit card, if you don't mind."

Harry looked down at Mykonos, who was staring up at him. Their eyes met and Mykonos let out a loud meow. Harry crouched down and peered at Mykonos through the bars of the kennel. He could see the bare skin under his chin where Mykonos used to have a thick ruff of fur.

"What happened to his neck?" asked Harry.

"Oh, they just needed to shave a little bit of fur so they could clean the skin before they took blood. He's got quite long hair, so it may take a couple of months to fully grow back. Now, I'm afraid he soiled himself and we didn't have time to clean him because it was getting late," explained Sandra.

Harry peered into the kennel. Mykonos looked a shadow of his former self. He was thin, he had a bald patch around his neck, and his tail was covered in faeces. Harry felt upset just looking at him.

"Athena's had some pain killers, so she should be alright, but it's better if she can't run around for the next forty-eight hours, just to give the wound a chance to start healing," continued Sandra.

"Okay," said Harry.

He peered into Athena's smaller carrier and Athena pressed her nose against the mesh panel and squeaked. She then rolled onto her side, and he could see the small area on her thigh where she'd been shaved. He could also see the loose ends of the thread from her stitches. Her skin was pink, but because she was short haired, the bald patch on her thigh was barely noticeable.

"Do I need to bring her back to have the stitches removed," asked Harry.

"Yes, the vet would like to see her in a week's time to make sure everything's okay. It will only take a minute," explained Sandra.

"It will have to be a Saturday. Can you book her in for this Saturday?" asked Harry.

"No need to book her in," replied Sandra. "I'll make a note that you'll bring her in. It will only take a minute or two if you don't mind waiting until the vet has a moment."

Harry picked up the kennels and managed to get a cab outside the surgery. Once home he released Mykonos and Athena. Both cats were overjoyed to be home, but still too groggy and too sore to roll onto their backs, stretch out, and flick their bodies from side to side, as would normally have been the case. The faeces on Mykonos' thighs and tail had dried. Whilst Athena sniffed it, Harry got their brush and started to gently remove it from Mykonos' fur. Once Harry had brushed the soiled areas, Mykonos continued to clean his fur with repetitious licks of his tongue. Harry prepared tuna and mackerel wet food in their bowls whilst they circled his feet, Mykonos meowing and Athena squeaking. They were both starving, and when Harry placed the bowls on the kitchen floor, they ate voraciously.

That night Mykonos curled in the hollow of Harry's armpit and extended arm. He had been traumatised by the day's events but now he was home with Harry, he felt safe. He was exhausted and fell into a deep sleep. Harry didn't want to exacerbate the cat's misery by locking Athena in the guest room, so he took the risk of giving her the run of the apartment, and no sooner had Mykonos curled up in his armpit, Athena placed herself between his legs and also went to sleep.

Once in bed, Harry wanted to check his work emails using his phone. Normally work would have been his priority, but this evening he decided not to check his emails because he didn't want to disturb Mykonos by moving his arm. The cats took precedence over his job. At least for a few hours that night. It was only when Harry woke up early the next morning that he found he had missed an urgent email from New York telling him that his boss, Hugh, had been dismissed, and that he (Harry) needed to attend a meeting at noon with the global human resources director who was flying in from New York that morning.

Harry had expected some changes, but he hadn't been expecting his boss to be fired. Hugh had sponsored Harry's promotions over the years and Harry had a great deal of respect for him.

Harry showered, shaved, and hurriedly dressed, whilst Mykonos and Athena looked on from the bed. Whilst on the subway Harry sent a text message to Hugh to say how sorry he was to hear the news, and to ask him what was going on. He sent another text to Maria saying that the cats shouldn't go into the garden that day because Athena was meant to be resting. When Harry came out of the tube it was raining. He hadn't brought an umbrella with him, and he got soaking wet whilst running to the office. Once in the office it became apparent that several people had been fired at around five-thirty the previous afternoon whilst he had been at the vets. Harry nervously awaited his fate, although he figured that if they were going to dismiss him as well, they would have done it the moment he got into the office. The fact that he had a meeting with the global human resources director who had flown in from New York suggested to Harry that the powers that be had different plans for him.

Chapter 18
The Love I Lost (and Found)

Even if Harry had not sent Maria a message saying that Mykonos and Athena had to stay indoors, they would have done so anyway. It was a cold, wet November day outside and both cats were still tired, so they slept on Harry's bed. Eventually Maria herded them off the bed so she could make it. Reluctantly, they stood up, arched their back and stretched, before jumping onto the bedroom carpet. The two of them went to the kitchen, had some kibbles and a drink of water, and then sauntered into the drawing room where they stared through the windows at the balcony outside, which was covered in half an inch of water, before finally curling up together again on an armchair.

Patricia collared Harry as soon as he got into the office and took him into a meeting room. She then recounted who had been dismissed the previous evening. She also told him that she'd heard that Amber Fudge, the Global Human Resources Director, would be arriving shortly, direct from the airport. When Patricia finally paused to draw breath, Harry told her that he had an appointment with Ms Fudge at twelve noon.

"That's good, isn't it?" Patricia surmised.

"I don't know," replied Harry.

"No, it must be good," insisted Patricia. "If they were going to dismiss you, they would have done it last night."

"I guess so," said Harry.

"The thing is, if they dismiss you, then they'll probably dink me as well," continued Patricia.

"Honestly, I have no idea what's going to happen," said Harry. "You work for four of us, so I'm sure you'll be fine. We all need to keep our heads down and just focus on the clients."

"Yes, but Hugh has gone, so that only leaves three of you for me to look after," Patricia fretted. "And what shall I say if clients call for Hugh?"

"I have no idea what we're meant to be saying. I assume they'll tell me at noon. In the meantime, just say Hugh's not in the office and that I'll call them back," replied Harry. "Okay?"

Harry's mobile rang. He recognised the number as the vet. *Mykonos' blood tests,* he thought.

"I need to take this, Pat. Try not to worry. Harry Parkman!" he yelled, answering the call.

"Hello Mr Parkman, Sandra here at Fulham vets. Have I got you at a bad time?"

"No. Hello, Sandra. It's a good time. Sorry if I sounded abrupt," replied Harry.

"I have Mykonos' blood test results. It's all fine. There was a very small issue with his liver function, but nothing that the vet's worried about. It could simply be something he'd eaten," said Sandra.

"He's been eating Athena's food, that's the kitten food," explained Harry. "I know it's a bit rich for an adult cat, but I can't stop him eating it. Could that be it?"

"It could be," replied Sandra. "Changes in diet can affect these results," she continued, "the main thing is that there's nothing to worry about. Keep an eye on him and let us know if anything changes. Bye for now." And with that, Sandra was gone.

Harry was too stressed out about the upheaval at work to be as relieved as he might otherwise have been to hear that Mykonos had no health issues.

At noon, Harry went to the assigned meeting room to meet the Global HR Director, Amber Fudge. The door of the meeting room was open, and he could see a man and a woman sitting at the conference table inside. Harry recognised the man to be Neil Vaz, the UK Human Resources Director. He assumed that the woman must be Amber Fudge. Harry knocked on the open door and Neil Vaz jumped up.

"Harry, come in!" exclaimed Neil.

"Thank you," replied Harry.

"Harry, this is Amber Fudge," Neil continued.

"Harry Parkman," said Harry reaching to shake Amber Fudge's hand.

"Please sit down Harry," said Amber. "Neil, can you close the door?"

"Yes, of course," replied Neil.

"Harry, it's a pleasure to meet you. I've heard great things," said Amber, turning her attention to Harry.

"Thank you," Harry responded.

"Neil wanted to give you a heads up last night on Hugh Matthew's departure, but I understand that you weren't around," continued Amber.

"That's right. Family emergency. Had to go to the…doctors," explained Harry.

"I see," said Amber, "I hope everything is okay?"

"It is, thankfully," replied Harry.

"I'm glad to hear it," said Amber. "Now," she went on, "we're downsizing London following the loss of our two biggest global clients in New York. The knock-on effect on London's revenue is going to be significant."

Harry listened attentively.

"Neil will take you through the re-structure, and who's staying and who's going, this afternoon," Amber continued. "New York consulted our key clients, and it appears that you are their valued partner, hence Hugh Matthews departure and, Erika, er…"

"Van Gestel," Neil interjected.

"Thank you. And Erika Van Gestel as well," explained Amber.

"Erika is going as well?" asked an incredulous Harry.

"Yes," said Amber. "Which means that you will be leading the business transformation practice and will be acting senior partner."

"Acting?" asked Harry, quizzically.

"Yes, we want to see a plan from you of how you intend to structure the downsized team. We want to agree some revenue targets. And we want to see how you get on. You'll report directly to Constantine Gianoutsos in New York. Do you know him?" asked Amber.

"No, I don't," replied Harry.

"Well he's a spectacular leader and has done an outstanding job in New York. He came to us from McKinsey two years ago. If all goes according to plan – and I'm sure it will – you will be confirmed senior partner for the business transformation practice in London and at that time we can also discuss a raise and your target profit share. All clear?" asked Amber.

"In as far as it goes," replied Harry, "but as I'm sure you can imagine, I have a number of questions."

"Neil can handle those this afternoon. He'll take you through everything and Constantine wants to see you next week in New York so you can take him through your plan. I'm sure you're going to do just great," concluded Amber.

"Harry, can we meet back here at four?" asked Neil.

"Sure. I'll see you at four then. Thank you…for the update," said Harry, leaving the conference room.

By the time Harry got back to his desk, news of his sort of promotion had already gone viral in the office and two of his clients had also emailed him to congratulate him and to say how happy they were that he was now leading the team. Patricia was excited and relieved.

Later that afternoon Harry met with Neil and was taken through New York's business plan, the revenue he'd need to deliver and the resources he would have in the downsized business transformation practice in order to do so. As a business transformation expert, Harry had serious doubts about the way in which New York was restructuring *its* business and the feasibility of achieving the revenue targets that were presented to him. But he made the decision to be pragmatic whilst he got his bearings and nodded along as Neil presented New York's plan. Harry told himself that stepping up would be good experience, even an opportunity, and in the absence of any other options, at least it bought him time to start looking for another job. Neil reiterated that Harry would have to be in New York the following week to meet his new boss, Constantine.

At home, Mykonos and Athena had returned to Harry's bed after Maria left the apartment at lunch time and they had spent most of the afternoon sleeping there together. Both of them were still physically and mentally exhausted from the previous day's events at the vet. Athena had not fully recovered from her general anaesthetic. Mykonos was relieved to have a day in which he didn't have to sprint around the apartment with Athena in hot pursuit. He made the most of the opportunity to spend an entire day resting.

The cats were still on the bed when Harry turned his key in the front door lock at around seven o'clock that evening. He always opened the door slowly because they would often be waiting for him on the other side. He didn't want to hurt them as he opened the door, and he also wanted to make sure that neither of them jumped out into the hall.

Maria had not left the hall light on, as she was meant to, so it was dark inside the apartment. Harry turned the lights on as Mykonos and Athena followed him from room to room. Mykonos and Athena still marvelled at Harry's ability to light up what had otherwise been darkened rooms. This seemed like a kind of magic to them. They were in darkness, and when Harry came home, suddenly there was light. It was even more magical than his ability to get water to flow out of taps. Athena had started to figure that one out.

Harry gave them their dinner and microwaved himself some spaghetti bolognaise. Once he'd finished the spaghetti, he spoke briefly with his mother on the phone and then ran a hot bath. He sat in the bath and stared up at the ceiling. Mykonos and Athena perched themselves at the other end of the bath, like a pair of sphinxes, with their tails elegantly wrapped around their feet. Of course, Mykonos' tail was considerably more elegant. It was beautifully bushy and shiny, with layers of brown, and grey and black. Athena's tail had short hair and was not as long. But it fitted her overall stature and look. Both of the cats were fascinated by water; water coming out of the tap, water cascading into the bath, water disappearing down a plug hole. And when the bath was empty they would climb in and lick the warm puddles that had not drained away.

Whilst Harry lay in the bath, he talked to Mykonos and Athena, as was his want. He told them that he would have to leave them for a few days the following week, he told them how much he was going to miss them, and he told them that Maria would come in every day to make sure they were okay. In return Mykonos and Athena blinked at Harry. He had read somewhere that when cats do a slow blink looking directly at you, that's their way of saying they loved you. He always blinked back in return.

It was whilst Harry lay in the bath that he got a text from Amy. His heart beat a little faster when he saw her name pop up on his phone.

Her text said that she was so happy to hear about his promotion, that she missed him, and that she wanted to see him. Harry guessed that Patricia must have told Amy about his 'promotion'. Amy had made a point of sending Patricia scented candles at Christmas and flowers on her birthday. Harry would never have remembered Patricia's birthday, but Amy was very particular about these things. Patricia, he surmised, had relayed a rose tinted account of his 'promotion' to Amy. It galled him to think that Patricia had kept in touch with Amy after they had split, but perhaps Amy had kept in touch with Patricia because she cared about him and wanted to know how he was doing. Or perhaps she had done so with the sole purpose of keeping an eye on him.

He didn't know how he really felt. He did miss her. A bit. He liked living with her. Or did he like living with someone, but not especially her? They had been together for four years and perhaps he shouldn't throw that away without giving it a second chance. He messaged her back to say that he'd like to see her too. She asked what he was doing on Friday, and he messaged back '*nothing*'. They agreed to meet at their favourite wine bar in Chelsea.

Harry spent the rest of the week re-structuring his team and re-booting the various client assignments they were handling with the resource that was available to him. He went home to shower and shave before he met Amy on the Friday night. It felt weird to be seeing her after two and a half months of no contact. He wondered where she was living now. As he recalled, she only had the place she moved to for two months. He was nervous, like he was on a first date. Christmas was approaching and there was no Christmas tree at home. He liked what she did to the apartment at Christmas. It felt rather sterile, and not in the least bit festive, without her.

He thought about how Mykonos used to climb the Christmas tree when he was a kitten, like a rat up a drainpipe, and how much Athena would love to do so if she had the chance. And she did have a slightly rat-like look about her, although she was growing out of this.

Amy was at the wine bar waiting for him. She looked pretty – prettier than he remembered. There was no awkwardness. They chatted and laughed, and it was a great release for Harry after the stressful week at work. Amy brought a framed portrait of a photo of Mykonos that she had taken the previous Christmas. She seemed interested in Athena, what she was like and how Mykonos got on with her. Amy told Harry that her landlord, Hugo, was returning from the States for a couple of months and so she was looking at other options for places to live. Harry mentioned that he would be in New York the following week and before he knew it, he'd suggested that if she wanted to use the apartment whilst he was gone, she was very welcome to. Amy jumped at it. They agreed that she would move in on Sunday, so he could introduce her to Athena and show her what she had to do to look after the two of them. They said goodnight with a kiss on the cheek and Harry walked home with a spring in his step. It had been a nice evening and it had been good to see her.

Sunday came and Amy arrived with a small suitcase and Chinese takeaway at around seven thirty in the evening. She very deliberately deposited her suitcase in the guest bedroom and then made an inordinate fuss of Mykonos. She was genuinely happy to see him, but Mykonos was not interested in her petting and stroking. His indifference was evident by the way that he ignored her. Harry wondered if Mykonos even remembered who she was. After all, it had been a couple of months since he had last seen her. But Mykonos did remember Amy, and her presence was not especially welcome as far as he was concerned. She had arrived carrying a suitcase, and suitcases made Mykonos anxious. The suitcase was a symbol of disruption. Of unwelcome change. Of Harry going away. *What did this suitcase mean?* thought Mykonos.

Athena, on the other hand, was delighted by the presence of a new person in the apartment. She rolled on her back and stretched out on the carpet as if to say, 'Rub my tummy.' And Amy did. Amy loved Athena's black mask and her white furry tummy. She loved the fact that you could pick Athena up and that she was totally compliant. Harry commented that Athena had started to become a bit podgy and Amy reprimanded Harry jokingly for body-shaming her. He explained that Athena's hormones would be going through a kind of menopause as a result of her being neutered. Amy felt a female bond with Athena and totally empathised with Athena's weight issues.

After the Chinese takeaway, Harry gave both Mykonos and Athena a good brush and cut their nails. Mykonos loved having his long hair brushed and arched his back as the metal teeth ran along it and up his tail. Athena hated the sensation of the brush on her short hair. She squealed and wriggled like a piglet, trying to escape. Athena, however, was totally compliant when it came to having her mani-pedi, whereas Harry had to wrap Mykonos in a towel so he couldn't scratch Harry with his back paws whilst the nails on his front paws were being cut. Harry had become an expert at pushing the claws out and cutting them quickly, so the entire manoeuvre took less than two minutes for each cat.

Harry packed his small suitcase for his New York trip. Mykonos feared the worst when he saw the open suitcase on the bed and climbed into one side of it, refusing to move. Athena didn't understand the symbolism of the suitcase yet, but she climbed into the other side of the open suitcase anyway. She thought it was a game. Harry lifted them out so he could pack his clothes, but every time he returned from the closet with a few more things, Mykonos had climbed back in and had to be forcefully removed.

That night Mykonos and Athena curled up alongside Harry and the three of them fell into a deep sleep. Athena got to the comfy 'V' shape in Harry's crutch first, so Mykonos took the armpit and Harry wrapped his right arm around Mykonos. Mykonos let out a high pitched sigh of contentment. Athena followed suit shortly afterwards.

Amy slept very well in the guest room across the hall. It felt like she had come home, and she liked it. She shut her bedroom door so that the cats couldn't get into her room and because she didn't want Harry to think that she had left the door ajar in the hope that he might pay her a visit. Of course she wanted to, but Charlotte had been coaching her. "Remind him of what he's missing, and when he asks you to move back in, only agree to do so if there's a marriage proposal and an engagement ring."

In the morning Harry walked Amy through the cat's feeding routine and sent a text to Maria to tell her that Amy was staying in the apartment that week whilst he was in New York, which meant she (Maria) only needed to come on her usual three days. As Harry wheeled his suitcase to the front door, Mykonos and Athena sat side by side in the hall looking up at him. Mykonos knew what the suitcase meant and gave Harry his *'please don't go'* look. But he knew Harry would be back. He always came back. Athena didn't understand what was going on. Harry pushed the suitcase outside the door, looked back at them, told them that he loved them and that he would see them soon, and closed the door behind him. This was all witnessed by an incredulous Amy, who got nothing more than a kiss on the cheek and a *'thanks for holding the fort. Have fun'*!

Harry took a cab to the airport and boarded his aircraft two hours later, happy in the knowledge that Mykonos and Athena would have somebody living in the apartment with them whilst he was away.

Amy was leaving for work just as Maria arrived that morning and there was a brief exchange of words between them. Amy was overly nice to Maria; *how was she? How were her children? It was so nice to see her.* Maria was polite but distant. Mykonos and Athena were thrilled to see Maria. She was like their nanny. She adored them and they knew that when Maria walked through the door, this would mean time in the garden and treats as an inducement to get them back indoors a few hours later.

Amy spoke to Charlotte that afternoon and they agreed that Charlotte would come to the apartment that evening to strategise on how Amy would turn this foot in the door into a ring on the finger. Amy duly fed the cats their wet food when she got home from work and changed their water. She decided to skip clearing their poos from their litter tray (something Harry did every day). She was certain that it could wait until Maria came again on Wednesday.

Mykonos and Athena were asleep on Harry's bed when Charlotte arrived at around seven. Mykonos assumed that it would be some time before Harry would return home but at least Harry's scent was on the duvet cover. This was a great comfort to both him and Athena.

Charlotte encouraged Amy to open one of Harry's best pinot noirs and after a few sips Charlotte exclaimed, "Darling, I *must* have a cigarette. Let's go outside on the terrace."

Charlotte promised her husband, Ed, that she had given up smoking many years ago, but she didn't miss an opportunity to have a cigarette or three when she was with a friend who could be trusted to keep her guilty secret. Amy had given up smoking before she started dating Harry. She'd heard that he didn't date smokers and it gave her a reason to stop. When she moved out of the apartment, however, she started to have the occasional cigarette, especially when she was with Charlotte. It was comforting.

"We can't open the terrace doors," said Amy.

"Why ever not?" asked Charlotte.

"Harry's rules," explained Amy. "The cats can't go out on the terrace. Athena's never even been on the terrace."

"Sod that!" exclaimed Charlotte. "Just lock them in a room whilst we're out there."

"Harry would freak out if he knew," said Amy.

"Well he's not going to know," insisted Charlotte.

Amy searched the apartment for Mykonos and Athena and found them curled up together on Harry's bed. They both looked up when she entered the room, but they didn't stir. Amy closed the bedroom door and returned to the drawing room, where she opened the terrace doors so she and Charlotte could step out and light up.

It was unusual for Mykonos and Athena to be locked in a room. As soon as Amy closed the door to the bedroom, Mykonos and Athena stood up, stretched, jumped down off the bed and walked across to the door. They both sat at the door, sphynx-like, staring up at the door knob, waiting for it to turn, for the door to open, and for them to be released.

On closer inspection, however, Mykonos discovered that the door had not been closed properly. It was very slightly ajar, and this enabled him to tug on the edge of the door, little by little, until eventually it was released. Once there was a gap big enough to put a paw through, it was a very simple exercise to open the door wide enough for both cats to slip out of the bedroom. They ventured down the hall and came to the entrance of the drawing room on their right. Mykonos and Athena's eyes lit up. They could see Amy and Charlotte on the terrace, and they could see that the doors onto the terrace were open, beckoning them to go outside.

It was night-time and the forbidding darkness beyond the terrace doors might have given the two cats cause to pause for more than just a moment. In any event, Amy turned on the spotlights that illuminated the terrace, so the world outside was suddenly bathed in light. Mykonos and Athena sprinted towards the terrace doors and once outside, they slipped through the balustrade on their left and disappeared into the darkness of the neighbour's adjoining balcony. Amy barely had time to put down her glass of wine and drop her cigarette.

"Shit!" exclaimed Amy.

"I thought you locked them in a bedroom!" sniped Charlotte.

"I did!" insisted Amy.

"They'll come back," said Charlotte.

"Athena's never been on the outside terrace. Harry will kill me. I need to get some treats," said a flustered Amy, running to the kitchen.

Amy returned a moment later with the treats and shook the bag vigorously. She knew it was a sound that Mykonos used to respond to. Charlotte shone the torch from her iPhone onto the neighbour's terrace, but there was no sign of the cats. The two women chorused, *"My-ko-nosss, A-thee-naaa."* But nothing.

Mykonos and Athena were, by now, two houses away. Mykonos was apprehensive about venturing onto the terrace of the third house down the street. That terrace belonged to Agro Atwood, and he had a vague recollection that he wouldn't be safe there. He decided to remain on the balcony of the second house.

Athena, however, had ploughed on and was sniffing around Agro Attwood's plant troughs. Mykonos was aware of the torch on Charlotte's phone flashing in the distance and he could hear the sound of the packet of treats being shaken. He decided to make his way back home, weaving his way through the balustrades that separated one house's terrace from the next. The apartment was a safe place for Mykonos, he had no interest in venturing too far, and treats did it for him every time.

Athena, however, had spent her entire short life longing to explore the outside world. She had no fear of the unknown. She continued to work her way along a further two terraces beyond Agro Attwood's, until she found herself on the terrace outside the big corner house that was being renovated. It was a building site with scaffolding that covered the entire front of the house. Indeed, the scaffolding rose above the roof and then down the rear of the building into the communal garden. The scaffolding at the rear of the building had wooden cladding around it from the garden level up to the first floor to prevent access to the site from the communal garden. Harry had successfully lobbied for the cladding at the rear to be cat proof so he could be certain that Mykonos and Athena couldn't get into the building site from the garden.

And so Athena sat on the first floor terrace at the front, staring through the open balcony doors into this building site. Although it was dark, the clouds broke every now and then to reveal a full moon. The combination of moonlight and streetlights meant that the interior of the building was not pitch dark. It would be easy for Athena to explore this adventure playground and she crept inside. Meanwhile in the street below, Amy and Charlotte were walking back and forth, shouting her name as they peered up at the first floor terraces, hoping to get sight of her.

Inside the building site, thick layers of dust covered the broken floorboards and assorted rubble. The stairs had been demolished and ladders were positioned to enable the workman to move from floor to floor. There was equipment lying around – toolboxes, drills, buckets and so forth. And there was also plenty of broken glass strewn across the surfaces. And there were mice. Athena saw a mouse disappearing up a ladder and she chased after it, her heart pounding as she climbed the ladder to the next floor. She lost sight of the mouse and stopped for a moment to look at her surroundings. She moved cautiously towards the back of the building, where she found an open window. She climbed out of the window onto the scaffolding at the back of the house. She was two floors high and looking down the full length of the communal garden below her. It was mysteriously bathed in moonlight. She sat down and surveyed the view. It was a moment of enormous satisfaction for Athena. She had triumphed. At last she was free to explore at her heart's content.

By now it was gone ten o'clock and Charlotte and Amy had given up searching for Athena at street level. Back in the flat, Amy sat on the sofa in the drawing room with her head in her hands.

"She's never been on the balcony before. What if she's fallen into one of the basements? Harry will kill me. He'll kill me," fretted Amy.

"Try not to worry, babe," said Charlotte. "We've checked every basement. If she'd fallen from a balcony, we'd have found her."

"I have a bad feeling about this," Amy continued. "Look at Mykonos, he knows something's wrong."

Mykonos was pacing back and forth in front of the now closed terrace doors, meowing loudly.

"Look," Charlotte continued, fixing her gaze at Amy, "remember what we said. They're only cats. Once you and Harry have children, he'll understand that they're cats."

"Try telling him that. He's just bloody texted me," said Amy, looking at her mobile phone. "He wants to know if everything's okay. Wants me to send him a picture of the cats. We should never have opened the balcony door. Everything is ruined!"

Mykonos continued to pace up and down, meowing loudly. His Athena was somewhere outside, and he was desperate to go outside to search for her.

"Shut up, Mykonos!" shouted Charlotte. "Listen Amy, send him a picture of Mykonos and say you're about to go to bed, long day, whatever, and I'm sure Athena will turn up in the morning. He'll be none the wiser."

It was early December, and the temperature was starting to drop quite quickly at night. Athena was a small cat with short hair who had only known the Summer and Fall. She was starting to feel quite cold on the second floor scaffolding, so she climbed back into the building and found a corner to curl up in. She had started to miss Mykonos and her warm home. She was starting to feel vulnerable in this strange place. She pushed her nose into her tail and tried to get some sleep, her ears constantly twitching in response to the strange sounds that echoed around the building site.

Amy did as Charlotte suggested and sent a picture of Mykonos. Harry received it in New York and sent a message back asking if Athena was okay. Amy ignored the message and Harry assumed that she had gone to bed and that everything was indeed okay, but he would have liked to have seen a picture of Athena as well.

Athena, who was used to sleeping through much of the night, got very little sleep in the building site. At one stage, she saw another mouse scuttling across the floor and chased it down the broken stairs, back to the first floor. She almost caught the mouse but carelessly lost her footing and slipped through a hole in the floorboard. She managed to cling on with her nails to prevent herself from falling into the dark abyss below and pulled herself back up through the hole. Her lungs had ingested quite a lot of dust and she was coughing. She couldn't find any water.

Amy also got very little sleep. She searched the street again at around half past seven in the morning and then got ready to go to a meeting with a client.

Athena was woken up at eight o'clock by the noise of workman opening the front door of the site. She could hear voices and the loud footsteps of several men on the ground floor beneath her. She jumped up, stretched for a moment, and then ran to the back of first floor where she climbed through an open window onto the scaffolding outside. Athena could see the men emerging one after another from the top of a ladder onto the first floor landing. They were shouting at each other, and their boots made a loud clumping noise on the floorboards. Athena was scared. She crouched low as she moved along an external platform supported by the scaffolding until she reached its edge. Her heart was pounding. Beneath her was the garden. It was probably a ten-foot drop. The men were now coming onto the platform. There was only one place for her to go. She edged her way along a single, narrow scaffolding pole that protruded from the platform over the garden until she got to the very end. Adrenalin raced through her body and her survival instincts kicked in. She jumped from the pole into the garden below. She landed perfectly. It was as if she had springs in her feet that cushioned her joints as she fell into the thick grass. She sat up. Having got her bearings, she wandered off down the garden she knew so well and towards the back door of her house. She was cold, hungry, and tired, but uninjured.

Amy finished her early client meeting and headed back to Harry's apartment. Harry had woken up at around five thirty in the morning in New York because of the time difference with London and he had started to go through his emails. He was both irritated and concerned that Amy had still not responded to his last text the night before (asking whether Athena was okay) and so he decided to give her a call. Amy saw Harry's number flash up on her mobile phone. She panicked and didn't answer. Charlotte had told her that under no circumstances should she tell Harry that Athena had 'escaped'.

"Darling," said Charlotte, "he doesn't need to know that she escaped. She'll be back before he gets home, and he'll be none the wiser."

Harry was now very concerned. He was angry that Amy wasn't sending him the re-assurance he needed, so he could get on with his day, safe in the knowledge that Mykonos and Athena were fine. He tried to contain his emotions. He told himself, "Don't be neurotic, everything's okay, you're overreacting."

Harry sent Amy another text:

'You haven't replied to my messages. Please let me know that Mykonos and Athena are fine'.

Amy broke into a sweat when she read that text. She could hear Charlotte berating her for telling him, but she had no choice. She had to tell him.

She replied, *'Everything fine. Mykonos in apartment but Athena got onto balcony last night. Have spent most of night looking for her. Am sure she'll turn up. Don't worry.'*

Harry felt sick in the pit of his stomach when he read Amy's message. He had known something was wrong. He called again. Amy saw his number pop up on her mobile phone. She took a deep breath. She knew she had to take the call.

"Harry," said Amy.

"What happened. Where's Athena?" he asked abruptly.

"I don't know. I'm sure we will find her," replied Amy.

"How did she get onto the balcony?" snapped Harry.

"I opened the balcony door. I know. I shouldn't have," confessed Amy.

"I can't believe it!" he interjected. "You need to knock on all the neighbour's doors. She could have climbed through a window. You need to get a photo of her and get Patricia to print some posters. Lost cat. Put my mobile on it. Put it through all the doors on the street. Pin it to the trees as well." His mind was racing.

"Okay, okay," she replied. "I don't have a photo."

"I'll send Patricia one now," said Harry, speaking quickly. "I'll ask her to bike copies of the poster to the apartment. You need to ring every bell in the street. You need to put the poster through all the letter boxes. You need to find her!"

"Okay, okay. I will, I will," said Amy.

"I can't believe you allowed this to happen. I can't believe it!" fretted Harry.

"Harry, I need to go, my cab is pulling up outside the apartment," said Amy. It wasn't. It was the other side of Sloane Square. But she had to get him off the phone. She couldn't bear to listen to him any longer. Reality struck at that moment.

Harry wanted to jump on a plane back to London. His imagination ran riot as he thought of all the things that might have happened to his precious, quirky Athena. He bombarded Amy with text messages;

'Have you checked all the basements to make sure she didn't fall off a balcony'?

'Have you rung the doorbells for every apartment yet'?

'Have you spoken to the builders in the site at 41? Maybe she got into that site from the balcony'?

Patricia printed twenty posters and biked them to the apartment. In the meantime, Amy worked her way up the street ringing doorbells.

Maria didn't come on a Tuesday, so Mykonos was on his own in the apartment. He was terribly distressed and had spent most of the night pacing up and down the length of the French doors in the drawing room, staring out at the balcony, hoping to catch sight of Athena.

In the garden, Athena had waited at the back door of the house for a while and then decided to climb down the iron ladder into the basement, as was her wont. It was something that drove Mykonos crazy because he was unable to do it. It also drove Puccini crazy because the basement was his home and his territory, something that Athena did not respect and regularly violated. Once in the basement she found a warm patch close to where the boiler was vented and curled up there. Sophia Pignataro spotted Athena outside her bedroom window and laughed. She was about to go out, so the window was closed to prevent Puccini from going into the garden. Puccini sat on the windowsill indoors, tormented by Athena's presence in the basement area outside and unable to challenge this incursion into his territory.

Sophia left the building and walked down the street, where she ran into Amy stuffing posters through a neighbour's letter box. She hadn't seen Amy since Amy moved out several months earlier.

"Ciao, Amy!" shouted Sophia. Amy walked up the street to greet her.

"Hi, Sophia. How are you?" asked Amy.

"I'm good, thanks. We miss you. Are you back with Harry?" she asked.

"No, not exactly," replied Amy. "I'm using the guest bedroom this week whilst Harry's in New York. And having a disaster. Athena has gone missing. Disappeared. Harry's having kittens. I'm knocking on doors and giving people these posters in the hope somebody sees her." Amy handed Sophia one of the posters.

Sophia took the 'lost cat' poster and looked at it. "But I just saw Athena," announced Sophia.

"Oh my God! Where?" asked Amy.

"In the garden. She is in our basement," replied Sophia.

"But how did she get down there? I need to go and get her right away," declared Amy, walking quickly back towards the house.

"I'll show you," said Sophia, following her. "Athena is a very clever cat. She can climb down the ladder into the basement. Mykonos cannot."

Amy and Sophia walked through the ground floor to the rear of the building and opened the door onto the garden. There, below them in the basement, was Athena.

"Thanks goodness!" exclaimed Amy. "She alright."

Athena looked up and saw Amy. She let out a squeal.

"How do we get her up?" Amy asked Sophia.

"I don't think you need to worry about that," replied Sophia, as Athena gingerly climbed back up the stairs and then ran through the back door into the hallway. Athena was ecstatic to be back indoors. She sprinted up the stairs and sat outside the apartment front door. Amy pursued her up the stairs. Athena was sitting close to the door and staring up at the lock by the time Amy caught up with her. Athena knew that when Harry and Maria put their hands on that shiny spot on the door it opened miraculously.

Amy opened the door and Athena shot inside the apartment. Mykonos was waiting in the hallway on the other side. He was elated to see Athena. They touched noses for a second and then he inspected her, sniffing around her body to see where she had been and to make sure she was okay. Athena was equally elated to see Mykonos. He started to preen her, removing the dust from her hair with his tongue.

Amy sprinkled some treats on the kitchen table. She figured that Athena would be hungry – and she was. The two cats jumped onto the kitchen table and after devouring the treats, they went to the kitchen sink and peered up the hole in the tap waiting for the miracle of flowing water. Amy turned the tap on, and they both drank voraciously.

Meanwhile, Harry was eating breakfast in his hotel room and trying to prepare for his meeting with Constantine Gianoutsos, but he couldn't stop thinking of Athena and what dreadful fate might have befallen her. When Amy's text message appeared on his phone saying that Athena had been found, it was the best news he had ever had. The message was accompanied by a photo of the cats drinking from the kitchen tap together.

Harry sent a message back asking Amy where she had found Athena, had she fed her and was she sure that Athena was okay? Amy replied saying that Athena was in the back garden and seemed perfectly okay, but clearly happy to be home. And she then sent Harry a video of Mykonos and Athena on his bed, preening each other. Harry was finally able to focus on his meeting with Constantine in just over an hour.

Mykonos spent almost fifteen minutes carefully grooming Athena. At one stage she rolled onto her back and stretched out in total trust and submission. When he was finished, she returned the compliment and preened his forehead and around his ears. They then curled up together and slept. It was good to be home, and although Athena's urge to explore hadn't diminished, she wouldn't spend a night away from Mykonos again.

Chapter 19
Under Pressure

Harry arrived at his firm's New York offices shortly before eight o'clock that morning, and after clearing security, he was sent to the twentieth floor. An assistant was waiting for him when the elevator doors opened on the twentieth and took him to Constantine's office.

"Harry, come in!" shouted Constantine, greeting Harry with a particularly firm handshake, whilst his left hand reached up and squeezed Harry's shoulder. "Would you like some coffee?"

"Yes, coffee would be good," replied Harry.

"Gina! Coffee for Harry!" shouted Constantine to his assistant. "How do you take it Harry?"

"Black, please," replied Harry.

"No cream!" shouted Constantine. "So Harry, how's it going in London?"

"Well, obviously there's been a lot of disruption over the last few weeks," explained Harry, "so I've been focusing on the clients, reassuring them, keeping the team motivated…"

"Yeah, yeah," Constantine interjected. "Listen Harry, something had to change. You know that, right? They've got to do better in London. Do you think you can do that for me?"

"Absolutely," replied Harry. "Did you have a chance to look at the report I sent you?" he asked.

"I did," replied Constantine, "and to be honest, Harry, I was disappointed."

"In what way?" asked Harry nervously.

"Your plan is all about risk management," explained Constantine. "There's no strategy for growing the business. Just what we need to do to hang onto the clients we got. I need somebody who wants to get out there and win clients. It's all about new business, Harry. You gotta play to win. You're playing not to lose."

Harry was somewhat taken aback. "I agree that we've got to win new business," responded Harry, "and I'm definitely in the business of playing to win…"

"I'm glad to hear that," Constantine interjected.

"I have some thoughts in terms of how we might better leverage the client base in the US," continued Harry, "and also the categories we should be targeting in Europe, but we do need to hang onto the clients we've got, and to be blunt, they're worried about the changes we've made."

"Well, I know you're going to re-assure them and take care of that, Harry. I'm going to send you some figures I've pulled together for you to look at. They're your targets for London. Take a look at them and let's hook up later today. Gina's gotten you a meeting room, so you have some privacy. Gina!" shouted Constantine. And with that Constantine stood up, as if to indicate that the meeting was over, and Harry was escorted out.

Harry studied the figures that Constantine had sent him and spent the rest of the morning responding to emails from clients and colleagues in London.

Constantine's figures made no sense to Harry. The revenue targets could never be achieved unless there was a significant investment in the London office, and they had just made a number of lay-offs. It was evident to Harry that Constantine would not be interested in why the financial targets were completely unrealistic, and if he rejected Constantine's plan outright, Constantine would most likely find somebody else who would sign up to it. Harry didn't want to set himself up for failure, but on the other hand, he didn't want to be out of job.

Later that morning he had coffee with a couple of partners in the New York office who he knew reasonably well from previous assignments. They told him that New York was under a huge amount of pressure and that costs had been cut left, right and centre. They also told him that Constantine was only interested in practice heads who had relationships they could leverage to bring in significant revenue in this time of need. He wanted 'hunters' and had absolutely no time for 'farmers'.

Harry reflected on this whilst reviewing the targets that Constantine had set his practice.

He had the hunter in him. He used to enjoy opening up new client relationships and pitching for business. But he wondered if he'd inadvertently slipped into his comfort zone at work and at home. Maybe his life had become all about the status quo. Just farming the same old field over and over again.

Harry had a further ten minutes with Constantine that afternoon. He told Constantine that he would focus his practice on new business and revenue generation. He said he would do his best to deliver against Constantine's targets. Constantine shook Harry's hand even more firmly, whilst squeezing his shoulder at the same time, and told him that he would come to see him in London in a few weeks to see how things were going. Harry then jumped in a cab with his bag and headed directly to the airport to take his flight back to London. It was four o'clock in the afternoon in New York and nine o'clock in the evening in London. As Harry sat in traffic waiting to enter the Holland Tunnel and leave Manhattan behind him, he sent Amy a message;

'Everything okay at home'?

She replied immediately with a picture of Mykonos and Athena eating from their bowls in the kitchen. He replied with a smiling emoji. He couldn't wait for the moment he would get home, open the front door and see the two of them sitting in the hallway looking up at him.

Amy paused for thought and then sent Harry an invitation;

'What time will you be home tomorrow? Fancy dinner tomorrow night? A x'.

Harry replied;

'Land at seven, so should be home by eight. Trip okay. Can't wait to get home and see M&A. Yes, dinner tomorrow night would be nice, but low key please. Will be knackered after the red-eye back. See you tomorrow morning'.

That night Amy lay in bed pondering the situation. Harry was looking forward to seeing Mykonos and Athena, but not her. She sent him a kiss and he did not reciprocate. But that could have just been Harry not clocking the kiss. He wants to have a low key dinner. Was that code for *'don't read too much into the dinner'*? Was he managing her expectations?

And worst of all, she had been super nice to those cats, and she'd left her bedroom door open so they could sleep with her, and they didn't want to. They'd rather sleep on Harry's bed on their own. The cats didn't like her. Harry obsessed about the cats and was evidently lukewarm towards her. The penny finally dropped. Charlotte was wrong. She (Amy) was flogging a dead horse and she was in danger of making a fool of herself. She had a moment of clarity. She knew that she had to move on.

The next morning Amy woke up early, packed her things, made the bed and put her used towels in the linen basket. She left shortly before eight o'clock.

Amy assumed Harry would be home shortly afterwards and she knew that Maria would come that day at around nine thirty. She had arranged to stay at her sister's in Richmond that night and she would move into another friend's house the next day whilst she searched for her own apartment.

Harry had slept for little more than three hours on the flight when the crew turned the cabin lights on and served a dry bacon baguette and a bland yoghurt for breakfast. The plane touched down in London shortly before seven in the morning. He decided that it would be quicker to get the express train back into town, and as he sat back in his seat, staring out of the window at the London suburbs, he thought again of Mykonos and Athena, and the moment he would open the front door and they would both be there waiting for him. He regretted having agreed to have dinner with Amy. He would only be able to get an hour's sleep at home before he headed to the office, and he knew that he wouldn't be in the mood to go out for dinner and make small talk with her by the time he got back home that evening. He was still annoyed that she had managed to let the cats onto the terrace. He could have lost Athena for good. It had caused him a huge amount of anxiety at a time when he needed to channel all his mental energy into preparing for his meeting with Constantine.

The express train arrived at Paddington Station, and he completed his journey home by taxi. He climbed the stairs of his building to the first floor, placed his bag on the half landing carpet and put his key in the lock to open the front door. The door wouldn't open. It was double locked. Either Amy had locked herself in or she had already gone to work and double locked the door behind her. He undid the bottom lock and then opened the door slowly. Mykonos and Athena were sitting in the hallway, side by side, exactly as he imagined. They both looked up at him. His eyes met theirs. They both blinked simultaneously, and Harry blinked back at them.

"Hello guys," said Harry, kneeling down on the carpet. "What a pair of cuties."

Athena rushed forward, making squeaky noises, and rubbed her torso along the side of his thigh as he ran his hand along her back. Mykonos had rolled over onto his back, and then flipped his body onto his side, and then flipped onto his back again. Harry had crawled over to Mykonos and rubbed his tummy. Mykonos was overwhelmed with happiness to see Harry. Athena had followed Harry and continued to squeak and rub her torso against him. She too was so happy to see him. She wanted to tell him about her horrible night away from home, and how she was cold and lonely, and how she missed Mykonos, and how she missed him. She tried to climb into his lap and push her head into his armpit, but he had to stand up and go fetch his bag from the half-landing.

Harry surveyed the apartment. Mykonos and Athena had water and food, and their litter tray looked clean. Amy had done a good job. The apartment was spotless, and the guest bedroom had been left with the bed made and everything in its place. None of Amy's clothes or personal possessions were in the guest bedroom or bathroom. The closet was empty – she'd actually taken the few things that she had left in the apartment when she originally moved out. He knew that she had gone for good.

It was half past eight in the morning and Harry had a bath and then climbed into bed. He set his alarm for ten o'clock so he would be in the office by eleven. Mykonos and Athena had sat patiently on the edge of the bath, watching him soak his tired body.

When Harry climbed into bed to get his sixty-minute power nap, they joined
him. Athena launched herself into the space on the duvet between Harry's legs,
so Mykonos had to settle for curling up in Harry's armpit. Harry wrapped his
arm around Mykonos and closed his eyes. For a moment everything was right in
the world. He fell into a deep sleep.

Power naps were one of Harry's talents and it meant that he rarely suffered
from jet lag when he travelled around the world on business. So long as he could
lie flat, he found it easy to fall into a deep sleep. So deep, in fact, that he didn't
hear Maria arrive or feel Mykonos and Athena jump off the bed and race into the
hall when they heard Maria closing the front door behind her. Maria put the cats
in the garden and took a look around the apartment. She too realised that Amy
had moved out. She wasn't disappointed. So as not to disturb Harry, she closed

his bedroom door and started to clean the drawing room. Harry woke up at ten, got dressed, had a brief conversation with Maria, and then headed for the office. He'd got enough sleep to sustain him through the day.

Harry returned home from the office at around seven that evening. He couldn't be bothered to cook for himself, and he had a yearning for Asian food, so he ordered a Thai meal which was delivered thirty minutes later. Whilst he waited for his dinner to arrive, he fed the cats, changed their water, cleaned their litter tray, gave them both a tummy rub followed by a good brush. He was too tired to cut their nails.

After eating the Thai food, he put his laundry in a pile for Maria to wash, showered and collapsed into bed. Mykonos and Athena both jumped onto the bed as soon as he was under the duvet. Harry sighed. He was glad that Amy had made the decision for them. He'd felt ambivalent at best about getting back together with her, and he had so many things that he was grappling with at work right now that he didn't have the energy to jump start their relationship. Mykonos made sure that he got the space between Harry's legs this time, so Athena propped herself up against his torso. Both stretched out and yawned. That night the two cats fell into the kind of sleep that a cat only allows itself when it feels totally safe and secure. They were beyond happy.

Chapter 20
The Unthinkable Road Ahead

Winter was fast approaching and by mid-December, the weather had turned decidedly cold. It had been a brutal year for Harry, both at work and at home. He'd said goodbye to a number of colleagues who'd become friends, and now he found himself in charge of an entire consultancy practice trying to deliver unachievable targets set by New York.

He'd also said goodbye to Amy, who had been a great support and continuum in many ways, but who he now realised had also been a source of huge pressure. Pressure on how the apartment needed to look, which restaurants they needed to be seen at, which people they needed to befriend. Most of all, though, pressure to get married and pressure to have children. And not just to get married and have children, but to have a certain type of wedding, and for the children to go to a certain type of school. He couldn't be doing with all that.

In a way, the unmeetable targets of New York and the unmeetable demands of Amy had converged, and Harry felt as though he needed to break free from his entire life. He had always been thoughtful and undramatic in the way in which he approached both his professional life and his personal life. He didn't relish drama. And yet now he felt this irrational and totally alien urge for drama, for liberation, and for emotional intensity. The disruption he was beginning to crave meant that sooner or later, he would need to act with real intent.

Harry reflected on the positive disruption that Mykonos and Athena had brought to his life and the impetuousness of his decision to bring them back to the UK. Mykonos and Athena had filled a void that he hadn't known existed and which he couldn't explain. He loved them. He loved them more than he loved Amy. He couldn't work out why this was, but he knew that it was true.

Harry decided that he would get a Christmas tree that winter and he would use the decorations that Amy had stored in the loft. It was Athena's first

Christmas, he thought, and she hadn't had the opportunity to climb a Christmas tree and tug at its decorations until they fell to the ground. He'd have quite liked to have got away over Christmas and New Year, and to have spent the ten days over the holiday season on a beach in the sun. But he was reconciled to spending the holidays in London and going to his mother's for Christmas day. He'd consoled himself in the knowledge that he would save the money he usually spent on Amy's tastes for exotic and luxurious destinations. And at least he didn't need to worry about who was going to look after Mykonos and Athena whilst he was away.

It hadn't escaped Harry's notice that Mykonos and Athena had both gained weight as winter set in and the weather deteriorated. Mykonos, who had become so skinny after Athena's arrival, had started to put on the pounds. Athena had slowed down a little, so Mykonos was no longer tormented by a hyperactive kitten. He didn't have to run a marathon every day. Indeed, Mykonos was back to his old self and the fur that had been shaved from his throat for the blood test had pretty well grown back. The corollary of Athena slowing down was that she *had* started to gain weight. This was compounded by the effect of her being neutered, which triggers a kind of early menopause in female cats.

As the weather got colder, Mykonos would go down the stairs, stick his nose out of the back door, sniff the damp air, and then retreat up the stairs and back into the warm apartment. Athena, on the other hand, was not deterred by the cold air and didn't mind being out in the rain. Whilst Mykonos would not cross a wet lawn, Athena was happy to get her paws soggy. She'd also roll around in the dirt until her white fur was a light shade of brown. Despite her time spent outside, Athena had got much larger around her haunches and she had also acquired what was best described as a paunch. She had a belly, and to make matters worse, she hunched her body up when she walked so that it looked like she had no neck. Harry loved her, but he thought she was growing into the oddest looking cat. On the other hand, Mykonos was a handsome boy. There was no denying it. A big, handsome cat.

Athena was aware that she was heavier. She felt slower and less agile. As a kitten, she would sprint up the stairs, race into the apartment, and jump from armchair to commode as if she was weightless. Now everything felt like such an effort. She didn't understand why she had gained weight, and she wasn't happy about it. The snow in January didn't help. Opportunities to go into the garden became few and far between, which meant Athena led an increasingly sedentary life.

For Mykonos, this sedentary life had its advantages. He didn't care about the size of Athena's tummy or her haunches. He adored her, and many an hour was spent lying next to her on an armchair or the bed, meticulously licking every inch of her face and her body. Athena was a grateful recipient and would reciprocate by carefully cleaning behind Mykonos' ears with her tongue.

Harry realised that he worried less about Mykonos and Athena when they spent more time in the apartment. He knew that this was silly, but when they were in the garden for hours at a time, he couldn't help being anxious that one of them might go through a window and get locked into a neighbour's apartment, or that somebody would let a crazy dog loose in the garden, even though dogs weren't allowed. He knew that his anxiety was ridiculous. He wondered how people could ever truly relax when they had children. Mykonos and Athena were cats, he would tell himself, and he worried constantly about them. In truth, of course, they were proxy children, and the only time he didn't worry about them was when they were curled up alongside him in bed at night.

In the second week of January, Harry ran into his super-model neighbour, Olga Dudin. They chatted on the stairwell about a new exhibition she had attended at the Tate Modern, and she invited him for dinner on the Saturday night – an invitation that he accepted. He liked Olga. She was an intimidating combination, he thought, of clever and sexy, and yet there was also a warmth and self-ease about her which put Harry totally at ease. If nothing else, dinner at Olga's would be light relief from work, he thought, and he needed to make more of an effort with his social life. The relentless work schedule had meant that Harry didn't feel motivated to do much else. He had come to realise that Amy had been their 'social secretary' and without Amy, he would need to be more pro-active in staying in touch with friends and arranging to see them. And at some stage maybe he needed to start dating again, he mused.

The pressure at work was getting even more intense. Constantine would fire off emails day and night and expect an immediate response. Harry's team was winning new projects, and Harry had managed to keep the show on the road, but there was no recognition from Constantine that he was doing a good job. Harry assumed that his position was unsustainable and that eventually Constantine would fire him for not delivering against the targets that had been set.

That Saturday night, Harry climbed the stairs to Olga's apartment carrying a particularly fine bottle of Claret. He recalled that she had once mentioned in passing that she was a red wine drinker. He presented the bottle when she opened the door.

Olga was dressed casually, yet elegantly. She was barefooted and Harry realised that she was actually a couple of inches shorter than him out of heels. Olga had invited two Italian friends – Stefania and Allesandra – and an older American banker, whom Harry thought she might be dating. He had seen the banker leaving the building before.

Olga introduced Harry as 'my wonderful neighbour and a very successful management consultant who has a fabulous lateral conversion on the first floor, ladies, you should see it, really beautiful'. Stefania was an attractive and intelligent banker in bond sales. Her line of questioning was direct and unsubtle.

"So Harry, you split with your girlfriend recently, I heard. Did you live together?" she asked.

"Yes, we did," replied Harry.

"But you didn't want to marry her?" asked Stefania.

"I wasn't ready to get married," confirmed Harry.

"To her or to anybody?" asked Stefania.

"Good question," replied Harry, dodging the question.

Allesandra was a stunning blond who worked in marketing for a power tool company.

"Who cares about marriage!" she interjected. "You just wanna have some fun, right Harry?"

"Exactly," said Harry, grabbing what he thought to be the lifeline that Allesandra had thrown him. "I'm sure I will get married. One day. But I want it to happen naturally…"

"And what do you mean by 'naturally'?" Stefania enquired.

"I mean not as a result of an agenda," replied Harry.

"I know, I hate people with an agenda," Allesandra interjected. "So you live on your own?"

It was at this point that Harry paused to reflect. He didn't live on his own. He lived with two cats. But, he concluded, telling a potential date that he had two cats was probably not a good idea.

"Yes, I live on my own," confirmed Harry.

"Nice," replied Allesandra, taking another sip of her Aperol spritz.

Harry had expected to see Olga's cat, Niki, that evening. He was sad to hear that Niki had died very suddenly whilst being transported to Moscow earlier in the year. Harry imagined how devastated he would be if anything happened to Mykonos and Athena.

Olga told Harry that Dimitri had taken the Niki's passing very badly and Harry suggested that perhaps Dimitri might like to play with Mykonos and Athena some time. Olga thought it was a great idea.

At the end of the evening Harry extricated himself before Allesandra had the chance to invite herself downstairs for a night cap.

"Must dash. Have an early start tomorrow. Lovely evening. Thanks so much," Harry enthused as he exited Olga's apartment.

Harry's social safety net came in the form of his evenings playing bridge with three friends from his time at Oxford. His bridge partner, Jenny, was a mathematician who had gone into fund management. She had married an entrepreneur and after having two children, she moved out of London and commuted into the city four days a week. On bridge nights she would stay in town and use Harry's guest bedroom. Although she was a dog person, Jenny was totally comfortable with Mykonos and Athena. Jenny and Harry had been playing bridge against Leon and Antonia since they were undergraduates. Leon and Antonia had met at Oxford and married shortly after graduating. He was a journalist and political commentator. She was a successful novelist. They lived just ten minutes' walk from Harry's apartment in Chelsea. They had two children and an old cat called Connor.

Antonia loved cats, and she loved Connor. This was something Harry couldn't comprehend until he had cats of his own. Connor was a handsome but rather unsociable cat. Antonia and her daughter were the only two people who Connor would allow to pick him up. Antonia's latest project was an anthology of cat literature, and as they chatted over bridge, Antonia pointed out how surprising it was that there hadn't been a blockbuster cat novel, given the huge popularity of anything containing 'cats' on YouTube, and social media in general.

"Think about it," said Antonia, "there are over two hundred and fifty million households with cats in the top twenty cat-owning countries alone."

"If I could write, I'd write a book about Mykonos and Athena," joked Harry. "The story of two refugees from the Greek Islands who make it to Chelsea. Narrated by me. Through my eyes and the cat's eyes. The only problem is, I don't read anything other than the business press and all I write are PowerPoint decks."

"You read my books, don't you, Harry?" quipped Antonia.

"I post online reviews of your books, Antonia. Excellent reviews," explained Harry.

"But we know you haven't actually read any of them, Harry!" exclaimed Jenny.

"I like Harry's reviews," said Antonia.

"Thank you, Antonia. Your book launches have become increasingly lavish over the years, which is always a good sign," continued Harry. "I'm sure that they are very good books. As per my reviews."

"Well I think you should write about Mykonos and Athena," suggested Antonia. "I like the idea of two refugee kittens rescued in the Greek Islands. It could be a children's book, with illustrations."

"Antonia! You've just trumped my ace!" Leon interjected.

"Shit!" exclaimed Antonia, as Leon scowled at her. She hadn't been concentrating on the cards. They all burst into laughter.

"More sauvignon blanc, Antonia?" asked Harry, gesturing with the bottle.

"I better not," she replied, giggling. "Why doesn't my bridge get any better after all these years of playing?" She tried to compose herself and focus on the game.

"So come on, Antonia, what's the secret of writing a bestseller?" asked Jenny.

"Jenny!" exclaimed Leon. "You're deliberately distracting Antonia."

"Oh, Leon!" Antonia interjected. "We're going down anyway, so it really doesn't make any difference."

"Antonia, we're vulnerable. They get a hundred points for every trick we go down," explained Leon.

"Oh dear. I've really messed up," said Antonia. "What were you saying Jenny?"

"The secret of writing a bestseller," repeated Jenny.

"Just tell the story. That's what I do," replied Antonia.

That night in bed, Harry couldn't sleep because Mykonos and Athena had both planted themselves between his legs and there were a lot of slurping noises as they licked themselves clean and then started to groom each other. It didn't sound very pleasant. To make matters worse, occasionally Mykonos would stop to chew the claws on his feet, biting them to make sure that they were completely clean. The slurping noise of the licking and the clicking noise from the biting of claws were keeping Harry awake. This was exacerbated by the moving around of eight kilos of cat on top of him. But all of this was also strangely comforting. When Amy had made half this amount of noise snoring, Harry had found it hugely irritating. But the familiar sound of Mykonos and Athena going through their ablutions made Harry feel like everything was alright with the world. He knew that eventually they would go to sleep, and so would he.

Before Harry finally fell asleep that night though, he got thinking about the unthinkable; that he might lose his job. It was unthinkable because he'd spent the last fifteen years getting promotions, raises and bonuses off the back of the projects he'd won and the client relationships he had built. He had felt totally secure in his employment until now. This hadn't made him complacent. He wasn't the complacent type. His career success had validated him and was what perpetually drove him to work hard and overachieve. But he had come to take for granted the hefty salary check that went into his bank account each month. The salary check which funded his lovely apartment and numerous luxury holidays.

Now everything had changed. His new boss, Constantine, didn't seem to care about the client relationships that were dependent on his being in the business and the damage it would do to the firm if he were to leave. Instead Constantine appeared to have set him deliberately unachievable targets as a stick to beat him with and an excuse to fire him, he thought.

Harry had been the youngest consultant to make partner in London office and generally regarded as the rising star. He was right in concluding that the financial woes of the London office were a direct result of a series of disastrous decisions made in New York. But if the unthinkable did happen, maybe that would be an opportunity to rethink his life. He couldn't afford not to work but he could afford to take a few months out. It might even take him a few months to find a new job, he thought, and maybe he could use those few months to explore how he might change his life.

Harry began to seriously consider whether his idea for a book could be the platform to launch an entertainment brand. After all, he'd spent fifteen years advising clients around the world on their strategies for developing entertainment platforms. He knew how to build an entertainment brand. The problem was that he didn't know how to go about writing a book and he was reticent about doing so.

He resolved his dilemma by telling himself that if he was thrown out of his job, he'd throw himself into his book. For the time being, though, the unthinkable didn't happen and Harry stabilised the business over the next couple of months as best he could. Constantine continued to set him unachievable targets and berated him for not delivering them.

Chapter 21
The Bullet

Harry travelled regularly on business for the first six months of the new year. Mykonos and Athena had got used to his comings and goings and were less distressed when they saw him packing his suitcase. Sometimes he would put them in the garden or lock them out of the bedroom in order to pack. He was never gone for more than a week and they would curl up together and wait patiently by the front door, hoping that when it opened it would be Harry, and not Maria.

Maria would text Harry every day when he was away to say that she had been and that they were okay. Three mornings a week, she would put them outside in the garden whilst she cleaned the apartment. It was spring, daffodils were poking up through the lawn, and Mykonos and Athena would skip around the garden like new-born lambs, stopping occasionally to chew some grass or to bask in the sun. On the other four days of the week, Maria would pop into the apartment for a few minutes to feed them, but they would be on their own for most of the time. And so they would curl up by the front door, waiting and hoping that Harry would be home soon.

For Harry, the best part of heading home from one of his trips was the anticipation of seeing Mykonos and Athena. This sense of anticipation increased when he landed in London and made his way to Chelsea. By the time he entered his building, he was bursting with excitement and would race up the stairs, open his front door lie on the hall floor so that Mykonos and Athena could walk all over him. Athena would squeak like a piglet as if she was asking him where he had been and telling him how much she had missed him. Mykonos would purr and roll over and over on his back, waiting to have his tummy rubbed. It would always be a euphoric reunion.

Athena's weight had steadily decreased during the spring and by June her belly had completely gone. She could feel the difference and it was liberating. The more weight she lost, the faster and longer she would race around the garden with Puccini, whilst Mykonos sat on a window ledge watching them. She had become a slim and agile little cat again, and what's more, she had grown a neck. It was as though her whole body and head had been elongated.

It was the last week of June and Harry had gone to stay with Robert Dibble in his weekend home in Cap Ferrat, in the South of France, to celebrate Robert's birthday. It was an annual event, and although Harry felt guilty leaving Mykonos and Athena because he had been away most of the week before, he knew the break would do him good. Maria would look after the cats.

Harry returned to London on the Sunday night. He felt relaxed and looked well after three days in the sun, a lot of rosé, and plenty of sleep.

Harry, Mykonos and Athena slept together on the Sunday. Harry got up early on Monday morning, brushed both cats and cut their nails, made himself a fresh juice and set off for the office at around eight o'clock. It was a beautiful, sunny morning and he had chosen a lightweight summer suit and white open necked shirt to show off his tan. He was feeling good. As he walked towards Sloane Square tube station Harry ran into Olga, who was in her jogging pants. She told him how handsome he looked and before he knew it, he had asked her whether she would like to have dinner the following week, and she said that she would love to. Harry had an extra spring in his step when he jumped onto the train at Sloane Square and when he exited it fifteen minutes later at Blackfriars station. As he walked to his office, he checked his work email on his phone, but couldn't seem to get into his account. It had been fine earlier that morning, so there must have been some kind of IT problem.

When he got to his office building, he could see through the glass frontage that there were more security guards on duty than normal and that a large number of people had congregated around the turnstiles in the foyer. Harry walked up to the turnstiles and swiped his security pass, but it didn't work. The security guard stepped forward and told him that his pass had been cancelled and that he needed to go to the counter at the other end of the foyer. There he joined a line of employees and learnt that the company had closed its London operations and that hundreds of them had been made redundant. When he got to the front of the line he was given a letter that set out his rights and explained how he would be able to recover any personal possessions that he had left in the office.

Harry stepped out of the building and into the sunshine. He was in shock. Even though deep down he had kind of been expecting it, it was still a brutal shock. It was almost surreal. But he also felt a strange sense of relief. He was liberated. It was as if a lengthy stay of execution had finally been rescinded and the inevitable had happened. The injustice of it all made him angry. Not for himself. He was that close to telling Constantine what he could do with his job. But he was angry for his team. They had done well. They were profitable and they were viable. It was the mismanagement of the entire business by the global leadership in New York that had plunged the firm into financial disarray, and yet those who were responsible for its failure would ultimately keep their jobs.

The contrast between this beautiful, bright sunny day and the utter darkness so many of his work colleagues had been plunged into was not lost on Harry. He started to walk towards the river and then along the Embankment towards Chelsea. As he walked, he phoned his team one by one to make sure that they were okay. One by one, he made sure that they understood their rights and that they had somebody who could advise them. He reassured them that he would give them sparkling references and that he would help all of them find new jobs. He told them that they would be fine.

His own letter set out the company's offer to him. It amounted to his three months' notice plus another three months' money. Some of it would be tax free. In order to get his six months' money, he would have to spend three months on 'garden leave', which meant that he couldn't start a new job for three months, even if he had one. After fifteen years of continuous employment, and having never paused for breath, Harry suddenly found himself with no job and an enforced opportunity to do whatever he wanted to do. And what he really wanted to do was write his book. What he really wanted to do was date Olga. And what he really wanted to do was liberate himself from his previous life as a management consultant and boyfriend to Amy. He told himself that from this moment forward he needed to be excited about his work and he needed to be in a relationship that had real emotional intensity.

Before Harry knew it, he had walked the three miles back to his apartment. Maria was just finishing some ironing and was surprised to see him. Mykonos and Athena were in the garden.

Harry explained to Maria that he had lost his job, that he was being paid off, and that he would be taking a three months' sabbatical. Maria burst into tears and Harry had to re-assured her that it was fine and that she shouldn't be worried for him or for her.

He could afford to pay her and his change in his circumstances would not affect her position. He needed her, and Mykonos and Athena needed her as well.

Harry found himself telling his mother and his brother on the phone that afternoon that he was confident that he would secure another job in management consultancy. He was well networked, he'd turned down plenty of approaches in the past, and he had to believe that he was employable, even if it meant taking a cut in his salary. But he didn't want to do this. Most importantly, he wanted to use his three months in the garden to write his book.

And so Harry resolved to tell the story of Mykonos and Athena and embarked on writing his book.

Harry's new daily routine involved settling down on the bench in the communal garden at around ten o'clock with his laptop and a bottle of water. On the days when Maria cleaned, he'd write until she left at one o'clock. On the days when Maria didn't come, he'd go into the garden a little later.

The trees were in blossom and the lawn was green and verdant. The bench got the morning sun and sometimes Harry would sit there in swimming shorts and catch a few rays whilst typing away on his computer. Mykonos and Athena would chase each other around the garden or practice their special powers.

Athena's special power was going down the metal ladder into the basement where Puccini lived. She was now confident enough to go down and then back up the ladder at speed, whilst Mykonos looked on in dismay, frustrated by his inability to follow her. She was, indeed, a very clever cat.

But Mykonos did have a superpower of his own. There was just one thing he could do that eluded Athena. Mykonos could climb a particular tree in the garden by sprinting at it and wrapping his legs around the trunk, propelling himself to a height of over five metres. Once up the tree, he would survey the garden from this great vantage point, before slowly inching his way back to ground level. Athena would sit at the base of the tree, staring up at him in amazement.

After all of these exertions, Mykonos and Athena spent much of their time in the garden curled up next to Harry on the bench, enjoying the sun on their backs. The warmth of the sun felt like some kind of distant memory. It was comforting for them, although they did not quite understand why.

As the days got warmer, Puccini would make an increasing number of appearances in the garden, running around with Mykonos until they were both exhausted. He didn't play with Athena – she was far too wary of him – but occasionally, he would launch himself at her when she was on her own. Despite being much smaller than Puccini, Athena had no difficulty in fending him off with a hiss and an outstretched claw. And if Mykonos caught Puccini harassing Athena, he would intervene and jump on Puccini before chasing the Italian cat down the garden. This usually resulted in Puccini retreating down the metal ladder to the safety of his home in the basement.

Occasionally it would rain, and when it did, Harry would sit in an armchair in the drawing room and work on his book indoors.

Olga and Harry's dinner date had gone well, and Harry had subsequently spent the night in Olga's apartment. They were now 'an item'. She inspired him to write, and she cajoled him into being more disciplined when he lacked the motivation to open his laptop and get to it.

When Olga wasn't travelling for her work, they would go running together first thing in the morning, or they would go to the gym together when he'd finished writing in the afternoon. He'd forgotten how lean and muscular he'd been before his back-breaking, paunch enduring job had taken its toll. He'd always looked pretty good in a suit, but now he felt pretty good in a pair of swimming shorts. He tried not to worry about how he was going to pay the mortgage when his savings eventually ran out. He could probably survive until the end of the year before he'd need to take a job, so instead, he focused on his newly found mental and physical wellbeing, Olga, the cats and the book.

Schools had broken up for the summer break, so Olga's son, Dimitri, would also spend much of his time in the garden. When Harry couldn't bear to write another word, he took great pleasure in kicking a ball around with Dimitri and Mykonos. For his part, Mykonos would chase the ball as Harry and Dimitri kicked it back and forth. When he Mykonos did manage to intercept it, he would push it along the grass with his paws. Athena preferred to watch from her shady vantage point in 'Agro' Attwood's birdhouse. It was the ultimate insult to Agnes that one of Harry's cats would squat in her birdhouse all day and frighten the birds away. But Agnes did see the funny side of this juxtaposition and had shared pictures of Athena making herself comfortable in the birdhouse on social media. Athena had absolutely no interest in chasing a football. It seemed totally pointless to her. But she liked to watch Mykonos sprinting up and down the garden from her elevated position.

Dimitri loved to play football in the garden with Mykonos. Their friendship had helped Dimitri get over the loss of Niki, and Mykonos couldn't have been happier to fill that void.

And so by the end of the summer Harry had finished his book and Olga had introduced him to some agents and publishers that she knew. The book was published the following Spring, and such was its success, it was made into a movie just a year later.

Of course Mykonos and Athena didn't have the slightest inkling that they had inspired a book and a movie. They were totally oblivious of their global cat icon status on social media.

What Mykonos and Athena did understand is that Harry had saved them, loved them, and provided this wonderful safe haven of a home. What Mykonos and Athena would never understand is that they had saved him right back.

-THE END-